COVER FIRE

A Hawk Tate Novel

DUSTIN STEVENS

The woods are lovely, dark and deep.
But I have promises to keep,
and miles to go before I sleep.
—Robert Frost

Prologue

M y wife hated when our daughter slammed the front door. She despised the way the old wooden gate would swing back and smash into the frame. The way the aging screen, lined with vertical tears, a few stray streaks of rust starting to show, would vibrate. The way the sound of it would reverberate through the house.

She loathed it so much that some of the few real tirades I can ever remember her going on could be traced back to that front door.

Without fail our daughter, in all her youthful exuberance, would shoot straight out across the porch and into the yard. Not until she heard the crack of it swinging back into place behind her would she stop, a wince of realization crinkling her features. On cue, my wife would storm out a moment later, anger coloring her face a bright shade of crimson, wagging an angry finger out before her.

The times are still very few that I can think back on it without smiling.

Only once can I ever remember the scene playing out any differently. On that day, unlike most others, the door slamming was not an accident.

Alice, just five years old, pushed it as far as she could, trying to make a point the best way her young mind knew how. She opened it out as wide as the springs would allow, until it almost touched the side of the house, before letting it swing back into place.

The crash of it slamming shut echoed through the house as I stood in the living room and watched through the front window as she stomped to the edge of the porch and sat down on the step. She pulled her knees up to her chest and wrapped her arms around them, her chin resting on the scraped skin covering her kneecaps.

Tears streaked down either cheek, dripping from her jaw, as she sat and waited for the response she knew was coming. I could tell she wanted to turn around and look for my wife Elizabeth to come out hot on her heels, vindicating her actions, but she never did.

Instead she maintained her position, her tiny body aimed straight ahead.

"I got this one," I said to my wife, reaching out and patting her on the arm.

To my eternal surprise, she did not object. She offered no harsh words about the door slamming, didn't even try to stop me as I walked outside. What was normally an outburst of acrimony filled with threats of docked allowances or withheld desserts became only the slight creak of the door easing open, the sound of my shoes clicking against the wooden porch floor.

The sleeves on my sport coat pulled a few inches up either wrist as I took a seat beside my daughter and wrapped my hands around my knees. Already dressed for the road, the garment was too hot for the early fall weather, the seams on it straining slightly as I wiggled myself into a more comfortable position.

"Hey, honey," I said softly, my voice even.

"I'm sorry I slammed the door," she whispered, her voice thick. She snorted deeply, the sound wet and phlegm filled, the effort lifting her chin a few inches up off her knees.

"That's alright." Chancing a glance to the side I could see her gaze aimed at the ground before her, eyes focused on nothing in particular. "Believe me when I tell you, I feel the same way right now."

"Yeah?" she asked.

"Yeah," I replied, a touch of weariness permeating the single word.

"Then why?" she said. "Why do you have to go again?"

A moment passed, the only sounds the ambient noise of the world as it began its descent into evening. Somewhere in the distance a dog barked. In the opposite direction a cicada could be heard chirping out a steady rhythm.

Everything about the moment was like a perverse take on quintessential Americana, a cruel reminder of what I was leaving behind, what I might never see again.

"Because they called and said they need me," I finally responded.

Once more I ventured a look in her direction, seeing the worry lines etched on her tiny face. Not once did she meet my gaze as she stared off at some indeterminate point in the distance, her entire body rigid.

Only a few inches separated us on that front porch, but already I could tell she was pulling away, fearful as she envisioned what surely lay ahead.

"It isn't fair," she whispered, dropping her chin back onto her knees. The tears had stopped falling long enough for her cheeks to begin drying, the salt pulling her skin tight, tugging with each blink.

My own father was a man of very few words. His mere presence could be intimidating, reducing men to silence with his withering gaze, but very few times did he ever utter a single word that wasn't absolutely necessary.

For that reason, when he did speak, people listened.

That afternoon, I thought of him. I thought of how many times the same conversation had played out with the two of us in much the same way it now was with my daughter. Me, young and angry, not wanting him to put on his Army uniform and leave. Him, trying to let me know he had no choice, that everything would be okay.

"Alice," I said, dropping my voice just barely above a whisper, "there are a lot of things in this world that aren't fair, but this isn't one of them. People like you and me, we have a responsibility."

I reached out and placed a hand on her knee, her skin soft and smooth, her limb so small beneath my palm.

"They're not sending me away to be mean. They're sending me away to make sure nothing bad happens to good people."

For the first time since stepping out on the porch, my daughter shifted and stared straight up at me. She considered me a moment before placing her tiny hand atop mine and smiling, a gap showing between her front teeth. "You promise?"

A matching smile appeared on my own face. "I promise."

What I had no way of knowing at the time, and would think about a thousand times a day for years to come, was that was the last conversation I would ever have with my daughter.

Part One

Chapter One

The last few bits of pink, purple, and orange were clustered together on the western horizon as Lake Pawlak pulled her Jeep to a stop. The tires beneath her squealed slightly from the effort as the aging rig ceased its forward momentum and rocked back a few inches.

Remaining seated behind the wheel, Lake twisted her gaze to the left and held a hand to her brow, using it as a visor to examine the scene. She waited in that position, rigid, her visage bathed in a multicolored hue, until the image was exactly as she wanted it before reaching onto the passenger seat and hefting up her Nikon S3.

Without once taking her attention from the sunset she raised the camera before her and snapped out a series of shots, the auto focus clicking off one after another.

Not until the final few sprigs of light were just apparent above the horizon and the last of the ticking had died away from the cooling engine did Lake replace the camera onto the seat beside her and tug the keys from the ignition.

"Didn't expect it, but I'll take it," she said aloud, the desert breeze pulling the words from her mouth as she said them, the sound of sand slapping against her tires the only response.

It was her first time ever out in this part of the state, the trip planned in haste on a tip from a friend. Sunrise photos were getting top dollar in the freelance market and while any tourist in San Diego or LA could walk down to the pier and shoot a few over the water, it took a real pro to venture out into the sand.

Lake's hope was that the difference would be rewarded with ample compensation, an infusion her bank account was in dire need of.

Parked just off of the two-track beaten into the desert, Lake slid down from her Jeep, the ground hard packed beneath her. The treads of her running shoes crunched with each step as she shut the door and walked around to the back, dropping the tailgate and inventorying her supplies.

Stowed in a row on the threadbare grey carpet of the back were three items. On the left was a sleeping bag rolled tight, an all-weather article advertised to insulate inhabitants down to thirty degrees, though in her experience that claim was proved faulty at anything south of fifty.

Even at the higher altitude she didn't expect a night nearly so chilly, the early spring weather already starting its ascent toward summer.

The right side of the rear space was taken up by a canvas photography bag, a Nikon system with a pair of oversized lenses - one for wide angle, one for extreme zoom - stored inside. Various pockets and zippers stowed wipes, memory cards, and the usual accompaniment of replacement parts, everything she would need to snap off hundreds of shots before returning.

The final item in the trio, wedged tight in the middle, was a single cooler bag, the blue nylon exterior faded from years of exposure to the elements. Inside it were a quart of water and two Snickers bars, more than enough fuel to carry her through the next nine hours.

There was a time not so long ago she wouldn't have even thought to bring it along, but the omnipresent voice of experience in her head told her to just in case.

"Alright," Lake said, her native Texas accent contorting the word as it passed her lips. Pushing out a heavy sigh behind it, she took up the straps on the sleeping bag and slung it over either shoulder, bouncing in place a few times to settle it across her back. Once it rode even between her blades she hoisted the camera onto her left arm, her upper body naturally tilting a few inches to the side to accommodate the load.

The last item to come out was the cooler, placing it on the ground between her feet long enough to close the tailgate before hefting it up. She could feel the water inside sloshing around as it rested against her thigh, swinging gently by the handle as she set off into the gathering darkness.

Putting her back to the Jeep she departed at a diagonal across the desert sand, the terrain extended up from her at a thirty degree angle. Underfoot the ground shifted from the hardpan trail to softer sands, her feet sinking a few inches with each step. Tan powder spilled over the tops of her running shoes as she went, sliding in along the sides of her bare feet, grinding into her skin.

Mere minutes after sundown, the sand was already beginning to cool, pushing feeling from her toes. Despite the numbness in her feet and the persistent breeze blowing across her, her body began to warm as she trudged along, dutifully lifting each foot and placing it back down again.

Lactic acid built in her calves and quads as she pushed on, her breath growing shallow in her chest. Casting a glance over her shoulder she could just make out the Jeep parked far below, nothing more than a shadow in the darkening world.

"Just a little further," she grunted, feeling the weight of her supplies grow heavier with each step. She trudged on another few minutes before the ground began to mercifully level out a tiny bit, the night sky opening up above.

The location was not one she had planned ahead of time, the entire undertaking put together in a matter of hours. If left to her own devices she would still be at home plowing through the first season of *True Detective*, though an angry visit from her landlord had put an end to those plans.

Somewhere in the midst of the tongue lashing she had recalled the tip from her friend, spending fifteen minutes on Google Earth before setting out. The thought of staying within shouting distance another moment made her skin crawl and the only thing she had to pack was the cooler, the rest of her gear already stowed.

The camera bag always remained ready by the door, set to be grabbed at a moment's notice at any time. The sleeping bag stayed on the driver's side in the rear of the car, easily deployed whenever necessary.

The drive from her place near Huntington Beach had taken just over two and a half hours. She had eschewed the traditional Palm Springs and Joshua Tree to push further south, aiming her sights on the Anza-Borrego. No information had fueled her decision beyond an intense desire to get out of town and the hope that the more remote location would provide something nobody had seen before.

The sunset she witnessed upon arrival only seemed to confirm that hope.

Sweat dampened the back of her polypropylene shirt and matted the blonde hair dyed pink along her temples as she inched her way up toward the ridgeline. Wind whipped down from the top of it, hitting her square in the face, pelting her skin with waves of sand. She could hear it slapping against her canvas pants and taste it in her mouth, her eyes pinched tight.

Overhead, stars began to dot the night sky, a waning gibbous moon providing ample light to guide her forward.

Twelve minutes after leaving the Jeep, the trail finally relented. Lake was able to straighten her body from the forward lean she had adopted, covering the last thirty yards to the top of the ridge. Feeling her pulse race through her temples, she dropped the cooler by one foot, her camera bag alongside the other, and worked the pack from her back. She removed the bottle of water and took a small swig, working it around inside her mouth.

The grit of the sand brushed along her tongue and against her teeth as she swirled it twice before turning over a shoulder and spitting it out. She felt the cool breeze pick at the perspiration on her skin as she stood and surveyed the scene before her.

Situated on the western rim, the desert floor stretched out below in a bowl more than a mile in diameter. The sides of the oversized crater descended almost thirty feet to the desert floor, gentle slopes funneled inward from all directions. Scads of cacti and sagebrush dotted the ground, the entire area bathed in moonlight.

Nowhere was there a sign of civilization, not the slightest hint that a human had ever even set foot on the ground. Peering into the distance she couldn't make out a single light of any kind, couldn't hear a stray noise drifting through the night air.

Combined with a weather report that promised clear skies, it would be the perfect place for a sunrise.

Or, more importantly, to capitalize on one.

Chapter Two

Thiago Ruiz ran the end of the match along the front dashboard, the phosphorous and potassium chlorate igniting with a spark. An orange flame blossomed from the end of it, a whiff of smoke sprouting above, as he held it to the end of his Honduran cigar and pulled in three long breaths.

On the final drag the tip of the cigar caught fire, the end glowing red in the darkness of the truck. Keeping both lips wrapped tight around it he drew in a mouthful of smoke, savoring the sweet flavor as he quashed the match between his thumb and forefinger.

"Damn, that is good," he whispered, flicking the match out the window and pulling the cigar from his mouth. Twin streams of smoke billowed from his nostrils as he stared down at the roll of tobacco in his hand, the only remnant of his native country he still claimed loyalty to.

"Smells like ass if you ask me," Hector Ortega said from behind the wheel, letting no small amount of derision show in his voice.

The comment did nothing to sour Thiago's mood. "Too bad I didn't ask you."

"It takes me a week to air out my truck every time you ride in here," Hector persisted, glancing over twice at the man sitting shotgun with him.

Giving no indication he was aware of the man's stare, Thiago regarded the cigar for another long moment before placing it back between his lips. Using his tongue he rolled it into the corner of his mouth, a steady pillar of smoke rising from the tip.

Waiting a few extra moments to make his point, letting the haze fill the cab, Thiago jerked on the handle beside him, a rush of cool night air flooding in around him. It pushed the smoke into a swirl about his head as he stepped out onto the desert sand, the treads of his boots sinking a half inch into the soft powder.

Opposite him Hector did the same, his truck door whining in protest with an angry screech of bare metal rubbing against itself.

"You ever going to grease that damn thing?" Thiago asked, letting the sour look on his face show in his voice.

"What for?" Hector replied. "Not like there's a soul out here to hear it."

Shaking his head, Thiago shoved the passenger seat forward and extracted a cloth gun case from the space behind it, the implement more than three feet in length. Propping the base of it between his feet he tugged on the zipper, starting by his ankles and pulling it up toward his waist.

Reaching inside, he grasped the barrel of his HK416, sliding it free. Holding it in one hand, he tossed the empty bag back behind the seat before slamming the door shut.

"How many are we expecting tonight anyway?" Hector asked. As he did so the sound of him checking a twin set of Sig Sauers could be heard, the slides working in exact precision.

"Don't know," Thiago said, "boss just said it would be big. Well over a dozen."

"Damn," Hector muttered. "We going to have enough room in the flatbed?"

Pushing a loud breath out through his nose, Thiago removed the banana clip from the bottom of his HK. He hefted it twice in his hand to ensure there was a full load before jamming it back into place and wracking one into the chamber.

In his experience an unloaded gun was worthless, even at times like this when it was just for show.

"How the hell should I know?" he said. "And what's with all the questions tonight?"

Hector appeared on the opposite side of the flatbed, his face lit up in the ambient glow from the interior of the cab. He placed the pair of guns down on the rusted metal before him and rested his palms on the edge of the bed, leaning forward.

The position caused his triceps to bulge, his arms unencumbered by another in his never-ending supply of classic rock t-shirts without sleeves, this one in support of the Eagles. A wide Mohawk of dark hair framed a square head, a tuft of matching fuzz extended down three inches from his chin. A heavy necklace and matching earring caught bits of errant light as he stared across at Thiago.

"Just curious, *mijo*."

The word brought a scowl to Thiago's face as he lifted the assault rifle to his shoulder and peered the length of it before placing it down on the flatbed beside him.

"Do *not* call me that," he said.

Across from him Hector raised his palms in a gesture of appeasement, though remained silent, just as he always did. Thiago knew his partner was only trying to get a rise out of him, but didn't much feel up for the banter.

Maybe after the exchange, but not a moment sooner.

"You know what I'm curious about?" Thiago asked. "When you're going to trade in those popguns for a real weapon."

An oversized grin creased Hector's features. He grabbed up the guns in either hand, jamming his index fingers through the trigger guards and spinning them like a modern day Doc Holliday.

"Popguns?" he said, a twinge of hurt in his voice. "These are my babies."

He rotated them once more, bringing both back to their original starting positions, before dropping them into place. The sound rolled out through the still desert night, echoing off the surrounding crater walls.

"Besides, they're American made. When in America..."

An eye roll lifted Thiago's face toward the sky as he shook his head from side to side. "So? Neither one of us are American."

That seemed to be the magic response, Hector finally running out of retorts.

Thiago turned and placed his back against the edge of the truck bed, feeling the cool of the metal pass through his tank top. A light breeze continued to push from east to west across him, pulling the smoke from his cigar, drawing it on toward the ocean eighty miles away.

Overhead an almost-full moon showed bright and clear, a few stray wisps of white drifting just beneath it. Acting as a natural spotlight it drenched the bowl in a ghostly pallor, the entire world still.

"What time is it?" Hector asked. All traces of the previous conversation were gone from his tone, his voice settling into the demeanor reserved exclusively for business dealings.

Thiago didn't bother to check his phone for a response. Instead he cocked his head toward the south, the slightest hint of a rumble finding his ear.

"They're here."

Chapter Three

A random shaft of light caught Lake's attention, poking her subconscious, pulling her from her slumber. Laying completely still, her body cocooned inside the sleeping bag, she opened her eyes to see the source of it a quarter mile away.

On the valley floor below a truck sat motionless, the light coming from the front cab.

"Oh, shit," Lake whispered, rotating her head just a few inches at the neck.

The confines of the sleeping bag grew ten degrees warmer as her heart began to pound. Her breath reduced itself to shallow gasps as she pressed herself hard down into the sand and narrowed her eyes, trying to make herself as small as possible.

There was no way to know for sure what time it was, though the sky above still seemed impossibly black. The moon and stars stood out bright against the inky backdrop, not even a hint of dawn yet encroaching.

Positioned high above with a direct view of the passenger side of the truck, Lake watched as doors swung wide from both sides of the cab. A pair of men emerged, though from such a distance she couldn't get a clear look at either.

There was no way of knowing for sure who they were, but the odds were whatever had called them into the desert in the middle of the night wasn't good.

And wouldn't be allowing for witnesses.

Every muscle in her body seized tight as Lake watched the men move about, the one closest to her reaching behind the seat for a long black object. For a moment his body blocked it from view before rotating just enough for her to see the oversized weapon gripped in his hands.

Sweat lined her forehead as she laid in paralytic fear, watching the lamp from inside the truck catch the polished steel of the gun, glints of bright light flashing into the night.

Just as fast the doors were pressed closed. The single orb of illumination was extinguished, the world seeming somehow even darker than it had minutes before.

"Breathe, breathe," Lake mouthed, no sound passing her lips. She could feel her pulse surging through her eardrums, the sleeping bag feeling like a polyester coffin as it wrapped around her.

In the darkness below she could hear the men talking, their voices drifting across the empty sand. The voices were too low to make out anything definitive, the accents too vanilla to ascertain much for certain.

Five long minutes passed as she watched the men assume stances on either side of the truck. There seemed to be little conversation as they stood, clearly waiting for something.

The thought of anybody else appearing pushed a renewed fear through Lake. Sweat dripped from every pore, soaking her clothes and the inside of the sleeping bag, her entire body straining to see or hear something.

Lifting her head from the ground, she rotated her neck to look in either direction. She had dug a shallow trench into the sand a few feet down from the top of the ridge. The original hope was to position herself out of the worst of the wind, though she now saw the move might have saved her life, preventing her from being a smudge on an otherwise clean horizon profile.

The sleeping bag she was in was charcoal grey, a color that

wouldn't stand out. The camera bag was faded green and the cooler dingy blue, none of which should draw attention.

Somebody would have to be looking to see her.

Whatever the men were waiting on would be coming sometime soon. The odds were they too would be arriving by truck, presumably with lights and many more people.

Both presented a major concern to Lake.

Drawing in a deep blast of air through her nose, Lake felt her thorax expand. She held it there long enough to count to five before easing it out, forcing herself to calm down, trying to gain some control of her faculties.

As it stood, she had two choices. She could lay right where she was. She could remain completely motionless, not chancing a single sound. Sweat would pour from her and her nerves would work themselves into a frazzled mess, but unless someone just happened to shine a light in her direction a full quarter mile away, she would survive unnoticed.

On the opposite side, she could inch her way out of the bag. Leave everything behind that wasn't absolutely necessary. Get herself back to the Jeep, hope they didn't hear the engine turn over, and put as much distance between herself and this place as she could.

Ticking the pros and cons of each off in her head one by one, Lake felt the anxiety within subside. She forced her mind to inventory what she knew, relying on instincts honed many times over to help her decide.

This was not the first time she had been in a precarious position before. No photographer worth their salt hadn't found themselves on the wrong end of a gun or had the full weight of Mother Nature's wrath threatening to do them harm at some point.

Feeling her heartbeat slow, Lake continued to watch the men below and she reasoned her way through her next step.

To her horror, every last thought was ripped away as the men began to move, the sound of another vehicle approaching in the distance forcing them into action.

Chapter Four

T hiago saw it the moment it crested over the opposite side of the bowl. A near copy of the truck they were standing in front of, it sat low and squat, a dark rectangle silhouetted against the horizon line. Moving in a slow and even gait, the front end rose as the tires made the final peak of the rim before plunging itself down the sandy slope.

Riding with its lights off, the only signs of its presence were the persistent rumble of its engine, a slight plume of sand and dust rising in its wake.

Hefting the HK from the bed of the truck, Thiago nestled the stock of it into the crook of his arm, leaving the barrel pointed toward the sky. He could hear Hector take up the Sigs across from him, shoving both into the rear waistband of his pants.

Together they walked around to the front end of the truck, both silent.

It took the approaching vehicle the better part of a minute to close the gap, driving straight at them and pulling to a stop with twenty yards to spare. Thiago and Hector remained motionless as it did so, the engine growing quiet, the sound of the cooling engine block sputtering finding their ears.

The runs had started four years before, the location just one in a half dozen located throughout the bottom half of California.

Despite the rote repetition of the activity, Thiago couldn't help but feel a bit of adrenaline enter his bloodstream as he stood there. His heart rate increased and sweat rushed to the surface of his skin, his brown arms shining in the moonlight.

The burst of trepidation wasn't so much from the exchange, or even the men he was meeting. It was from moments like this, standing out in the open, feeling exposed. Even with the gun in his hand, a full clip at the ready, he didn't like the notion of being a stationary target.

He could see two silhouettes in the front cab, knew exactly who they belonged to, but he still couldn't shake the idea that he was on display.

"What the hell are they waiting on?" Hector whispered, his head never wavering as he stared at the truck before them.

Thiago grunted a response in the negative, his body motionless. Stabs of uncertainty began to dance deep in the pit of his stomach as he stood there, the sweat on his skin starting to bead up and streak down his arms.

For a moment he considered extending his free hand and motioning for the others to get on with it before deciding against it. Both sides had been through the exchange enough times to know how the drill worked.

If one side was taking an extra moment or two, there must be good reason.

"Man, something's not right here," Hector mumbled.

The same feeling emanated through Thiago, though again he remained silent. Every instinct in his body told him to move, either forward to incite action, or backwards to enact a retreat.

Just standing, waiting, was not something he was good at.

In total, seven minutes passed between the truck's arrival and the driver's side door opening. Unlike Hector's, it was well oiled and moved without a sound, a solid black implement swinging wide.

A pair of feet appeared beneath it as Thiago felt his heart rate rise again, his right hand squeezing tight on the stock of his weapon. It stayed that way as fingers appeared on the edge of the door and pushed it shut, Felipe Soto appearing from behind it.

"Good evening, my friends," Felipe said, extending his hands out wide to either side. Two rows of even white teeth flashed in a quick smile as he stepped forward, swinging one foot out in the front of the other.

Across from him the passenger side door opened, Thiago feeling Hector tense beside him. This door too made no sound as it rotated out in a quarter arc away from the truck, returning in total silence.

From behind it emerged the other half of their counterpart team, Dante, a man with skin so dark he was barely visible under the night sky. To accentuate the effect he wore only black cargo pants and boots, his entire torso left bare.

Striding to the front of the truck, he fell in beside Felipe, both men stopping with ten feet separating the two groups.

"Thought we saw something on the way in," Felipe opened. "Wanted to make sure it was clear before we got out."

Thiago cast a glance to his right, nothing meeting his gaze but scrub brush and barren sand, before shifting his attention back to face forward, assessing the men across from him.

On the left, Dante was his normal stoic self. In the previous years of making scheduled pick-ups, Thiago had yet to hear the man say a word. Instead he always kept his lips mashed together in a tight line, his oversized eyes rotating constantly, never missing a thing.

Taking the lead, always, was Felipe, a man Thiago had come to loath in their time together. Dressed in a sleeveless flannel with nothing underneath, he made a point of perpetually showing off as much of his abdomen as possible and insisted on having three or four days of facial hair, but never a full beard.

As evidenced by his nearly neon smile, he also had a strong proclivity for teeth whitening treatments.

Neither man visibly carried a weapon, but Thiago knew they were both well armed, their guns never more than a few inches from their grip. To not be in their line of work would be a major faux pas.

"How many you got?" Hector asked, eschewing the apology and cutting straight to business.

The corners of Felipe's mouth turned down a bit as he glanced between them. "Eighteen."

The earlier feeling of trepidation returned to Thiago's stomach, roiling within. "Eighteen? That's more than we were told. I don't think we have that kind of space."

"Had to," Felipe said, shaking his head to the side, "most of the mules are kids. Any less and we wouldn't have been able to get all the product here."

Thiago cast a glance to Hector, his partner catching his eye before turning back. So far the largest load they had received was fourteen, which was extremely tight. Trying to squeeze another four on the flatbed could be a problem, especially given the uneven terrain of the desert floor.

"Besides," Felipe said, "we gave most of them a nice shot in the ass a few hours ago. Knocked them out cold. You can pile them sky high back there, just like we did."

The abhorrence Thiago felt for Felipe rose another notch as he stood rooted in place. It settled behind his eyes as he glared at the cocksure man across from him, saying nothing.

Even with a load as large as eighteen, it still meant that each person was carrying eight packets or more. Every last one of them was extremely fragile, even a single one breaking meaning the death of the host and no way of extracting the rest of the product inside.

"You know that isn't smart," Thiago said. "We've discussed this before."

A tense moment passed, all four men staring at each other, before the same conceited smile appeared on Felipe's face. He extended his hands before him and patted the air. "Relax, my friends, they're all safe and secure. Come on, you can see for yourself."

Chapter Five

L ake dug her heels into the soft sand beneath the sleeping bag. Once the indentation was deep enough for her to gain some tiny bit of purchase, she used it to leverage herself backward. Inch by inch she slid her body out the top of the bag, never once raising herself from the surface of the desert floor.

Sweat poured from her skin as she nudged her way back, the dry sand clinging to the droplets of moisture, grinding into any exposed flesh. Her lungs fought for precious air as her heart rate hammered away, her waist followed by her knees coming free from the material enveloping her.

The arrival of the second truck had changed everything. At first she had believed she might be able to wait things out. Whatever the men were doing far below, it was apparent they did not want to be doing it under the light of day. If she could just remain where she was, stay silent, perhaps even pile up some sand around herself and her belongings, there was a good chance she could skate by unseen.

There was still the issue of her Jeep parked on the trail below, though it appeared they had traveled in from a different route. Perhaps they would turn around and follow the same trail right back out, bypassing her completely.

It wasn't an ideal plan, far from infallible, but given the circumstances there were worse situations Lake could find herself in. She was positioned on a good vantage point, well beyond a direct sightline. She was tucked away nearly a quarter mile from them. The moon was out, but it was still nowhere near full visibility.

Bringing a second vehicle into the mix changed things though. It brought with it at least one more person, possibly many times that. Each of those people came with their own eyes and ears, scouring their surroundings for any interlopers such as her.

Even more troubling was what the second automobile itself represented.

A single truck could be written off under several different explanations. It could have been a pair of campers, two buddies from San Diego out for a few days in the desert. Just as likely was the chance that someone had gone off-roading in the park and gotten lost.

Two trucks coming together in the dead of night eliminated all such possibilities. All that it left was something illegal, the kind of thing that didn't allow for spectators.

Running the list of items she had on hand in her head, the only thing she absolutely could not leave behind was her camera bag. In sum total the goods inside cost several thousand dollars, more than her Jeep, damn near more than the tiny renovated cottage she lived in.

More than that, the bag represented most of her identity. It carried with it her career, her aspirations, everything she was and hoped to become.

There was no way it was staying behind.

Beyond that, while losing the sleeping bag and the money she had invested in it would sting, it wasn't worth the risk. The thought of getting injured or even worse over something as ridiculous as a damn bolt of nylon was just too big a stretch to even consider.

That left only the cooler sack, which was long past needing replaced anyway.

Bending her knees to a sixty degree angle, Lake forced her body the last few inches out of the bag. The cool night air kissed her sweat drenched skin, every article of clothing she wore clinging to her.

For a moment she lay still, staring down at the meeting below. On one side she could see the men that had arrived first, both out of the truck and standing before their vehicle. Across from them the opposing truck sat silent, no sign of movement of any kind.

Feeling her lungs draw tight, Lake thought for a moment they had spotted her, that maybe that was the cause for delay. She lay motionless, pressing the small of her back into the sand, until finally the cab of the second truck opened.

A burst of light matching the one that had awoken her shot out from the front cab, bathing the first two men in illumination as a second pair emerged. Lake watched for a moment before recognition dawned on her, bringing a string of explicatives to mind.

The light below was not only blinding all four men from seeing her. It was also destroying their night vision.

If ever she was going to make a move, this was her chance.

With one last breath, Lake used her hands and feet to rotate herself ninety degrees. Clawing at the ground, she could feel sand working its way beneath her fingernails and lodging itself inside the waistband of her pants as she moved. She continued to shift until the strap of the camera bag was just inside her reach, clasping her left hand around it and instantly rolling over onto her stomach.

For a moment the thought of rolling herself over the ridge crossed her mind, but disappeared just as fast. Doing so could be noisy and would almost certainly produce a puff of dust in her wake.

Instead she raised her bottom just a couple of inches off the sand and began to army crawl forward, her knees and elbows chewing up the distance as she passed over the top of the ridge and disappeared from sight.

Chapter Six

T hiago Ruiz was fifteen years old when he first came to America. Three weeks removed from the death of his mother, he had accompanied his father and younger sister north out of Honduras, settling into the low income section of Maywood. Nestled dead center of East Los Angeles, the neighborhood boasted a demographic of more than ninety-eight percent Hispanic, something that should have made the Ruiz family feel right at home.

Instead it only exacerbated their plight, every other immigrant in the area hating them, the Hondurans somehow ending up even lower on the social totem pole than the Mexicans or handful of African-Americans that called the place home.

Just four months after arriving, Thiago's father was killed by a stray bullet in an attempted convenience store robbery, another statistic in a story that had become so commonplace in Maywood it was almost cliché.

It was at the funeral, standing in the rain next to an unmarked grave, that Thiago first met Arturo Molina.

Dressed in shorts and a black t-shirt, two of the only five pieces of clothing he owned, Thiago had stood beside the open trench cut into the ground and watched as the rickety pine box containing his father was lowered out of sight. In his right hand he held a carnation one of the diggers had given him, no doubt pilfered from a nearby grave.

In his other was clutched the trembling hand of his nine year old sister Luanna.

"How old are you, *mijo?*" a voice had asked, appearing beside him as if from thin air. Low and graveled, it conveyed both a sense of sadness and deep understanding.

The sound of it caused Thiago to flinch as he turned to find a man approaching forty by his side. Dressed in a solid black suit with a matching tie, his coal colored hair was combed straight back from his forehead. Already his cheeks were beginning to sag on either side of his mouth, the skin scraped completely free of facial hair.

Above his head was an oversized umbrella, a young girl beside him holding it in place, the run-off spilling down onto her face.

"Fifteen," Thiago replied, his voice breaking just a bit.

"Hmm," the man had replied, nodding thoughtfully. "And her?"

"Nine."

Again the man nodded. "Do you have anywhere to go?"

Thiago shook his head. "No."

"Anywhere to stay?"

"No."

"You do now," the man replied.

More than twenty years had passed since that day, Thiago rising from a young messenger for the Molina enterprise into now a trusted security specialist. It was a position he took no small amount of pride in manning, a culmination of decades of repaying the old man's faith in him that one fateful fall morning.

The ascendance had not merely been a lesson in nepotism though, his life marked by an education of the purest form. The first time he had ever fired a gun was less than a year after his father's death. The first time he ever took a life just six months after that.

What those combined experiences had left him with were some very particular assets, both of which he could feel rising to the surface as he stood in front of the truck staring back at Felipe and Dante.

The first was a keen ability to read a situation, to assess a set of circumstances, to foresee what was going to happen long before it did.

It was obvious how the nervous smile lingered a little too long on Felipe's face, the way Dante shifted his weight from side to side. Never before had either man seemed so stilted, making the deliveries with a nonchalance that edged into boredom.

Something had them spooked.

The second asset Thiago he had on his side was the ability to act whenever things didn't seem right.

Pulling the Honduran cigar from the corner of his mouth, Thiago stubbed the end of it out against his weapon. Bits of white ash flaked off as he pressed it against the matte steel finish before tucking the remainder of the smoke behind his ear. He kept his movements slow and easy, giving no indication that anything was out of the ordinary.

"We're not doing this," he said, watching as the faces across from him registered surprise. To his left he caught a glimpse of Hector's gaze swinging toward him, just as fast returning into position.

"What? Why not?" Felipe said, his features falling flat. He took a step forward, reaching for the small of his back, but Thiago gave his head a terse shake.

"Don't," he said. "Stay right where you are, give no indication anything is wrong."

His gaze never left the men across from him, watching anxiety seize their bodies tight, each of them looking from him to one another for some indication what was going on.

For all of the shortcomings of Felipe and Dante, and Thiago had come to be intimately familiar with every last one of them, they weren't ones to rattle easily. Both had been to jail before, had gotten through their share of scrapes. They had decent enough instincts when the time called for it, otherwise they never would have been entrusted with such a task.

"We're going to clear the area before we do anything," Thiago said. His first, more rational response to the situation was to call the exchange off for the night, though doing so without reason was a decision far beyond his pay grade. "You still have that spotlight on your rig?"

All ten of Felipe's fingers twitched in slow, striated movements, beginning to dance by his side. His chin rose a half inch as he stared at Thiago, clearly trying to determine what was happening.

Seeing the thoughts play out on the man's face, Thiago tapped the barrel of his HK with the tip of his right index finger. "If I was trying to pull something here, I would have already shot you. We need to make sure we're the only ones here before we do something stupid."

Thiago watched as Felipe's gaze tracked from the tip of the weapon pointed to the sky and back down. There was no way the younger man could draw a weapon before Thiago had the gun lowered and fired, nothing he or Dante could do if their time was at an end.

Realizing this Felipe nodded slowly, his gaze remaining in a fixed position. "We have the light."

"Good," Thiago said. "Real slow and natural, go around and aim it in the direction you thought you saw something."

All four men remained in position a moment, specks of sand slapping the bodies of their trucks the only sound.

Felipe was the first to move. He kept his hands a few inches from either hip and walked around to the side of his truck, snaking a hand through the open driver's side window and using it to leverage himself up onto the bed. The top half of his body appeared above the cab as he hoisted a silver light fixture into place, moonlight flashing off the glass bulb.

"Ready?" he asked, aiming it toward the western edge of the rim above them.

Shifting himself to the side so that he, Hector, and Dante were in a line three across, Thiago raised his weapon to his shoulder. He paused a moment, waiting as the other two readied their weapons and braced themselves alongside him.

"Hit the light."

Part Two

Chapter Seven

Nestled tight against my cheek, I could feel the cold steel of the barrel passing through my skin, slowing my breathing. In and out I drew the brisk Montana air, the scent of pine needles and gun powder easing through my nostrils, filling my lungs.

The air, the scents, felt good as I pulled them in, paused, and pushed them back out, my left eye closed. My right was pressed tight against the Leupold VX-2 scope fastened to the top of the Winchester bolt action 30.06, my attention focused on the trio of green digital hashes lined one atop the other.

Lying flat on my stomach, I could feel the cool from the ground passing through the front of my jeans, pressing against my thighs as I sighted in on the target, the butt of the gun flush against my shoulder. Waiting an extra moment I made sure my breaths were even, my heart rate normal, before drawing back on the trigger, my body absorbing the kickback of the weapon as it recoiled against me.

The spongy orange plugs shoved deep into my ear canals deflected most of the sound as the weapon barked, a plume of white rising from the end of the gun. The acrid scent of smoke passed over me as I remained in position, waiting for the air to clear, using the scope to determine the success of my shot.

Thirty yards away, a tuft of red fabric fluttered from the front of the target, a jagged hole ripped through it by the oversized shell.

Content with the morning's work, I placed the gun on the ground and pulled my knees up under me, working the plugs from my ears. Around me the sounds of the forest flooded back in, the familiar dins of water rushing by in the stream below, the wind rattling the tree branches overhead.

Getting fully accustomed to the rifle was still a work in progress, though I couldn't help but be pleased with the way it was coming along. The purchase had been a rare impulse buy for me three months prior, something I had seen as a year-end closeout special in Billings.

Never much of a gun fanatic the way many of my brethren in both the navy and the DEA had been, weapons to me were an object of purpose, nothing more. On the job they had meant either personal protection or the threat of violence, both functions little more than a means to an end.

In my life since transitioning back into the civilian world five and a half years before, guns had begun to take on a bit of a different meaning. As a licensed guide in Yellowstone National Park, I made sure to always have a handgun available just in case. Most of the time there was no call for one, but in the event I found myself going deep into the backcountry where grizzlies and mountain lions were known to roam, it was nice to know I could bring something down if I needed to.

Rising to full height, I gripped the weapon by its polished walnut stock and lifted it from the ground, collecting my shell casings and heading back toward the cabin. Above me the sun could be seen trying in vain to push through the cloud cover enveloping eastern Montana, appearing more like a white disk than the golden ball I knew it to be.

Picking my way through the clumps of snow still dotting the forest floor, I followed the stream back over a quarter mile to my cabin. A heavy blanket of dead pine needles swallowed the sound of my footsteps as I pushed on, blending seamlessly with my surroundings.

Spring, such little of it that existed in Montana, was still a month or more away. Much of the world remained shrouded in a heavy coat of snow, bringing with it temperatures capable of plummeting dozens of degrees below zero, fierce winds that could rage for weeks on end.

For some, the lingering effects of winter were what ultimately drove them away. The forced isolation could bring on cabin fever for even the heartiest of souls, causing them to search out warmer locales.

Personally, the winter had been one of the easiest in recent memory, for the first time ever finding my cabin to be a welcomed retreat instead of a self-imposed exile. Six months before, I had finally done away with the men that had killed my wife and daughter, the first tiny cracks in the cloud that had hung over me for five years appearing.

The going was slow, but for the first time since their passing I felt like my trajectory was tilted slightly upward instead of straight down.

Ahead of me the single story structure I had built myself came into view. Constructed entirely from old growth pine, the cabin stood ten feet high before sloping upward beneath an insulated aluminum roof painted green. Heavy chinking filled in any remaining cracks between the logs, their ends laced together like fingers on every corner.

Aesthetically speaking it was far from the prettiest thing I had encountered since coming to the mountains years before. In truth it was closer to flat-out ugly, a visual abomination that was almost an insult to the forest it was tucked away in. Sitting low and brooding along the bank of the stream, it more resembled an angry and brooding bullfrog than a home.

The faint hint of smoke played across the breeze as I approached, the source of the smell rising from the far back corner of my place. It twisted upward in a lazy curlicue, a tuft of white against a green canopy, before disappearing into the sky above.

Pausing by the front door, I slipped my feet out of my insulated boots and stepped inside. Warm air rushed to meet me as I shut the door, bringing a flush of color to my cheeks.

Out of pure habit I gave one quick glance around as I stood just inside the door, surveying my surroundings.

To my left was a makeshift kitchen - a gas stove, a sink, and a refrigerator reclaimed from the sixties all sitting silent. Beside them was a table and chairs I had constructed from some split top pine logs, the seats of the chairs padded with squares of an old Indian blanket.

Off to the right was my living area, a wooden-framed sofa and matching armchair clustered around a roughhewn coffee table. Atop it was a collection of Louis L'Amour and Lee Child novels, all of which I had read at least three times apiece.

Beside it sat an old box television that couldn't pick up a single channel, but worked fine for playing DVD's. This winter I had finally taken the suggestion to begin watching *Friday Night Lights*, all five seasons stacked neatly across the top of the device.

In the far corner rested my bed, constructed from the same design as everything else in the cabin, varnished blonde wood providing the frame. A thick layer of blankets I had picked up in various places was piled atop it, everything tucked in tight.

Just one of many habits acquired as a military brat.

Comprising the final corner of the room was the wood-burning stove I used for heat and a small restroom, both functional if not ornamental in any way.

From start to finish the entire sweep of the place took less than ten seconds, a practiced movement born of rote routine. Every last thing in its place, untouched since my departure, inventoried and dismissed in a glance.

Stepping forward into the room, I placed the Winchester down on the kitchen table and shrugged my coat down off my shoulders, the heavy canvas article falling to my waist. Catching it with both hands, I tossed it on the rack alongside the door and did the same with the fleece vest beneath it.

Inside the small, silent confines of the house, the sound of the phone ringing went off like a shotgun blast. It sent a thunderbolt of adrenaline through my system as it sounded out sharp and shrill, my body crouching into a shooter's stance as I instinctively reached for the gun beside me.

My mind rifled through the locations for ammunition that was stored inside the cabin before pushing the notion aside. A small smile crossed my lips as I stood, feeling my pulse race. Shaking my head at the foolishness of my actions I crossed the floor toward the bed and took up the satellite phone from the nightstand beside it.

Flipping the bottom of the device open, I pressed it to my face and said, "Hello?"

The phone was so old it didn't have caller ID, not that it would matter much anyway. Only a small number of people in the world even had the number, not enough to fill a single hand.

Of those, none were the type that would be calling unless it was important.

Still, even from such a small group of possibilities, the voice on the other end of the line surprised me.

Chapter Eight

D aniel Guzman closed his eyes and inhaled deeply. The scent of the freshly ground coffee wafted up from the handheld grinder, his hands operating the antique machine from pure muscle memory. Once the smell made its way up to his nostrils he gave it exactly ten more revolutions on the wooden crank, careful not to crush the beans too fine.

Guzman could feel the eyes of all three men on his back as he worked, making no effort to speed up his movements. This was his process every single morning and nothing, no matter how large, would take from him one of the few remaining joys in his life.

Lifting the top from the grinder, Guzman transferred the pulverized beans to his French press. Taking up the folded towel on the counter beside him, he lifted a kettle of steaming water from the stovetop and poured five ounces of water. He paused, watching as the beans bloomed for half a minute, before adding the last ten ounces and replacing the pot.

Each person in the room waited in silence as he counted off the final two and a half minutes in his head, savoring the rich aroma, before straining out the grinds and pouring his drink into a mug.

The bottoms of his slippers scraped against the Spanish tile underfoot as he shuffled from behind the bar. A white silk robe fluttered about him, a sharp contrast to his dark brown skin, kept toned from an early morning swim every day.

Aside from the coffee, it was the only thing he did with religious consistency.

Routine was a vice of the unimaginative.

"I tell you," he said, walking past the three men and settling himself onto the thick white cushion atop a black rattan chair. The implement protested just slightly under his weight as he slid his feet from his sandals and propped them on the matching ottoman before him. "I don't understand how anybody can live in Ecuador and drink instant coffee."

Taking the cue, all three men assumed their places.

On the right, Ramon Sanchez dropped into a matching rattan chair, facing forward to look at Guzman. Despite the early hour he already wore a tan suit with a light blue shirt, his thick dark hair gelled to the side.

Positioned three feet to his left in another duplicative chair was Martin Morris, a stark contrast to Sanchez in every way. Standing no more than a few inches over five feet tall, most of the hair was gone from his head. What remained was buzzed into a short ring around his scalp, matched by facial hair of equal length.

Heavy smudges of dirt and grease lined his clothes and fingernails, his hands never stopping their fidgeting in his lap.

The final man in the room was Rafa Willis, Guzman's oldest associate, a man that had played no small role in building the business into what it was. Standing back a few feet from the others, he was positioned directly across from Guzman, allowing the two men to exchange facial cues whenever necessary.

Now a year or two over fifty, his hair was just beginning to travel from black to salt-and-pepper. A matching goatee encased his mouth, growing right up to the edge of a battle scar on his cheek earned in a knife fight years before.

All three waited for Guzman to take another drink of his coffee, sighing appreciably at the taste, and set it on the small end table beside him. A persistent breeze blew in through the open veranda doors lining the walls around them. Plenty of early morning sun poured in, illuminating the room, glowing off the floor tiles.

Outside, row after row of neatly trimmed coffee trees were extended in all directions.

"Okay, begin," Guzman said simply.

Taking the lead, Sanchez motioned to the man seated beside him. "Mr. Guzman, joining us is Martin Morris, our pilot. He has some information I think you should hear before we get started."

It was the first time Guzman had ever seen the man in person, though he could recall the name from several prior discussions. At the time of his hire Guzman had not been especially keen on employing an American for such an important role, feeling that his presence might attract unwanted attention.

The lack of any suitable local hires though had necessitated overlooking his skin tone.

Thus far, it had been an arrangement that had worked well for everybody.

"Um, hi," Morris said, opening and closing his mouth a few times in false starts. "I mean, uh, good morning, Mr. Guzman."

Holding up a hand, Guzman let a smile cross his lips. "Martin, you have no reason to be nervous. Please, just tell me what business you have here this morning."

Whether or not those words were true Guzman did not yet know, though he needed to put the man at ease if ever he was going to get what he needed from him.

A brief flash of relief passed over Morris's face as he matched the smile, glancing down to his hands. For the first time he seemed to realize how nervous he appeared, pulling them apart and stuffing them under either thigh.

"As you all know, each time we have a shipment I fly the mules from here to Mexico," Morris said, his voice displaying a tiny bit more confidence. "I help Felipe and Dante get everyone loaded up, then I wait until first light before returning the next day."

Every man in the room knew the schedule Morris kept wasn't quite so innocent, a watering hole he and Felipe liked to frequent a few times a week being the chief reason he insisted on staying over whenever possible.

Placing his elbows onto the arms of his chair, Guzman chose not to call Morris on the discrepancy. He raised his hands and brought his fingertips together just inches from his face, nodding for the pilot to continue.

"Last night, when they returned though, they still had a full load with them," Morris said. He delivered the line quick and low, shifting his gaze to the ground. There it remained, his body seeming to shrink back a few inches.

Guzman's eyes narrowed, his gaze flicking to Rafa. "A full load?"

"Yes, sir," Morris replied.

Shifting his attention to Sanchez, Guzman asked, "How many?"

"Eighteen," Sanchez replied without consulting his notes.

The number jogged Guzman's memory, his head rising and falling a few inches. The decision to use so many children on this particular run was less than ideal, but given the circumstance it was the best they could do.

Making three runs a week required a vast number of willing bodies. Sometimes those coming forward skewed a bit younger.

"Have you tried to contact Felipe?" Guzman asked.

"Not yet," Sanchez said. He left the response open ended, the implication clear.

Given the recent uptake in interest from Federales regarding border crossing activity, all communication with Felipe was to be kept to a minimum. That was no doubt the reason Morris now sat before him, the reason Sanchez had not made any calls yet.

A small nod shifted Guzman's head less than an inch, his attention rotating back to Morris. "Where is the shipment now?"

"At the safe house," Morris said, a slight wince drawing up the skin tight on either side of his eyes.

Guzman didn't have to bother asking about the response. By now the mules would be passing the product they were carrying, dozens of marble sized bags exiting their rectum in a viscous sludge of blood and feces. More than once he had seen a similar scenario, his reaction much the same as Morris's.

In a perverse sort of way, the ones that suffered a rupture and died actually got off easy.

A moment passed as Guzman contemplated the information in silence. One question after another entered his mind, ranging from Felipe to Arturo Molina. His eyes glazed as he shifted his attention out through the window, watching as the morning sun danced off of the bright green leaves.

Bringing the shipment back across the border was an extreme risk. Felipe was not the most intelligent man in the system, but even he knew not to take such an unmitigated gamble without good reason.

"What happened?" Guzman asked.

Twice Morris opened his mouth, pulling his hands from beneath his thighs and raising his palms to the ceiling. "All I know is, Felipe said somebody was there waiting for them."

Another glance was cast between Guzman and Rafa, the larger man's eye narrowing slightly.

"An ambush?"

"I don't think so," Morris replied, "but again, I don't have all the details. By the time they made it back things were starting to get a little ugly with the supply. Felipe was running around, trying to take care of things, and Dante, well..."

"Doesn't talk," Guzman finished, nodding in understanding.

Another moment passed before he lowered his feet from the ottoman and placed them back in his slippers. He stood, crossing his left hand over his waist to hold the robe in place and extending his right.

"Please feel free to come to me with anything like this in the future."

It took a moment for Morris to understand he was being dismissed. Once the realization arrived he scrambled onto his feet, shuffling forward and meeting the handshake.

"Thank you, Mr. Guzman. Anything I can do to help."

"Of course," Guzman said, smiling. "Rafa will see you out."

The big man appeared instantly at Morris's elbow, extending a hand toward the door. Together they walked out, neither saying a word, the only sound their footfalls as they departed.

Once they were removed and the door closed behind them, Guzman lowered himself back into his seat. He extracted his feet from their plush bindings and returned them to the ottoman, the morning breeze playing over his exposed toes.

"I think it was a safe assumption he had reached the endpoint of his usefulness," Guzman said.

"Agreed," Sanchez said, nodding. "Shall I set up a meeting with Felipe and Dante?"

"Yes," Guzman said. "We need to determine what exactly happened."

Sanchez flipped open his notebook, going to work with an ink pen. "I'll have them here by tomorrow morning at the latest."

"No," Guzman said, resuming his previous stance, his fingertips raised and focus aimed out the windows. "I'll send Rafa to them. We need to make sure the product is safe, and we'll need to be in Mexico anyway."

He didn't bother adding anything more to the final statement. There was no need to.

"Of course," Sanchez said. "Shall I make the call?"

"No," Guzman said, his eyes losing focus as he stared at nothing in particular, his mind working to put together everything he had just been told. "You know the rules. The old ways dictate that one falls to me."

Chapter Nine

M ia Diaz stepped out of her car the moment my front tires turned from the pavement onto the gravel of the parking lot. Her gaze never left my truck as she slammed the door shut and thrust her hands deep in the pockets of a long black overcoat.

Behind her was the familiar sight of my second home five months out of the year. Standing a single story tall and formed entirely from flat-front pine boards, it was painted dark brown. Forest green covered the front door and lined the windows, providing the lettering for the roughhewn sign stretched across the roof.

Aside from Diaz standing in the parking lot, nothing seemed to be out of order.

The call from her had been a thunderbolt from a clear blue sky. I was more than a little surprised to hear her voice on the other end of the line, completely shocked when she said she was in West Yellowstone waiting for me.

Not one other word of what had brought her here was shared, though I knew enough from our previous time together not to question it. Whatever had pulled her up from sunny California to the cold of Yellowstone in March must be important.

The fact that she wasn't offering a single detail about the nature of the visit only confirmed that.

Easing to a stop at an angle before her, I pulled the keys and stepped outside, a burst of cold air wrapping around me. Despite the ski cap atop my head it managed to push hair around my face in a swirl, carrying with it the omnipresent Montana scents of ice crystals and pine needles.

"Damn," she muttered as she walked toward me, her shoes biting into the gravel, leaving small divots in her wake. "Hawk?"

The better part of six months had passed since we last saw each other, standing outside of the Drug Enforcement Administration headquarters in Washington, D.C. It was at the conclusion of the case that had put my family's killers down for good, and had earned Diaz no small amount of fanfare within the organization.

At the time we had parted on good terms, each thankful for what the other had done, ready to move on in our respective directions. We had left each other with an open invitation should the need arise in the future, though I'm not sure either one of us had much real intention of taking the other up on it.

As far as working partners go we had gotten along even better than could have been expected.

We also both just happened to be fiercely independent people, neither especially prone to reaching out.

That single thought occupied my mind most of the drive down from my winter cabin outside of Glasgow. The fact that she was doing so meant something large was afoot, something with enough force to cause her to both need outside assistance and to come for it in person.

"Diaz," I said, knowing exactly what her question was referring to but refusing to acknowledge it just yet. Instead I allowed a wry smile to cross my features, stepping forward with arms outstretched.

She met me exactly halfway between our respective vehicles, a quick embrace and release, each side appraising the other.

In the months that had passed, not one thing had changed about her. Dark hair hung in ringlets to her shoulders, framing a heart shaped face with prominent cheekbones. A well-defined jaw line sat below full lips. Dark half-moons still underscored both eyes, maybe even a bit more pronounced than the last time we spoke.

Apparently the drug trade had not relented at all over the winter.

"You look good," I said, nodding for emphasis. "Though I see despite living in southern California year round you still haven't bothered to see sunlight."

Her eyebrows tracked a quarter inch up her forehead as she nodded in faux mirth, a trio of horizontal lines appearing. "Or it could be this place is so damn cold I don't have any circulation in my face."

Stifling a laugh, I moved toward the front door of my shop. "Could be that, I suppose."

Diaz remained behind as I tracked up the three short steps onto the front porch, twisting the key ring in my hand to find the proper one.

"*Hawk's Eye Views, West Yellowstone's favorite private guide*," Diaz said behind me, reading the sign that sits along the top awning of the building. "Subtle."

Again feeling a smile grow across my features, I managed to unlock the deadbolt on the front door and push it open. The bell above the door jangled slightly as the wooden gate passed, the weather stripping around it moaning in protest as it swung wide for the first time in months. Stale air came out to greet me, flecks of old coffee and cleaning solution riding with it.

"Subtle doesn't pay the bills," I said, turning back to face her.

"Ahh," she said, accepting the explanation without further comment as she stepped forward, taking the stairs one at a time. "Tell me this though, how does a man with a barber shop right next door show up looking like you do?"

My cheeks bunched tight as I tried to suppress a smile, my entire upper body quivering with the effort. Since our last meeting I hadn't touched a single bit of growth on my head. My hair, which was already growing shaggy, now hung well past my collar, sandy brown throughout.

The bigger surprise though was no doubt the beard, several inches of grizzled whiskers, streaked with auburn.

"Told you I go off the grid in the winter time. This is the first time I've been to any town in two months, first time I've been here since November."

"Ahh," she said again, nodding slightly as she stepped past me into the shop.

"And it keeps my face warm," I added.

Swinging the door closed behind her, I fumbled for the light switch on the wall, a pale yellow fluorescence passing over the space. The fixtures buzzed slightly as electricity pulsed through them for the first time in ages, taking a moment to warm up.

"You'll have to excuse the place," I said, half explanation and half apology. "Nobody's been here since we closed for the season. I usually don't come back until mid-April, my secretary starts the first of May."

Without saying anything, Diaz kept her hands shoved deep into her pockets and walked forward, surveying the set up.

The building as a whole was cleaved into two equal parts. The front half was comprised of one open room, a waist-high wooden counter spanning the majority of it. On the left end of it was a door leading to a restroom, a basic toilet and sink affair. On the right was the entry into my office, which formed the back half of the building.

To either side of us were provisions for the rare occasion when we had customers waiting in person. One side held a small sitting area, four chairs grouped around a table, a random assortment of travel magazines strewn atop it.

The other held two oversized racks of brochures and pamphlets, a drip coffee maker on an end table between them.

Every item in the shop was chosen from an entirely functional standpoint, whatever few touches of character or aesthetics there was being added by my secretary over time.

I was sure a psychologist would have a field day assessing what exactly that said about me, though I was long since past caring.

Continuing to pace, Diaz finished a complete loop of the room before coming to a stop directly in front of me. Despite our earlier embrace and the friendly banter we had already partook in, the strain she was under was plain on her features. Her mouth was turned downward into a frown, folds of skin forming along her neck from the position.

Again I couldn't help but return to the same thoughts I'd had in the truck on the way down, though I knew better than to pry. She would get to whatever had brought her here in her own time.

I just needed to stay out of the way until she did so.

"Nice place," she said, giving a tiny nod of her head.

"Nice enough," I said, casting a glance around. "Like I said, we've been closed for the winter. In the summer, I'm out in the park ninety percent of the time anyway."

Again she nodded, seeming to accept the explanation.

"I turned the heat up," I added. "Shouldn't take too long to get warm in here."

I had no idea of knowing how long we would be, still not the slightest clue why we were having a conversation that was fast becoming awkward.

At the same time though, not that long ago she had gone out on a limb and helped me when she had no earthly reason to do so. If there was anything, anything at all, I could do to return that favor I would.

"It's okay," Diaz said. "Just being out of the wind helps."

I nodded in agreement, again casting a glance around. "Get us some coffee going while we wait?"

Diaz paused until my gaze returned to her, her eyes meeting mine for a moment. Finally she sighed, the effort raising her shoulders an inch, her hair shifting with it.

"Yeah," she said. "That would be great. This could take a while."

Chapter Ten

"Lake Pawlak."

I gave no reaction at all to the words as I leaned back in my desk chair, the familiar groan of the metal springs rolling out as I leaned back as far as I could. Raising my right foot up, I rested an ankle on my thigh and buried my fingers into my beard, scratching at my chin.

"Never heard of it," I replied.

My immediate reaction upon hearing the name was to rifle through my internal Rolodex of locations in the park, a conditioned response from years as a guide. After ticking off the big ones in my mind – Yellowstone, Shoshone, Heart – I gave up on the task.

There weren't but a handful of actual bodies in the park, most of the water found in rivers and streams.

Besides, something told me she didn't come here to plan a trip. Whatever reservoir she was referring to was probably much further south.

"Not it, *her*," Diaz corrected. "Lake Pawlak is a person, a twenty-eight year old photographer from Huntington Beach."

Again I forced my face to remain neutral as I lifted the Styrofoam cup from my lap and took a long pull. The only coffee in the place I could find was from a Folgers can with a fast approaching expiration date, the taste a bit off as it slid down.

All things considered though, it was hot and caffeinated, far from the worst I'd had.

I watched as Diaz took a drink of her coffee as well before placing her cup back on the edge of the desk between us. The lack of a grimace told me she was probably of the same mindset, just thankful to have something warming her from within.

"Two nights ago she camped out in the Anza-Borrego Desert hoping to, as she put it, score some killer sunrise photos." Diaz glanced over to the bookshelf along my wall at the photos of the sun appearing above Old Faithful and Morning Glory pool. "I guess they go for a real premium these days."

Photos like the ones she referred to went for a premium in any day. Nature enthusiasts loved anything that conveyed pristine beauty and weren't afraid to indulge in that affection.

"Anyway, she was out there hunkered down in the sand, had all her gear and everything with her, just waiting for daybreak. Middle of the night though, she was woken up by two trucks coming together for a meeting."

She couldn't see my eyebrows rising behind the thick curtain of hair hanging down, but I'm sure she could see my eyes grow larger. My own experience with the Anza-Borrego was limited, though at one point my family and I made our home not far from there.

I knew the area well enough to know there wasn't a damn thing for eighty miles in any direction.

Certainly no legal reason for multiple vehicles to be having a rendezvous in the middle of the night.

"Okay," I replied, scads of thoughts and questions already springing to mind.

After five years, with the lone exception of the single case last fall, I had been completely removed from the DEA life. Not once had I even taken part in a local grassroots search for a missing hiker. The only time I had smelled so much as marijuana on some teenagers at Arby's after a football game I deliberately got up and walked out.

Despite all that, it was almost alarming how fast many of my previous instincts returned to me.

"Scared the hell out of her," Diaz said. "By the time she got to the park ranger station she was a complete mess, barely able to keep herself together."

"She survived?" I asked, cutting her off, putting more force onto the question than intended.

Still, that didn't mean it was wrong. In my experience, people like those she was describing had a wanton disregard for human life and never, ever left survivors.

"Mhmm," Diaz said, the expression on her face letting me know she thought the exact same thing. "The desert is a national park, which meant once the ranger got her calmed down enough to tell him what happened-"

"Immediately turfed her to the FBI," I finished, knowing all too well how jurisdiction worked on federal lands.

Once upon a time I had used such stipulations to the fullest of my abilities. Now, I had to wave and be friendly whenever I saw the federal agent assigned to Yellowstone poking about.

"Yeah," Diaz said. "They talked to her yesterday morning. Long story short, they got a full briefing from her, piled her into one of their patented black sedans, and drove her straight down to me."

For a moment I almost smirked at her dig about the FBI's choice of vehicles. Rare was the day that a DEA agent didn't take an opportunity to undercut the bureau when they had the chance, almost every last one of us believing in the acronym *Famous But Ignorant.*

"So she arrived on your doorstep yesterday," I prompted, lifting my coffee to take another drink. No longer having the benefit of being piping hot it tasted close to battery acid, but still I took it down anyway.

"By that point she was a real wreck," Diaz replied. "Had been shuffled through three different branches of law enforcement, all original fears she had gone."

"So by the time she got to you she was just flat out pissed."

"Beyond," Diaz said, nodding her head. "Gave us the usual shtick about wishing she'd never said anything, that she hadn't seen that much, the whole nine."

My head rocked back and forward a couple inches, knowing exactly what she was referring to. On average, at least a third of witnesses we encountered ended up saying something similar.

"Okay," I repeated, "so what did she see? I'm guessing out in the desert, middle of the night, had to have either been people or drugs that were being traded. Since they sent her to you instead of INS, I'm assuming the latter."

For the first time since arriving, Diaz unbuttoned the front of her overcoat. She stood for a moment and shrugged it down off her shoulders, letting it fall back across the chair. Beneath it she wore black slacks and a blue v-neck sweater, no jewelry visible of any kind.

"Not exactly," she said, lowering herself back into the chair. "Remember I mentioned her being a photographer?"

"Yeah," I said, already sensing where this might be going.

"Well, for whatever reason she decided to snap a few shots before she left."

I kept the coffee cup in my right hand as I raised my left toward my brow. My eyes slid shut as I pushed my fingers back through my hair, feeling the dampness that was beginning to cross my forehead.

"Why?" I whispered. "Why would she do that?"

"Beats the hell out of me," Diaz said across from me, "but at the moment I'm not especially complaining."

The last comment was deliberately left as a bread crumb for me.

Fortunately for her I was too vested in the story, even if I had no idea how or why I fit into it, not to press for more details.

"She saw the transaction?" I asked.

"No," Diaz replied, "she saw what was supposed to be a transaction before they spotted her."

A sharp pang of tension rippled through my stomach. The wind slid from my lungs as I imagined this young girl in the desert being spotted, who-knows-what peering back at her through the dark.

Even knowing how the story ended, that the girl did survive, did nothing to ease the apprehension roiling within.

"And she still made it out?"

Diaz raised her eyebrows, nodding slightly in explanation. "The first couple muzzle flashes she actually got on film. Wasn't until the damn bullets starting hitting the sand nearby that she even realized what was going on."

Air wheezed between my teeth as I drew in a sharp breath, my face twisted up just slightly, imagining the scene in my head. Never had I seen the girl or the location Diaz had described. I had no idea who was on the other side or how many there were.

Still, I could depict the entire affair in my mind with vivid clarity, imagining her face as the reality of the situation set in.

"So she's not terribly bright, but she's lucky as hell," I whispered.

"Oh, she's pretty damn bright," Diaz corrected, raising her eyebrows in an expression I didn't pretend to understand. With her left hand she waved off the question on my face and said, "Obviously the photos aren't all-encompassing, and she didn't exactly stick around to get the full interaction, but what she got puts together a pretty complete scenario."

For a moment I remained silent, pondering what little I already knew. Just based on the information she had shared, it was clear that a mountain load of questions and investigating remained to be done.

At the same time, if I was reading things correctly, she had just been handed a major player in the drug trade along the border. While that location would never be used again, there were photos and a breathing witness. Years removed or not, I didn't have to have a picture painted for me to know how monumental that could be.

What I still didn't have the slightest idea of was how I fit into any of it.

"Understanding that we could discuss this all afternoon," I opened, holding up the cup in my hand, "and believe me, we have half a container of grounds left out there, I'm happy to do so."

The small attempt at levity earned me a half smile from Diaz, but nothing more.

"But out of respect to your time and the enormity of the situation you're now describing, what role do I play in any of this? Everything sounds very above board right now, so you have no need for anything covert.

"My time in the region was spent mostly working international, so I'm afraid I don't have much to offer on the way of insight."

Even as I outlined the various possible scenarios, I knew neither one could be why she had made the trip north. Those types of things could be ascertained with a simple phone call.

A moment passed as Diaz stared back at me, seeming to decipher my exact train of thought. She remained silent until she had worked out exactly what I was thinking before pushing forward, tailoring her response in the best way possible.

Just as I had spent the entire drive down wondering what drew her north, I'm sure she had spent the entire trip up thinking of the best way to answer the question I had just posed.

"Before sending her our way, the FBI ran her pictures through their database," Diaz said. "One of them came back with a positive ID on a Felipe Soto, low-level guy that did a nickel at MCC for running drugs a few years ago."

MCC was the Metropolitan Correctional Center outside of San Diego. It was a federal facility, meaning the offense must have been as well, most likely involving international exchange.

The time frame also meant that while the name meant nothing to me, it was possible our paths had crossed.

"Who was he affiliated with?"

"Don't know," Diaz replied. "He was apprehended alone the first time, never turned on anyone despite whatever he was offered."

I nodded, the corners of my mouth turning downward. "If you're here asking about him, I'm sorry I don't remember. Besides, I'm sure you have better access to those files than I ever did."

"No," Diaz said, shaking her head. "I'm here about the girl."

For the first time since our discussion began, the name returned to my mind, though I still had no idea how we were tied together. "Lake Pawlak."

Twice Diaz opened her mouth to say something, closing it before any words came out. From the look on her face it was clear this was the big ending, the final crescendo she was here to deliver, though she still wasn't quite certain how to do it.

"She needs protection," Diaz finally said, blurting the words out without a trace of eloquence. "She's threatening to walk. I can't hold her against her will, but she is a witness. To who or what we really don't have any idea yet."

"Which means there are no charges."

"And without charges, we can't put her in witness protection," Diaz finished.

My initial reaction was to chuckle. Not at the situation, which was beyond harrowing for all involved, but at my own stupidity.

There were only a handful of reasons why Diaz would go to the time and financial expense of coming to see me in person. One was because she feared a mole in her department. After sniffing one out the previous fall, I was willing to bet that was certainly not an issue.

The other was because she wanted as little physical trail between the two of us as possible. If this arrangement came to pass, the threads connecting our respective sides needed to be microscopic, if not non-existent.

"You'll be considered a special consultant again," Diaz said, "the only difference being we will compensate you handsomely for the effort."

This time I didn't hold back the laugh, a short, sharp sound that seemed to echo through the empty building.

"That's not what I'm concerned with," I said, shaking my head just slightly. I tilted my cup to look down at the last dregs of coffee before placing it on the desk and lacing my fingers before me.

There was so much I still didn't know that it was laughable. If we were to try and hash out every last answer we would be here all after-noon and well into the night, no doubt constructing even more questions we had no possible way of answering yet.

None of that really mattered though. What mattered was the most fundamental tenant of the entire situation, the reason that had caused Diaz to climb into a car and make the trek.

After that, if the answer was sufficient, everything else would find a way to work itself out.

"Why me?"

I had a pretty good inkling what the answer might be, but I still had to ask the question. Not in some form of misguided attempt at stroking my ego, and certainly not just to make her say the words out loud.

If what I was hearing was correct, and my interpretation of it accurate as well, right now somewhere a thousand miles south of us sat a young woman in a room. Someone that had done nothing wrong, that was only working to advance her career, to maximize the potential she'd been born with. In doing so she had seen something she shouldn't, and people that weren't worth half what she was could be circling in, willing to snuff her out for the sole purpose of furthering their own lecherous enterprise.

The thought alone was enough to make my skin crawl. It permeated through every fiber of my being, nerve endings tingling, sweat forming a film over my skin.

A young woman's life was in danger, and I was being asked to help keep her alive.

Across from me Diaz stared back, her lips pursed slightly. At a glance I couldn't tell if the pose was from considering the answer to my question or in surprise at my asking it, but either way didn't much matter.

I needed to know her response before the conversation went another word further.

The silence between us lasted a moment, both sides of the desk sizing up the other, considering the proposition that was on the table.

"Last fall," she began, the look on her face relaying she was choosing her words carefully, "everything that happened – San Diego, Mexico, Russia – was that you, or was that the situation?"

She cut herself off there, choosing not to explain any further. There was no need to, both of us understanding exactly what she meant.

The impassive look on my face remained as I met her gaze, the same burning sensation still roiling through my body. Hundreds of times since then I had asked myself that very same question, almost always coming back to the same conclusion.

"Yes."

The left corner of Diaz's mouth turned up just slightly, enough that I knew the answer was the correct one, the exact thing she antici- pated from me.

"*That's* why you."

Chapter Eleven

Twenty-eight hours had passed. Every last one of them Thiago Ruiz had spent alternating between pacing the front room of his home and checking his messages. Twice in that span Hector had called seeking an update, his voice relaying he was just as agitated with the situation.

Otherwise there had been no real communication with anybody in the organization, everyone waiting to hear back from the head man before making a move.

At exactly noon on the second day after the incident, a knock sounded at the front door. Two distinct beats, they came in low and even, stopping Thiago in his tracks across the threadbare carpet of his front living room.

Despite his nerves already being stretched taut, he felt anxiety ratchet a bit higher within him as he stared at the solid wooden door painted white across the room. For a moment he stood, making no movement at all, before taking one quick step to the coffee table and snatching up his Luger.

Bending his arm at the elbow, he extended the barrel of the gun toward the ceiling and looped out wide away from the door. He pressed his cheek against the outside wall of the house and rose onto his toes, gaining just enough perspective to see out through the curtains of the front window.

There, parked on the curb, sat a familiar Lexus SUV. The glossy black finish was polished to a mirrored shine and the wheels were void of any debris, the windows tinted as dark as the law would allow.

More than once Thiago had heard Molina describe it as a car unique enough to be recognizable without drawing attention.

Lowering himself from his toes, Thiago deposited the gun back on the coffee table and made his way to the front door. He didn't bother to check the peephole before swinging it open and standing off to the side.

"Please, come in."

The first person to pass through was Arturo Molina, dressed in exactly the same manner he was every time Thiago saw him. Regardless of time or temperature he was always adorned in a black suit, slacks and jacket both. Beneath it he wore a white shirt, on his feet polished black wingtips.

The only thing that ever varied at all was what he wore around his neck, the options limited to a solid black tie or nothing at all.

On this particular morning he had opted for the latter, the top two buttons undone.

Second in line behind him was Jasmine, his newest assistant. Appearing just a couple of years above twenty, she wore a form-fitting black tube dress and three-inch heels, the shoes giving her difficulty on the uneven carpet underfoot.

She was the sixth such woman to occupy the position since Thiago had come into contact with Molina, fitting the exact specifications the old man required. She was young and beautiful, knew to keep her mouth shut at all times. Some day she would turn thirty, at which point she would be let go, replaced with another just like her.

As Thiago had long since learned, appearances went a long way with Molina.

The final person to step inside was Declan, private security for Molina wherever he went, the internal counterpart to Thiago on the outside. A former soldier with the South African National Defence

Force, his posture and build still strongly hinted at the man that had received an entire chest's worth of medals in his previous career.

Standing three inches shorter than Thiago's six feet, he carried on extra ten pounds on his frame. His blonde hair was cropped close to his skull, his face void of any stubble. Bright blue eyes peered out from a sloped face, a deep tan splashed across his skin.

Thiago closed the door behind Declan without checking for anybody else, knowing the only other person to ever travel with the group was the driver, who would stay with the car. Once the door was shut he turned to find Molina already situated on his sofa, Declan and Jasmine standing together on the far side of the room.

Between them all sat the coffee table, the Luger in plain sight for everybody to see.

"I didn't know you had returned," Thiago said, focusing his entire attention on Molina, ignoring the other two. "I would have met you at the house."

Three times a year Molina was forced to take his wife on a trip, the down payment for her looking the other way on everything else that he partook in for both business and pleasure. This one had been on the books for months, nobody having any reason to believe his absence would cause even the slightest problem.

The old man raised a hand to dismiss the comment, his skin dotted with sun spots. "Nonsense, *mijo*," he said, his oversized jowls shaking as he spoke. "After the trip, I needed to get out for a bit, stretch my legs."

Thiago knew the words were code for needing a break from his wife, though he gave no indication to such.

"What happened?" Molina asked, a simple inquiry, two words and nothing more.

Every moment of the previous day and a half Thiago had spent trying to make sense of what took place.

As far as he could tell Felipe and Dante were just as surprised by what happened as he was. The location was too remote for encountering someone to have been coincidence. The spotlight sniffing out a camera lens had only confirmed that.

They were being watched, though by who or for what purpose was anybody's guess.

"We arrived at the spot a few minutes early," Thiago said. "This time we were down in Anza-Borrego, the desert bowl we've used a half dozen times."

On the couch Molina nodded, his stiffly oiled hair not budging with the movement.

"They showed a few minutes later, but instead of climbing out like usual they sat in the cab for a good while."

"How long's a good while?" Molina interjected.

"Five minutes or more," Thiago replied. "Long enough Hector and I both had our suspicions raised."

From the corner of his eye Thiago could see Jasmine shift, trying to balance on her heels.

"Once they finally emerged, Felipe said they had caught a glimpse of something on the drive in," Thiago said. "Claimed they were staying inside to keep the interior light from coming on while they scoped the surrounding area."

A momentary cloud seemed to pass over Molina's face, a frown accentuating the deep parentheses on either side of his mouth. "Did you see anything when you drove in?"

"Nothing," Thiago said. He felt his pulse rise a fraction of an inch, knowing that whoever was out there had gotten past him. There was no reason to believe anybody was watching them, no call for him to have scoured every inch of the surrounding desert, but the fact remained that it was his job to ensure things didn't come to that.

"Didn't matter though," Thiago said. "I called off the transaction right then, told Felipe to get in his truck and fire up his spotlight."

He paused for a split second, long enough to allow his employer to admonish him in any way if necessary. Stopping the deal mid-stride had been his call entirely. It was the first time he had ever done something like that, acting from pure reflex, no forethought applied.

No comment came.

"He turned the spotlight on high while the rest of us readied our weapons," Thiago continued. "Took less than a minute before a glass winked back at us."

The old man grunted once, his eyes narrowing just slightly. "Scope?"

"No," Thiago replied, shaking his head. "No shots were fired. It was just a quick flash, but I got the impression it was a camera lens. Singular, definitely not binoculars."

The look of concern grew deeper on Molina's face. He glanced over to his support team, Declan remaining stony while Jasmine seemed to still be preoccupied with balancing herself on the platform heels.

"What did you do?"

"We emptied every round we had," Thiago said. "Over a hundred shots between the three of us. Once we were all out of ammo I sent Felipe and Dante back home, Hector and I took off in pursuit."

There was no reaction of any kind as Molina waited for him to continue.

"By the time we crested the ridge there was nothing left but a dust cloud," Thiago said. "Not even brake lights were visible."

How the patriarch of the organization would act to any new situation was never a given. The vast majority of the time he hid behind an impassive visage, not allowing anybody to see his thoughts.

On occasion though, especially when dealing with staff, he allowed his inner feelings to bubble upward. Only twice had they ever been directed at Thiago, though in retrospect both were deserved.

Neither was very pretty.

"Just one person?" Molina whispered.

"Yes," Thiago said, his entire being still pulled into a half-cringe. "We stayed until daylight, scoured the entire area. No other tracks of any kind, vehicle or human."

"Law enforcement?"

Thiago had asked himself the same question dozens of times throughout his pacing. He couldn't imagine any reputable group, state or federal, sending a single person with a camera out into the desert.

Even less though could he imagine a solo private individual being foolish enough to do so.

"I don't think so."

Silence fell over the room as Thiago kept his arms by his side, fighting the urge to cross his arms as he stood and waited. He knew the stance would appear imposing, something Molina did not abide by.

Instead he tapped his fingertips against the outside of his thighs, alternating a quick glance between Declan and Jasmine and Molina on the couch.

Ignoring everyone around him, Molina sat and stared straight ahead for several long moments, digesting everything that had just been shared.

"Goose and I, we've been doing business a while now," he finally said, keeping his focus on the table before him. "This venture in particular for what, almost three years?"

The number was actually four years, though Thiago remained silent.

"Always," he said," always we have abided by the old ways." He paused, shifting his attention up to Thiago. "Honest reaction, do you think he had anything to do with this?"

Once more Thiago thought back to two nights before. The handling of the mules was less than optimal, but they were all present and accounted for. Remaining in the truck had been unusual, but had turned out to be the right call.

More than anything though, the surprise each man wore, both at his decision to forego the exchange and to finding someone watching, was genuine.

"If there was something going on," Thiago said, "it was occurring a lot higher up the ladder than Felipe and Dante. That much I know for sure."

There was no reaction at all from the old man for a moment, his features going slack as he stared at Thiago. He remained that way, borderline meditative, for a moment before stating, "And if they weren't made aware, it's very unlikely that anything originated on their side."

Thiago agreed with the statement, though he gave no indication either way. Making such decisions was the purview of Molina exclusively, something he was more than adept at.

When Thiago first met him, the old man would have burned all of

Los Angeles to the ground at the mention of a mishap. The fact that he was now willing to be a bit more methodical spoke volumes to how far he and the business had both evolved over time.

"Allow me to reach out," Molina said. "There are procedures, proper channels, for handling this sort of thing."

Thiago nodded, having been an accessory to the life for long enough to know how matters were conducted. "In the meantime?"

"In the meantime, nothing," Molina said. "You and Hector, you boys did a good job. Go about your business, just don't worry about any runs for a while."

Again Thiago nodded, having expected that at the very least. He waited a full beat to make sure Molina was finished before taking a half step forward and nodding to the blue lunch sack sitting on the coffee table beside the Luger.

"There's something else. Might change how you want to proceed."

Chapter Twelve

W hen Diaz called the day before, I had gotten the distinct impression I might be gone longer than just the drive down to West Yellowstone to meet with her. Anything important enough to drag her north so early in the spring most likely also carried with it an urgency that would last more than a few hours.

Sensing that, I packed a duffel bag for the trip. In addition to the jeans, boots, long sleeve Henley and flannel I already wore I brought along a second pair of jeans and a pair of cargo pants. For my upper half I stowed a second flannel, a long sleeve Dri-fit, and a trio of non-descript t-shirts, just in case I had to head south in a hurry.

Since no mention of being brought back into the fray was made on the phone I didn't bother with anything more formal. I didn't want to be presumptive about the reason for the impromptu visit and certainly didn't want to have to put on a tie unless I absolutely had to.

In addition to the clothes I brought a toiletry kit and my MK 3 knife, one of the few holdovers from my life in the navy. No additional weapons of any kind made the cut. If a gun was needed for anything that might lie ahead, I knew Diaz would cover it, just as she had in the past.

I was also sure neither one of us wanted the potential of

answering a bunch of questions about a shooting from a private weapon, licensed or not.

The bag was wedged into the bed of my truck as Diaz and I crested over the Laguna Mountains. Tucked in tight beside it was a small overnight bag Diaz had brought up with her. Both were strapped down with nylon bungee cords, held in place in an otherwise empty truck bed.

The decision for us to drive was equal parts logic and utilitarian. There was still a great deal of intel I needed from her before getting on-site, the kind of thing we wouldn't be able to do while crammed into adjacent seats on a plane and wouldn't want to do in front of Lake.

We both knew it was important that I walk in completely up to speed, able to jump right in to any pertinent conversations if for no other reason than to put the girl at ease. More than once we had each encountered flighty witnesses before, knowing how vital their testimony could be and how easily it could be dissuaded.

The second part of our decision was to further the blind trail Diaz had already started to lay out. The first thing we did after leaving my office was drive her rental to Bozeman, returning it at the airport counter. From there we had tracked west to Butte before jumping onto I-15 and going straight south in my truck, completely invisible from anybody that might be watching.

What gas and supplies we needed we bought with cash. If we needed to use the restroom, we used out-of-the-way rest stops.

The first six hours I drove, taking us into Salt Lake City as Diaz painstakingly went through everything she knew. The sum total to that point was that Felipe Soto, a known drug runner, had been present at a clandestine desert meeting. A young photographer just happened to be nearby when the meeting took place, acting against better judgment and taking some pictures of the entire affair.

Doing so had pissed off Soto and his cohorts enough that they not only spotlighted her, but unloaded every bullet they had trying to bring her down. Who they worked for or the full extent of what they were meeting about was anybody's guess, though the supposition of a drug deal was strong enough to send it straight to the DEA.

I wished I could say the entire thing seemed a fool's errand. Without knowing who Soto or the other men were affiliated with, there wasn't much chance at apprehending anyone. No crimes had actually been witnessed, making any testimony the girl provided just a piece of a much larger tale, not the entire story itself.

At the same time, there was a reason those men had been meeting in the middle of the night. People that are just looking to swap recipes didn't drive out into the desert to do so, and they damned sure didn't wait until cover of darkness.

I could tell by the tension rolling off of Diaz that she too sensed how tenuous the entire thing was, but the truth was I had gone after leads just as ethereal over the years. We all had, with the arrests to justify them.

That's what made our division the best at what we did.

Just outside of Salt Lake City I relinquished the wheel, staring out into the darkness for over an hour, processing what I knew. Once I was content I had a reasonable, if not patchwork, framework for everything, I stayed up a few minutes longer to make sure Diaz was okay behind the wheel before drifting off.

A few miles outside of Henderson, Nevada, we again traded places, Diaz this time falling fast asleep as I took us the rest of the way in.

In total the trip took fifteen hours, fourteen accounting for the hour of time difference we gained en route. The sun was just rising in the east as we crested over the Lagunas and headed toward the DEA Southwest Headquarters, the blinding light smashing into my tailgate and sending a long shadow over the ground before us.

I allowed Diaz to rack out as long as possible, waking her with a gentle shake ten minutes before we arrived. One moment her eyes were closed, her body completely powered down as she slumped against the window. The next she was awake and alert, ready to start the new day.

Impressive.

Neither of us said a word as I maneuvered away from the freeway, the traffic beginning to thicken the closer we got to civilization.

Behind us the sun rose a touch higher in the sky, the clock on the dash stating it was half past eight in the morning.

Using the thumb and forefinger of my left hand, I rubbed a bit of crust from the corners of my eyes as I directed the truck over a two-lane road. Operating from memory, I came upon the building that had served as my employer for years, not one thing having changed in the time since.

A single story tall, it was made entirely from red brick, practically screaming government bureaucracy. At a glance the place could have housed a DMV or schoolchildren, the shrubs out front manicured into uniform lines and the gravel beds raked as neat as a Japanese garden.

Eschewing the visitor stalls out front, I pulled into the side lot and slid into a spot along the back row. Compared to the myriad of various sedans parked in tight rows my aging rig was an eyesore, though neither of us said a word as we climbed out.

Most likely, the truck wouldn't be there long anyway.

I left my bag in the bed, grabbing up Diaz's and handing it across to her as we headed toward the front door, matching each other in stride. We both drew our faces tight as we went, wearing grim expressions as we passed inside. A blast of warm air pulled at my hair and beard as we walked under the vents and out onto the foyer.

Despite the early hour, a large handful of agents were on hand. Several had already discarded their jackets for the day, their sleeves rolled to mid-forearm. For a moment they all paused as we entered, openly staring.

At which one of us was anybody's guess, though I felt reasonably certain nobody was that surprised to see Diaz show up.

It was exactly the same response I had gotten upon arrival six months prior.

Ignoring every last one of them Diaz walked to the front desk, a young blonde woman with a wide headband holding her hair back seated behind it. Her eyes grew wide as Diaz approached, glancing from her to me and back again.

"Good morning, Agent Diaz. We didn't know you would be back so soon."

Diaz completely ignored the salutation, walking right up to the desk and tapping at it with the nail of her right index finger. "Where's the girl?"

"Um, she, uh, is back in the sleeping quarters right now with Agent Lefranc."

"Get them both to the conference room," Diaz said, already turning back toward me. "Now."

Chapter Thirteen

The name was entered simply as Paul in Thiago's cellphone. For the entire time he had known him it was Paulie, harkening back to a previous time when he was just a low-level kid the organization occasionally used as a messenger.

To the rest of the world, he was known as LAPD detective Paulo Gomez.

Idling up to the curb on San Fernando Road, Thiago parked his truck in a yellow loading zone and left the engine idling. On the sidewalk beside him an older Asian man carrying boxes of onions into his ramen shop cast a sideways look his way, letting a sneer raise one side of his nose. Otherwise nobody glanced his direction as he sat behind the wheel and stared up at the gleaming glass and steel structure one block down from where he sat.

By all accounts, the Northeast Precinct of the East Hollywood Police Department was one of the more cherry assignments in the entire LAPD system. Tucked away on the northern edge of the city, it was miles from the urban warfare of Compton or Inglewood, a distinction that applied to more than just geographical distance.

Serving the posh surrounding neighborhoods of Echo Park, Silver Lake, and the like, it was the kind of place where a detective was as likely to be called to the home of a celebrity for a run-in with the paparazzi as an actual murder scene.

Lifting his iPhone from the seat beside him, Thiago held the black plastic device to his lips and said, "Call Paulie."

Despite his lilting accent the phone dialed straightaway, a shrill ring sounding out three times, echoing through the cab of the truck.

"Hello?" Gomez answered, his voice pinched and low.

Thiago could see him on the other end, somewhere inside the building across the street, hunkered down behind his desk, trying to cover the screen of his phone.

"Can you talk?" Thiago asked.

"Hey, honey," Gomez replied, raising his voice a tiny bit. "Sure, I can do an early lunch. Say, meet in ten at our favorite spot?"

A grunt was Thiago's only response as he cut off the call. The Asian man on the sidewalk continued to glare as he dropped the gearshift into drive and eased back into traffic.

Rolling slowly, he made his way past the police station and hooked a right, going three blocks before cutting a sharp left into a dog park. There he parked, remaining behind the wheel. He left the engine on, cool air blasting through the vents, as he watched a middle-aged woman slowly walk about the deserted park area, two Shih Tzu's circling her feet, yipping loudly.

His face remained impassive as he watched the diminutive woman try to corral the rambunctious animals, her best efforts falling short as they continued running around her.

Exactly ten minutes after ending the call, Gomez appeared on the opposite side of the park. He moved with both hands shoved into the front pockets of his slacks, the sleeves of his suit coat bunched up around his wrists. His entire body was pitched forward as he walked, staring intently at the ground, moving at a speed that was bound to draw attention from anyone nearby.

A frown tugged at Thiago's mouth as he watched him go around the perimeter of the park and climb into the passenger seat.

"Hey," he said, bouncing himself onto the woven seat cover and slamming the door shut behind him. The move was done with enough percussive force to rock the entire truck, the old woman glancing up from her dogs at the sound.

"Not exactly covert, are you?" Thiago asked, letting his displeasure show in his voice.

Beside him Gomez opened his mouth to respond before thinking better of it. He again cast his eyes downward and said only, "Sorry."

Ten years Thiago's junior, Gomez had already lost the majority of his hair. What remained was cut short and pushed to the side, his skin tone olive. A pair of wire-rimmed glasses rested on the edge of his nose, a new addition since their last encounter.

What interested Thiago most though was the series of faint scars on the side of his neck, the skin puckered just slightly, perceptible only to those looking for it.

Reclined behind the wheel, Thiago reached out with his right hand and ran a finger down the dimpled skin. "Hey, I remember what that used to say."

At the touch of his finger Gomez jerked away, his entire upper body pressing itself against the passenger door. A look of mortification passed over his face, as if he might bolt out of the truck at any moment, though he remained motionless, just as Thiago knew he would.

The scar was a reminder of a previous life, one that Gomez had left behind after watching his best friend get killed in a drive by.

Despite being a man that had amassed his fortune through nefarious means, Arturo Molina was not one to suffer street gangs. The entire enterprise he found counterproductive and foolish, a waste of human and financial capital.

Twelve years prior, Gomez had come to Molina. He had pledged to leave the street gang behind, but feared for his life should he try to get out. The decision to take the young man in was not made lightly, earmarked with the expectation of eternal allegiance, regardless where his life took him.

The fact that his path had landed him as a police detective was a stroke of good luck the organization was all too happy to occasionally lean on.

"Yes," Gomez said. "Mr. Molina did me a great service. I am in his debt."

The words brought a smile to Thiago's face, the exact thing he had been hoping to hear. "That's right, you do."

Raising his wrist, Paul pushed back the sleeve on his suit coat. "I am sorry, but I am running on a tight schedule."

The smile fell away as Thiago cocked his head to look across at the younger man. "I know. I just saw you practically sprint over here. If anybody was watching at the precinct, they would have smelled suspicion on you from a mile away."

The corners of Gomez's nostrils flared just slightly as he pushed a long sigh out through his nose. "Is there something I can help you with today, Mr. Ruiz?"

It was clear from the tone that Thiago was already working the kid's last nerve. For a moment or two the notion had been a bit amusing, but now it was time to move forward.

His reason for being here was certainly no joking matter.

"I need an address."

"For?" Gomez asked, not looking over, not showing the least bit of surprise at the statement.

"Lake Pawlak," Thiago said, picturing the name scrawled across the bottom of the blue lunch sack in magic marker.

A look of confusion passed over Gomez's face as he glanced across at Thiago. "Is that a person or a place?"

"A person," Thiago said. "P-A-W-L-A-K."

Gomez's face tightened just a bit as his gaze shifted, committing the name to memory. Both men were well aware that Molina had a rule about putting as little in writing as possible, a maxim that had served both sides well over the years.

Thiago watched as an internal debate took place, the evidence of it apparent on Gomez's features. He knew from previous experiences that the man wanted to ask what they had done, wanted to beseech him not to hurt anybody, but that he wouldn't.

The last time he had done so hadn't ended well for him.

"Just an address?" Gomez asked.

"Just an address," Thiago confirmed.

Another moment passed as Gomez pressed his lips tight together and stared out through the windshield. In the dog park before them the woman had finally managed to wrangle her small critters, pulling them toward the gate in the far corner. Overhead the sun shined down brightly, illuminating the small park, just another bucolic scene in what could be almost any city in the country.

"Give me until close of business," Gomez finally said, jerking his door open and disappearing without another word.

Chapter Fourteen

"Anything else I should know before we go in there?" I asked, stopping just outside the conference room door, my tone lowered. Inside we could hear voices, none of them sounding particularly happy to be there.

Diaz turned toward the sound drifting out and gave me a grim look, offering only a quick shake of her head. "Good luck."

The sentiment did little to quell my concerns as we stepped inside, Diaz leading the way. Upon our arrival both people in the room fell silent, staring our direction.

The space was arranged exactly the same as it had been six months prior, a mirror image of what it had been five years before when I was still under active employment. In total, the room measured almost twenty feet in length, the bulk of it filled by a long oval table. Constructed from some dark wood - cherry, perhaps - it was polished to a mirrored sheen, the overhead light reflecting off of it. Arranged around it on either side were a dozen chairs, high-backed and covered in burgundy leather.

Occupying a single one on the left side of the table was a man a few years older than me. His brown hair was shorn down and starting to recede at the corners, the first strands of grey beginning to show at the temples. The dark suit he wore was already rumpled despite the hour and his eyes were both red-rimmed.

"Agent Lefranc, Hawk," Diaz said, taking charge of the room without waiting for invitation. "Hawk, agent Lefranc."

I nodded at the introduction, choosing to remain near the head of the table. At this point I didn't want to be seen taking either side in what was clearly a standoff.

Lefranc returned the nod, but remained silent.

"And this," Diaz said, motioning toward the girl sitting opposite Lefranc, "is Lake Pawlak."

When Diaz had first mentioned a *young girl* was potentially in danger, I had envisioned in my mind a petite, mousy thing staring out at the world through oversized doe eyes. Why that was I'm not sure, perhaps based on societal conditioning, maybe even a tiny bit of unfortunate misogyny on my part.

What sat before me did not fit that image. At all.

From the way she was slouched in her chair, my best guess at a height was somewhere in the five-eight to five-ten range. That put her close to a half foot shorter than me, though still quite tall for a woman.

Dressed in khaki cargo pants and a short-sleeved navy blue t-shirt, the bulk of her arms were bare, displaying a vibrant array of tattoos covering most of the available space on her left arm. At a quick glance, I could see a pair of lips and tongue on her forearm that resembled the emblem of the Rolling Stones and a panda covering most of her bicep.

Not a trace of anything appearing satanic or gang related, though from a distance I couldn't get a great view.

A small stud sparkled from her nose as she turned to look at me, the sneer she'd been giving Lefranc still visible. Framing it was a head of blonde hair, thick stripes dyed pink on either side of her face.

Diaz had said repeatedly she was a photographer. I never would have guessed her appearance to be as extreme as it was, though I should have reasoned that it would be closer to this than the school-marm I was envisioning.

I definitely now understood what Diaz's comment about her being bright meant.

"What the hell?" she asked, her eyes widening as she looked me up and down, not making any attempt to hide the assessment.

"Likewise," I said, remaining in place. I stepped forward and gripped the top of the chair back in front of me, fighting the urge to walk over and shake her hand.

For the time being I needed to establish boundaries. She had clearly spent the last couple of days thrashing about, the look of Lefranc making it clear which side was winning. Right now I needed to bypass cordiality for professionalism, setting the tone for the rest of our time together, no matter how counterintuitive it might seem.

"Jeremiah Tate," I said, keeping my voice even, without a trace of warmth. "Call me Hawk."

Again she ran her gaze the length of me. "You don't look like a Hawk. More like Jesus Christ."

I ignored the comment entirely. It wasn't the first I'd heard over the years regarding my winter grooming habits.

"Hawk is a former agent of ours," Diaz said, again taking control of the conversation. "And is still one of the very best at what he does. Until we have a chance to investigate what you saw and determine how much - if any - danger you are in, you will be staying with him at all times."

In a flash Lake was on her feet, confirming my initial assessment of her height. She snapped upright and slapped her boots against the floor, her knees hitting the front edge of her seat so hard it was sent spiraling behind her. Leaning forward she smacked her palms against the table top, the sound echoing through the room, causing Lefranc to flinch across from her.

"No. No way in hell. Not happening."

Diaz and I both waited in silence. We'd seen enough of these tantrums before to know more was coming.

"I am a citizen," she said. "I have rights!"

It was all I could do not to roll my eyes, hearing her hit the familiar high notes.

"You've already kept me here two days," she said. "Forced me to wear the same smelly clothes, to have to put up with buffoons like this guy."

As she spoke she swung a finger across the table, Lefranc looking aghast as she did so.

"Miss Pawlak," Diaz said, raising her voice to be heard over the yelling, trying to stem the outburst before it really gained momentum. "I am sorry, but while we investigate, we need to ensure your safety."

"Oh, right," Lake replied, nodding bitterly, "to protect your case."

"And to protect you," Diaz said. "You witnessed a rather unique encounter that ended with you being shot at. Do you think those people would hesitate one second to do it again?"

The incredulity on Lake's face wavered for just a moment, a clear response to being reminded that not too long ago live ammunition had been fired her way.

"They don't even know who I am," she countered. "I could go home right now and never hear one word from anybody."

Beside me Diaz opened her mouth to respond, but thought better of it. I could tell the conversation was one they must have had multiple times before she came to see me, not wanting to rehash it again.

"We just need time to investigate," Diaz said. "Once we do, we'll know if there is anything for you to fear or if we need you to testify."

Leaning forward over the table, a disgusted smile crossed Lake's face. She stared down at her own reflection and shook her head, muttering something indecipherable.

"Until then, we can't put you in witness protection," Diaz said, her patience clearly growing thin. "That leaves you with either staying here-"

"No," Lake snapped.

"Or going to a safe house."

"Hell no."

Halfway down the table Lefranc held out a hand toward her. He looked our way, displaying the sheer exhaustion he felt from being around her, and let the back of his hand slap down against the wood.

"See what I've been dealing with?" he said, clearly looking for some sympathy.

Neither of us humored him even the slightest bit.

"See what I've been dealing with?" Lake echoed, glaring across at him before looking up at us. She settled her glare on me and said, "Let me guess, Mr. Big Former Agent, you fall directly in line with them."

My face betrayed nothing as I stared at her a moment. In my periphery I could see Lefranc looking my way, almost pleading for someone to validate the troubles he was having. Beside me, Diaz remained motionless, allowing me the floor.

"Him," I said, nodding with my chin toward Lefranc, "no. Her, yes."

The answer seemed to strike a chord with Lake, giving her pause for a moment. She stood to full height and folded her arms across her chest, the hostility fading a bit from her features. "Meaning?"

"Meaning I'm not sure what he's been telling you, but I'm reasonably certain it's wrong," I said. There was no way to know if that was true, but just watching the man's behavior and complete lack of decorum made it a fairly safe assumption.

Watching him wilt into his chair upon hearing it only confirmed my supposition.

A flicker of a smile pulled up at the corner of her mouth. "So I don't have to cut my hair?"

The question seemed from far afield, something I was not expecting. I forced myself not to react as I digested it.

"No," I said. "For the same reason I didn't bother cutting mine before I got here. Like Agent Diaz said, we're not even certain there is a threat right now."

The smug smile on Lake's face grew a little larger as she looked over at Lefranc.

"Besides," I continued, pulling her attention back toward me, "what was the first thing you thought when I walked in here?"

The smile faded as she turned back my direction. "That you looked like Jesus Christ. Or maybe one of those guys from *Duck Dynasty*."

"And I thought you looked like Rainbow Brite."

I could tell the words surprised her, pulling the air from her lungs, leaving her not quite sure how to respond.

"But that's kind of the point," I said. "If anybody is out there and sees us, they'll be looking for Jesus and Rainbow. Right now we're nothing more than caricatures, reduced to our single most distinctive features.

"Later on, if we have to, it'll be that much easier to change our identity."

I was completely making things up on the fly. Diaz would recognize it instantly, but was too vested to ever call me on it. Lefranc was already too browbeaten to bother, which left only Lake to take the bait. If she could be convinced that I knew what I was doing, that I wasn't looking to be another wet blanket agent, then the odds of her playing along became that much better.

In truth, both she and Diaz were right. Keeping the girl alive was most important, but preserving the integrity of the case was a close second.

If a play as big as the one Diaz described to me the day before was happening, it could be paradigm shifting for the entire region.

Lake looked at me a long time, seemingly weighing everything she knew in her head. Option A was for her to stay where she was, going to battle with Lefranc in an unending duel. Option B was to go to a safe house and potentially have many more just like him watching over her.

Option C was taking her chances with me. Even in my current grizzled state, there was no way of denying how attractive my presence must have appeared.

"Do I have any other choices?" Lake asked, seemingly having run the list in her head and coming back with nothing she especially liked.

On my side Diaz started to respond, but I beat her to it.

"Death," I said. One simple word that snapped the stares of all three people in my direction. I paused a moment to let the word hang in the air before adding, "What happened the other night wasn't random and it won't go away. I'm sorry, and I'm not merely trying to use scare tactics here. That is the reality of your situation.

"Either you let us help you or you die."

The statement was brutal, but it was entirely true. I watched as it hit her center mass, her lips parting as her body expelled all the air in her lungs. Rotating her head at the neck, she stared down at the table in front of her, the hostility of earlier having fled entirely.

This was no doubt the girl that had first showed up at the ranger's station in Anza-Borrego two days ago. She was frightened and in need of help.

There was no way to know for sure what Lefranc and his team had done to bring about such a standoffish demeanor from her in the time since, but I needed it to melt away, fast.

The reminder of mortal danger has a way of doing just that.

"Where we will go?" she whispered.

"We'll be nearby," I said, "but nobody, not even these guys, will know where."

She nodded once, accepting the answer. "Can I stop by my house for a minute before we disappear?"

Chapter Fifteen

The entire wrap-up took less than ten minutes. Diaz dismissed Lefranc, much to the relief of every person in the room. Once it was just the three of us, we outlined everything that would occur in the ensuing days, both so Lake could hear it said aloud and so we both could reaffirm everything in our minds.

Much had been discussed on the drive down from Montana, most of it in the dead of night, with one or both of us not far removed from slumber.

The plan was for Lake and I to walk out through the front door, climb into my truck, and disappear. We would not leave the greater Los Angeles area, taking cover in the larger metropolis, never being more than three hours away, not accounting for traffic.

Beyond that we would not tell Diaz one thing about where we were going. Open phone communication could occur, but nobody from the office would be following us. I would ensure Lake stayed hidden and that we both stayed alive, allowing the DEA to conduct their investigation.

Twice a day on the eight's I would call Diaz so both sides could provide an update. If at any point it appeared our identities or location was under duress, I had the latitude to do whatever was necessary.

Two consecutive missed check-ins and the administration would send everything they had to find us.

The plan, as it were, had a great many gaps. Diaz and I both knew it, but more importantly knew there was nothing we could do to close all of them. Situations like these were just too fluid, with too many moving parts, many of which we didn't even know of yet, to hammer down every detail ahead of time.

I got the impression Lake picked up on that too as we were explaining things, though to her credit she didn't voice it.

Once we were done going through things, Diaz shook each of our hands. She provided me with a Glock 17, the larger of the two standard issue weapons used, designed for a man's grip, and enough ammunition to reenact Beirut. She also handed over a small box with a half dozen phones in it, all burn phones, the plastic covering still on them, to be used for the check-in calls.

Tucked away in the bottom of the box were two stacks of cash, all twenty dollar bills, both banded up tight, a thousand dollars each.

There was no way of knowing for sure how that much cash just came to be lying around, though I didn't press it.

Disappearing without it would be a prospect almost impossible to pull off.

An hour later we found ourselves halfway between San Diego and Los Angeles, the first signs for Irvine just beginning to show up. Having ducked the morning traffic coming out of San Diego we made good time headed north, taking the I-5 the entire way, before the sprawl of the larger city began to slow us down.

"So, Hawk?" Lake said, the first conversation of any kind between us since leaving. It was apparent as we climbed into my truck that she was less than sold on things, seeing my appearance and choice of automobile as an overarching indicator of what she could expect in the days to come.

"Yeah?"

"No," she said, her head turned to stare out the window, "that was the question. Hawk? How does one pick up a nickname like that? You have great eyesight or something?"

A hint of a smirk tugged at my features, rocking my head back an inch. "Not a nickname. I go by my middle name."

Her head turned a few inches toward me, a look of confusion on her features. "Your full name is Jeremiah Hawk Tate?"

"Hawkens," I corrected, changing lanes of traffic to get past a Matson shipping truck. I glanced over her direction and added, "My pop was a big *Jeremiah Johnson* fan."

Much like with Diaz when I first explained it to her, and most anybody outside the state of Montana, the look on her face told me she had no idea what I was referring to.

"It's a mountain man movie from the 70's," I said. "Robert Redford in his prime."

The look remained on her features, though I didn't bother to inquire if she knew who Redford was.

Some questions you just don't want to know the answer to.

"You don't look like a Hawk," Lake said. "A grizzly maybe, but not a Hawk."

I kept my attention aimed out the window, saying nothing. It was the third different moniker she had assigned to me in an hour and a half, all of them based on my appearance.

None were especially amusing, though I couldn't argue with any of them.

Still, I remained quiet. I'd certainly been called worse over the years.

Five miles of silence passed, my attention aimed straight out the front windshield, one hand looped over the wheel as I processed the coming days. This was my first stab at a protection detail, something I was only nominally qualified to do. I had been trained by the navy and the DEA both, the vast majority of that preparation spent on being the aggressor.

Keeping the opposition at bay wasn't an idea I was entirely sure I was comfortable with, though I reasoned at least I would have good insight into how they would act.

All I had to do was mount a credible defense.

My selection by Diaz showed a tremendous amount of faith in my skills, something I would do every last thing in my power to vindicate.

It also displayed the precarious position she found herself in, one she knew I would be able to identify with.

The justice system was designed for those that were or had been a direct asset to the apprehension of a criminal. The size of the catch often directly dictated the lengths to which the government was willing to go to help witnesses.

For someone like Lake Pawlak, they were in the proverbial gray area. At some point they may become a tremendous ally, but until then they were basically on their own.

"You know, I spent the last two days solid in that place," she said, pulling me from my thoughts.

I glanced over in her direction, not sure where the statement was going. "And? You hungry or something?"

She dismissed the question with a shake of her head, meeting my glance before again staring out the passenger window. "I heard a lot of whispering about you in there. Seemed once Diaz disappeared they all knew where she was headed."

The statement could be taken in several different ways. I remained silent, trusting she would fill in the blanks.

"All those things they were saying..." she began, her voice trailing off. Just from the sound of it I knew what she was alluding to, but still offered nothing to help her. "All that stuff true?"

There was no way of telling what had made its way around the office. Diaz had told me shortly after we met that most agents there were familiar with the murder of my family. It was tied to a case I was working and had led directly to my early retirement.

I'm certain even more people had heard what happened last fall, the way in which I had finally been able to exact revenge.

If she was alluding to any one of those things, I didn't especially want to get into it. If she wasn't, there was no way I wanted to prompt any further questioning.

"Aw, probably not," I said. "You know how things can get blown out of proportion after the fact."

"Diaz seems to think pretty highly of you."

I considered responding that the feeling was mutual, that Mia Diaz was a damn fine agent, but I refrained, choosing to remain silent.

"Anything ever go on with you guys?"

Had I not been expecting the question, I'm sure it would have caused anger to surge within me, bringing a flush of blood to my cheeks. Instead I remained completely calm, giving no outward sign.

Women, especially young ones, can be predictable at times.

"Absolutely not," I said. "And if anybody said as much, I want you to point them out to me next time we're there."

Lake raised a hand in silent apology as we bypassed the split for the 405, staying on I-5 North. She stayed motionless a moment, staring out at nothing, before realizing what was occurring and sitting up. She craned her neck to watch the green road signs passing by before extending her left index finger out across the cab of the truck.

"Hey, you forgot to turn. My place is in Huntington Beach."

My body clenched a tiny bit. Again I could foresee an explosion on the horizon, knowing it was just seconds away.

"We're not going to Huntington Beach." I kept my gaze aimed forward, seeing her head whip toward me in my periphery, feeling her angry glare on my skin.

"Why the hell not? You said this morning-"

"I said we would go to your house," I said, keeping my voice even, on the border of placating, "but I never said when."

Glancing over I could see fire flash behind her eyes, her face growing crimson, offset by the pink hair on either side of it. "What the-" she snapped, cutting herself off just short of the punch line. "What kind of shit is this?"

Already I could see what Diaz meant when she wished me luck, could understand the look on Lefranc's face as we walked into the conference room. How I handled the next five minutes could determine the rest of our time together, whether she would come to trust that I knew what I was doing or would continue throwing fits every time something didn't go her way.

"We will go to your house," I repeated, looking over at her. "Tomorrow morning. Right after rush hour, when the sun is full overhead. You have my word."

My response did nothing to quench the frustration on her face, her entire body turned to face me. "I didn't have to say anything, you know. I could have just gone home that night, never would have met you or Diaz or that dipshit Lefranc."

I let her vent, watching signs as we pushed forward. A handful began touting Disneyland and Angels Stadium of Anaheim, the freeway becoming clogged with scads of drivers all looking like they would rather be anywhere else in the world. Overhead the sun seemed to have lost some of its luster, a thick layer of smog hanging over the city.

"And who knows," Lake continued, undeterred by my lack of reaction, "I could be anywhere else right now. I could be down on the beach, or up in the mountains, or even back in the desert with my camera, which by the way, you guys stole from me."

"Dead," I said, seeing the sign I was looking for and drifting toward the exit, cars immediately fighting for the twelve free feet of space in our wake. "You'd be dead."

The statement cut her off mid-tirade, a finger raised before her as she prepared to continue. "What?"

"You would be dead," I said, turning to look her square in the face, making sure she saw how serious I was. "Trust me, no matter how clean you think your getaway was the other night, these guys have some lead on you."

Her eyes widened a bit as she stared at me, saying nothing.

"You might have dropped something, they might have gotten a glimpse of your license plate while you were leaving, they might have even been able to hack into the security camera at the Anza-Borrego guard station and pull your picture."

All color receded from her features as she stared at me, her body still perched on the front edge of the seat. I alternated glances between her and the road ahead, pushing two blocks off the freeway and following the directions posted on the blue signs along the road.

"They can do that?"

"You damn right," I said. "And if they can't, you can bet your ass they have someone in one of the police precincts on the payroll that can."

Her body seemed to wilt before my eyes, slumping back to lean on the seat.

"And don't think you could have just left the area," I added, "for all the same reasons. If somebody wants to find you bad enough, they will."

Ahead of me I could see our destination on the right, a square gleaming structure rising two dozen floors high. The hazy morning light refracted off of it as we approached, the mirrored images of the neighboring building reflecting from its surface.

"So then what good are you?" she asked, turning to face forward.

"I'm here to make sure Diaz finds them first," I said, turning off the roadway into the parking lot of the Marriott Anaheim. Swinging through the front gate I circled around to the concrete awning, pulling up behind a Buick Escalade being loaded by a trio of bellhops.

Shifting low in her seat, Lake looked up at the sign on the marquee above us. "This isn't exactly inconspicuous you know."

"I know," I replied. "That's the idea."

Jamming the gear shift up into park, I twisted behind the wheel and reached over the front seat, my fingers finding the nylon strap of the pouch I wanted. Hefting it straight upward I placed it on the seat between us, the top gaping open.

Unable to curb her curiosity, Lake used her thumb and forefinger to spread the top open a bit wider, glancing at the muddied trail cameras stowed inside. Confusion crossed her face as she studied them a moment before looking up at me.

"Come on," I said, "let's go set a trap."

Chapter Sixteen

"You sure we're good here?" Hector asked, leaning back behind the wheel to check the side mirror. He remained there, his body cocked at an angle, for a moment before returning to his normal position and staring into the rearview mirror.

Thiago blew a long sigh out through his nose, making sure it was loud enough to be heard, his point getting across.

The two of them had been sitting for over half an hour, staring at the small cottage five blocks in from Huntington Beach. So far in that time they had seen a handful of evening joggers getting in a quick run after work and a trio of older couples walking their pets, but nothing that resembled who they were looking for.

Three hours earlier Paulo Gomez had sent them an email containing the driver's license for Lake Pawlak. The name was unique enough to be the only one in the state, the picture displaying a blonde girl in her mid-twenties, her face narrow and pale. The stats on it listed her as five-nine and a hundred thirty five pounds, not needing glasses or corrective lenses.

The body of the email had indicated the given address on the license was no longer valid, a more recent listing coming up for her at the house they now sat outside of.

"I'm just saying," Hector began again, agitation plain in his voice.

"I know what you're just saying," Thiago snapped, cutting him off. "And I'm saying we're fine. Paulie called an hour ago and said he ran her through the system. Earlier today she booked herself a room at the Marriott in Anaheim."

Some of the trepidation seemed to bleed from Hector as he leaned forward over the wheel, a half-smile revealing his top row of teeth.

Of everything Thiago had encountered since taking on Hector as a working partner four years earlier, his extreme deference to tight urban surroundings was by far his biggest shortcoming. Out in the open of the desert or floating on the water in a boat, there was not a calmer, more self-assured companion to be found. Once he was placed inside the tight confines of a city though, with eyes and ears and cameras all around, he became jittery.

Thiago knew it could be traced back to the time he had spent in prison and his deep-seated deference to ever return, but that didn't necessarily make the habit any less annoying.

"You ready?" Thiago asked, checking his own mirror to make sure nobody was out.

"We going in?" Hector replied, the smile melting away.

"Yeah," Thiago said. "We already know she's not here. Let's just go have a look, then take a drive down to Anaheim."

Without waiting for Hector to reply, Thiago jerked on the handle of the Toyota four-door they had procured for the evening, just another in an unending string parked nose-to-tail along the street. Stepping out onto the curb he raised his hands above his head and made a show of stretching, rotating at the waist to check in either direction.

From where he stood he could see lights on in several of the houses nearby, televisions playing and families sitting down to eat. Somewhere in the distance he could hear a dog barking, the sound of laughter.

Thiago waited as Hector circled around the front of the car and together they walked down the sidewalk, passing a pair of houses before coming up on their target.

Out front was the main house, a two story home with yellow wooden siding and white trim. A concrete porch extended most the way across the front of it, a matching driveway snaking down the right side of the house.

As they approached Thiago could feel his pulse pick up slightly, watching the house for any signs of life. From his vantage in the car all he could see was the single lamp burning in the front living room, no other movement of any kind occurring since they'd began surveillance.

In even steps he and Hector walked forward and made a hard right into the driveway, the space void of any cars. A still-damp spot of radiator coolant in the middle of it proved that somebody had been parked there recently, forcing another surge of adrenaline through his system.

"Five minutes," he hissed, pushing the words out through his teeth without looking over at Hector.

"Roger that."

Their pace increasing a tiny bit, they walked back the length of the driveway and found what they were looking for, a standalone structure that had been renovated into a single unit cottage. Built to match the main house, it was covered in wooden siding and painted yellow, white boards trimming out the front door and windows.

A welcome mat sat on the concrete landing right outside, flower pots to either side of it already having some sort of growth Thiago couldn't identify, despite the early month.

Seeing the thin wooden door and the aging casing surrounding it, Thiago's first instinct was to jam his heel through the wood beside the handle. Tucked away as they were it wasn't likely that anybody would hear the breech, but should someone return later to the place it would be a clear sign of forced entry.

Instead he paused for just a moment to see if Pawlak was foolish enough to leave a key under the mat. Finding the concrete beneath it barren, he stood and extracted his pick gun from the small of his back. Easing a single steel pin into the locking mechanism, he fired the gun once, the implement making a small popping sound, and felt the locking cylinder seize tight, the pins falling into place.

From there it took only a simple twist, the bolt clicking open, and they were in.

Heavy shadows shrouded most of the place, which was nominally more than a studio apartment. To the right was a kitchenette and small table for two, the laminate on the tabletop cracked and peeling. A myriad of female knickknacks lined the window above it and adorned the cabinets over the sink, most of them sunflowers and the like.

The left side of the room gave way to an open living area, a futon splicing the place in half. A shag rug sat on the floor before it, covering the narrow alley between it and a television on a stand. A bookshelf sat just under the front window, a row of potted plants across the top of it.

Most of the wall space in the cottage was covered in photographs, the majority of them black and white. They depicted scenes of outdoor landscapes, ranging from waves crashing on the beach to the sun rising behind mountains.

In just a handful of them were there people, Lake Pawlak the only one to appear with any regularity.

Pacing forward, Thiago crossed his arms and studied the wall. He remained in that position, barely noticing Hector as he brushed past him through the open doorway, disappearing into the bedroom that comprised the back half of the structure.

His gaze remained on the images as he thought back to the desert, to the position of the items they had found, of the single orb flashing under Felipe's spotlight.

"She's a photographer," Thiago whispered, the thought drawing a smile to his lips.

For over a day now he had been trying to make sense of what they had found. The sleeping bag, the cooler tote, the fresh tracks stumbling through the sand all confirmed they were being watched. That much Thiago knew for sure.

Beyond that though, he couldn't quite nail down why the person was there. Clearly no effort had been made to apprehend them. The leaving behind of items, especially something with a name scrawled across the bottom of it, seemed to indicate it was somebody scared and fleeing fast.

Who such a person would be though, out in an extremely remote part of the desert, camped in an odd location, had mystified Thiago. Now he understood.

The girl wasn't a threat, was certainly not a federal agent looking into their affairs. She was a photographer, a young girl that had simply chosen the wrong spot to wait for sunrise.

The smile grew a little larger as he stepped away from the photos and turned his gaze back to the room. The girl would still need to be eliminated, she had seen too much not to be, but the task had just gotten infinitely easier for them.

"Cameras," he called out, already moving back into the living room to check the bookshelf.

"What?" Hector asked, appearing in the doorway, a look of confusion on his face.

"If she comes back, she's going for the cameras," Thiago said. "Find them."

Chapter Seventeen

Three weeks of validity remained on the old passport I had used in my time with the DEA. Made especially for situations in which I needed to move about without fear of a paper trail, the picture inside it was mine but not much else.

The name was a combination of my two favorite football players, the address a parking lot on the outskirts of Dallas. Inside the pages were stamps from ports spanning the globe, the vast majority of them appearing in a tight three year window representing every country in Central and South America.

The young man behind the counter at the LaQuinta Inn barely looked at it, only needing something to ensure that the credit card I was handing him under the same name was valid. Once he had gone through the required steps he handed the items back to me with a room key, directing me to the third floor without another comment.

If my appearance, or that of Lake behind me, concerned him in the slightest he didn't let it show.

Based on some of the folks I saw on the drive in though, I wasn't especially surprised. A little facial hair and some tattoos weren't that bad, considering.

The room was a very standard hotel accommodation, matched by no less than a hundred thousand just like it in the greater Los Angeles area. Some, like the Marriott we had been at earlier in the day, were much nicer. Others, like the Budget Inn that I had voted for, earning myself an awful tongue lashing from Lake in the process, fell on the opposite end of the spectrum.

A pair of double beds covered most of the square footage, both tucked down tight and lined with pillows, everything in white. Against the opposite wall was a dresser, a flat screen television atop it. In the back corner was a desk and chair, a window facing out over the parking lot allowing a faint orange glow from the security lamps outside to shine in.

"The Marriott was nicer," Lake said, complete indifference in her voice, a statement and not an accusation.

"It was," I agreed.

The idea had been to rent someplace nice, a national chain with a networked database. It was also deliberate to use her name and credit card, making sure that anybody using traditional tracking methods would be sure to find her.

As things now stood, I figured we had two ways of approaching our situation. The first was to go as close to underground as greater Los Angeles allowed, staying in total shit boxes, paying cash for everything.

Without knowing exactly who Lake had seen though, total invisibility wasn't without drawbacks. As much as I would like to keep her completely concealed, Diaz and I had also discussed the possibility of chumming the water a bit in our wake. Every move had to be calculated, but it also needed to be done with an eye toward drawing whoever she saw out into the open. If ever Lake was going to have a hope of ridding herself of this mess, of stepping outside her door and not worrying what might be in the shadows, we had to be proactive.

Otherwise we were all just sitting and waiting for an attack that was someday coming, our senses dulling in the meantime.

"I'm going to take a shower," Lake said, turning straight into the bathroom and closing the door behind her. A moment later the overhead exhaust fan came on, pushing out a loud and persistent rattle.

Stepping forward, I dropped my duffel on the floor by the first bed and lowered my laptop bag to the mattress. I contemplated moving immediately to set up the computer system and begin surveillance but noticed the glowing red digits on the clock beside the bed.

Unzipping the side pouch on my computer bag, I extracted one of the burn phones and dialed Diaz's number from memory, walking past the foot of the bed to check the window. Standing off to the side, out of a direct sightline, I peeled back the curtain and peered outside.

The parking lot was more than half full, a few clusters of people walking toward the street in sets of two and three. All groups were of mixed gender and well dressed, appearing to be headed out for the evening. None seemed to glance at the faded truck parked in the back corner, nose pointed out in case a quick getaway was needed, a shadow thrown across the front hood.

"Hawk," Diaz said, her voice sharp.

I could tell by the tone and cadence she was in front of others, allowing her a moment to step away before saying a word. Not until I heard a door click shut did I say, "This a bad time? I can call back."

"No," she replied, letting out a sigh. "Just been a long day."

"But a productive one?" I asked.

"Yeah, something like that," she replied, her tone sour. "What's going on with you?"

I watched the parking lot for another moment before stepping back from the window. In the bathroom I could hear the water kick on, the shower curtain being pulled along its rod.

"We're in for the night," I said. "Everything is quiet."

She remained silent, seemingly waiting for more that wasn't coming.

"How's it going with her?"

Out of reflex I glanced back to the bathroom, the door still pulled closed. "A little touch-and-go at times, but it's alright. Scared and confused being masked by lashing out. You know the drill."

"I do," Diaz agreed. "What's the plan looking ahead? You going to roam or hunker down?"

Leaning my back against the wall, I crossed my free arm over my stomach, propping my opposite elbow on it, the phone resting against my ear. "Depends what happens tonight. I set a little trap just to see how far out ahead of them we might be."

I left the ending vague, knowing I didn't need to explain further. Diaz would pick up that my next option would be directly linked to the results of that trap.

"Okay," Diaz said. "Keep me posted on how that goes."

"I will," I replied. "Have you had a chance to check her place yet?"

"Earlier today. Didn't find anything there, but told the owners of the property to clear out for a few days just the same. They left a few lights on to give the illusion of occupancy, but it won't be hard to figure out if someone is watching."

I nodded to myself, filing away the information. Part of the reason for delaying Lake earlier was to give our guys a chance to look everything over first.

The fact that Diaz hadn't mentioned anything meant the search had turned up nothing.

"You staying on the property?" I asked.

"No," she replied. "We have no reason to think anybody knows who she is. There was no sign of entry, no earmarks of surveillance. Right now our presence would do more harm than good."

Again I nodded. Anybody that happened to be nearby would take the presence of agents as a sure sign.

"How about Felipe Soto? You been able to turn anything up there?"

Again a sigh passed from Diaz, the same exhaustion as earlier entering her tone. "Not a damn thing. His old cellmate is dead, none of the guys he served with have heard from him in years."

A stab of disappointment passed through me. For most people like Soto, prison only served to reinforce criminal behavior, not rehabilitate it. It placed them in an enclosed area with hundreds of like-minded individuals, all of them with special skills and affiliations. By the time they were ready to reenter society they had graduated from common thugs to master criminals.

Finding out the most obvious starting point was a dead end would have incited in me the same exact reaction I could hear in Diaz.

"I'm guessing he wasn't kind enough to leave a forwarding address or a list of new associates," I added.

"Ha!" Diaz barked, the sound sharp and loud. "Heck, I'd be happy with a phone number or his name tattooed on some bimbo's arm right now."

Without realizing it, the corners of my mouth turned down into a frown. "Nothing, huh?"

"Not a whisper anywhere," Diaz said. "It's like the guy walked out of prison and just disappeared."

My vision blurred over a bit as I digested the comment, staring at the plain white comforter before me. As automated as today's world was, nobody just evaporated. I had spent most of the previous five years trying to do just that, only to discover how many people were intimately familiar with everything I was doing.

If Felipe Soto was that non-existent, it meant somebody was scrubbing his back trail.

"Okay," I said, blinking myself back to attention. "If I come across anything that will help, I'll be sure to pass it on. If not I'll talk to you in twelve."

"Thanks," Diaz said. "Be careful out there."

"You too."

We both disconnected without another word.

Chapter Eighteen

The wheels on the dented and dusty SUV moaned once in protest as it came to a stop in front of the dilapidated dwelling, the entire body rocking forward a few inches. It remained there suspended for a moment before returning to its natural position, jostling Rafa and Martin Morris in the front seat.

The headlights bathed the exterior of the house in bright fluorescent light, the structure the only one around for miles. Located off a dirt road eight miles outside the closest town, it gave the distinct impression of being a squatter's den more than a primary residence.

"You sure this is the place?" Rafa asked, staring out through the front windshield. It appeared at first glance that nobody was inside, the entire place dark. The front door was closed but the only two windows on the front of the adobe structure were open, the remains of curtains fluttering in the breeze.

"This is where they said they were going," Morris said. He raised his hands from the steering wheel and added, "That's all I know."

Rafa grunted at the explanation, leaning forward and taking up his weapon from the floorboard between his feet. Unsnapping the leather holster, he slid it away from the .45 ACP and checked to make sure a round was chambered.

More than once he had walked into a place thinking it friendly only to find hostility waiting for him.

It seemed to be the nature of their business.

"Stay here, keep the lights on," Rafa said. He took up a second matching .45 from the same place as the first and slapped it down on the dash. "If you hear shots, grab that and come running."

He wrenched open the door and extended a foot to the ground before pausing. "Just don't shoot me."

Morris grunted in understanding as Rafa stepped out and closed the door behind him. He paused for a moment and cocked an ear to the wind, listening for any sounds.

So far from the nearest town, no stray noises came to him. In the distance he could see the faint glow of lights and on the breeze he could smell cactus flower, but he could hear nothing.

Picking his feet up to avoid scraping them over the sandy ground, Rafa walked to the front door and pressed his body to the wall alongside it. Raising the gun in his right hand, he used his left to knock twice, the sound carrying out through the quiet night.

A moment passed before the door eased itself back just a few inches. Rafa's entire body tensed as he stared into the void inside, seeing nothing but darkness.

Not until Dante blinked did Rafa even realize he was standing there.

Pulling the door open wide, a stench of equal parts vomit and feces passed over the threshold. It engulfed Rafa in a heavy cloud, drawing the air from his lungs, bringing tears to his eyes. The back of his throat burned as he turned to the side and bent at the waist, trying in vain to cough the acrid taste from his throat. His face grew red and spittle hung from his lip as he remained folded in half, collecting himself before rising to full height and stepping inside.

The floor underfoot was nothing but desert sand as he entered, the place resembling more of an old west hangout than somewhere anybody in modern times would live. In one corner was an ancient potbellied stove, a pot and pan sitting atop it. Beside it sat a simple wooden table with four matching chairs, all made from wood polished by time and bodily oils.

Situated along the back wall was a bunk bed, the top frame empty. On the bottom was a thin mattress, a threadbare blanket tossed upon it in a heap.

None of the scattered furniture items caught Rafa's attention though as he stepped inside. Instead his focus went to the row of native blankets lined up on the floor against the wall, each one containing a single child. Including both girls and boys, all were laid on their sides, their knees pulled up to their chests.

None of them looked up at him as he entered, their faces bathed in sweat. Several appeared to be sleeping fitfully, the others having their visages contorted in pain.

In the far back corner stood Felipe, his shirt off. Light from the car out front gleamed off of him, streaks of mud and assorted fluids on his skin. A pair of yellow rubber gloves encased his hands, stopping mid-forearm, and a round white mask covered his nose and mouth.

Seeing Rafa enter, he lowered the bucket in his hand, the tin implement pinging as he placed it on the ground by his feet. "Rafa."

"Felipe," Rafa replied, nodding once. He tracked his gaze around the room a second time, taking in the hellish scene. "How bad?"

Felipe turned to face him full, leaving his arms hanging by his sides. "We lost two. The rest passed what they were carrying. This is the last of them."

The original load had carried eighteen in total. Losing two was bad, but with so many on hand it also meant they weren't out quite as much product as it could have been.

The more important thing now was getting everything out of the remaining six.

"How much is left?" Rafa asked.

"The two that are sleeping have pretty much passed everything," Felipe said. He made no attempt to remove the mask over his face, the words coming out a bit stilted.

Nodding once, Rafa glanced to Dante. "You take over here for a few minutes." He motioned with the top of his head toward the door, not waiting for a response from Felipe as he stepped back outside.

The cool night air hit him in a rush as he made his way out, pulling away the smell he didn't realize had collected on his shirt. The stench from within faded as he took several steps, motioning for Morris to kill the lights.

A moment later they blinked out, plunging the world into an exaggerated darkness.

"My apologies for not delivering the news myself," Felipe said, his voice arriving several seconds before he did. He waited until he was well clear of the home before removing the mask from his face, allowing it to hang from a rubber cord around his neck.

Rafa shook off the apology, waving a dismissive hand at Felipe. "You did the right thing. We all know the rules."

In the four years Felipe had been with the organization, Rafa had only encountered him a handful of times. His initial reaction - that the man was arrogant and self-absorbed - had not wavered one bit in the time since, though he had to admit he had proven a better employee than originally expected.

The fact that he was still with them confirmed that.

"What happened?" Rafa asked. He stayed a few feet away as he did so, making sure he was downwind from the odor that had permeated Felipe's skin.

Raising his palms toward the sky, the rubber gloves squeaking slightly, Felipe recounted what had happened. He started with their initial suspicion that someone was waiting for them, filled Rafa in through the end, when the two sides parted ways.

"Did anybody follow you?" Rafa asked, processing the information.

"Nobody," Felipe said, not a shred of doubt in his voice. "And we would have easily spotted them coming over the border. It was just us."

Rafa grunted, nodding in agreement. "Any trouble since you've been here?"

"Just them," Felipe replied, rotating at the waist and pointing back inside. "Most of them were nine kinds of pissed when they woke up still in Mexico."

More than once Rafa had considered that very thing. He could only imagine enduring what they had to still find himself on the outside looking in. "Any problems?"

"No," Felipe said. "Dante's good at what he does."

Again Rafa nodded in agreement. Felipe's partner indeed served a very specific purpose, one that was not at all inhibited by his shortcomings as a conversationalist.

As best Rafa could tell, there were only a few viable explanations for what had taken place.

The first was that Felipe and Dante had simply become greedy, falling victim to some misguided avarice. It still would have looked bad for the Guzman enterprise - his employees being his responsibility - but it wouldn't have been an irrecoverable black mark.

Standing here now though, he knew that to not be an issue. Had the problem been in any way attributed to them, he never would have seen them again. There was no way they would still be at the safe house, slogging through the worst human defilement he had seen in quite some time.

Knowing that, it left Rafa only to believe that either Molina's men or a third party was making a move.

On most nights, a shipment would have anywhere from ten to twenty mules, though usually it was more in the twelve to fourteen range. Each loaded with one hundred capsules of product, they represented a kilo of pure grade cocaine per person, ten to twenty kilos in total. On the street the substance was selling for sixty thousand dollars apiece, as much as a million dollars arriving over the border three times a week.

The exchange location was still fairly new, not one they had ever seen anybody else near before. The odds of somebody finding them in the middle of the desert in the dead of night were just too negligible to really believe.

That left only their business partner himself, a conclusion Rafa wasn't quite yet ready to jump to either.

Rules were in place to govern men like Arturo Molina and Daniel Guzman. They still clung to the old ways even after it was long past worth their time to insist on doing so. The fact that a rendezvous was planned for the following night proved that.

There had to be something Rafa wasn't seeing, he just wasn't quite sure what it was yet.

Nodding once, he turned to Felipe and said again, "You handled this like pros. I'll be sure to let Daniel know."

Felipe lowered his head in a sign of appreciation, remaining rooted in place as Rafa made his way back toward the SUV.

"Also," Rafa said, turning at the waist, "we'll need you on hand tomorrow in the capitol. You know how these things go."

A single wave of understanding was the only response as Rafa opened the passenger door and slid inside. Grabbing his holster up from the floor, he pushed his .45 into it and paired it with the matching gun still resting on the dash. "Drive."

On command Morris's hand shot up to the gear shift, jerking it down into reverse. "Where to?"

"Somewhere downwind."

Chapter Nineteen

Thiago stood on the edge of the tiny airstrip outside of Palmdale, a Honduran cigar stuck in the side of his mouth. The rich flavor of the smoke barely registered with him as it funneled out through his nostrils, his thoughts in a dozen different places.

Chief among them was the fact that he was now standing in Palmdale, the strip a private one on some land owned by a family farming organization. The company had installed it a number of years before to accommodate a trio of crop dusting planes, even erecting a mid-sized hangar for storage and upkeep.

Arturo Molina had two private planes in his possession. The first was a Cessna Citation Encore that was stored at the Bob Hope Airport in Burbank. Large and comfortable, it was capable of taking off on short runways and traveling long distances, ideal for the trips he took with his family or the times his wife wanted to go shopping in New York for a few days. Kept in pristine condition with a regular crew, it was completely up-to-date on all paperwork.

The second aircraft was the Raytheon Premier 1A that Thiago now stood beside. While still quite posh and attainable only to the elite, it traded out some of the basic comforts of the Cessna for economic practicality, both in maintenance and fuel usage. For quite a handsome annual cash fee, Molina stored it in the corner of the farming operation's hanger, covered and out of sight ninety percent of the time.

The choice to obtain the plane was steeped completely in business reasons, Molina knowing that once his enterprise with Guzman began he would be needing to make the occasional hop across the border. Not wanting to have to deal with the litany of red tape tied to flight manifests and the like, the second mode of transportation was obtained under a false identity for emergency outings such as this.

Thiago was not especially keen on leaving the country at the moment. He had no particular problem with Mexico, had been many times since immigrating to the United States years before. One of the first things Molina had seen to for he and Luanna both was full naturalization, ensuring that the threat of deportation never existed.

The concern was with leaving Hector behind to deal with finding Lake Pawlak.

The increased agitation in Hector's voice as Thiago stood with his phone pressed to his ear only heightened that unease.

"I'm telling you, *mijo*, I don't like this," Hector said, his voice drawn taut.

"Do not call me *mijo*," Thiago said, the words spit out in a quick burst, a directive made so many times he was tired of repeating it. "And I don't like it either, but this is what we have right now."

"Man, I don't see why you couldn't have been on surveillance and I went for a little day trip down to Mexico," Hector said.

More than once Thiago had thought the same exact thing. If his presence was merely meant to be a show of force, Hector was infinitely more qualified for the role. With his Mohawk and chains, his sneering bravado, he cut a much more imposing figure than Thiago. If he was only going to vouch for what happened a few nights earlier, Hector could handle that as well.

Molina would not hear of it, though. He countered that Guzman knew the important players in the operation and it would be an insult to walk in with underlings.

There was no way to know if any of that was true or the old man was simply saying what he had to so as to quell concerns, but Thiago had let it go just the same.

"Look, it is one girl," Thiago said, allowing his voice to take on a dismissive tone. "We've been inside her house. She's a damn photographer. All you have to do is sit tight and see if she returns."

A moment of silence passed over the line as the twin engines on the Raytheon came to life. The sound rolled out over the grass clipped as short as a putting green, Thiago turning perpendicular to the noise. With his right hand he jammed the phone down tight against his face, the index finger of his left going into his ear canal to block out the sound.

"What the hell is that?" Hector asked.

"The plane," Thiago replied, "we're getting ready to take off." He glanced up at the top of the stairwell leading into the cabin of the plane, Declan atop it, motioning him inside. "Look, just sit tight, we'll be back late tonight."

A string of low grumblings rolled out, though Thiago couldn't decipher any of the words.

"If she returns," he pressed on, "and you have a clean opening, grab her. If not, tail her."

"Okay," Hector said, his voice leveling out a bit under the clear direction. "You want me to take care of her?"

"No," Thiago said, "not yet. We need to see what she knows and more importantly how much she got on film."

"Ahh," Hector replied, a bit of dawning in his tone, "then we get rid of her."

"Then we get rid of her," Thiago replied, ending the call without another word. Turning on the ball of his foot he tossed his cigar to the side and jogged over to the stairwell. He took the steps two at a time, the upended door bouncing slightly under his weight.

The engine, just feet from his head, roared as he knocked out the last few strides and stepped into the cabin, cool air and the scent of flowers hitting him in the face. His pupils dilated, trying in vain to adjust to the dim light of the cabin as he stepped past a young cabin stewardess they had rented for the day. She nodded politely and eased around him, lifting the door into place and securing it.

In whole, the cabin area was roughly fifteen feet in length, less than half that in width. The right side was outfitted with two captain's chairs, a table between them. One of the seats was occupied by Molina, a fresh whiskey on the table beside him.

The other side was fashioned with a single bench seat stretched ten feet in length, the surface padded and covered in charcoal grey leather. Jasmine and Declan had already taken up positions on either end of it, the chasm between them showing a clear lack of personal affinity.

All three stared at him as he stood in place a moment longer, allowing his eyes to adjust before moving further.

"Everything alright, *mijo?*" Molina asked. For the trip he had opted back into his usual look, a solid black tie knotted at the neck.

"Yes," Thiago said, walking in exaggerated steps to keep his balance as the plane began to roll forward. He fell into the second captain's chair and allowed his body to recline a tiny bit, propping his left elbow on the shiny wooden tabletop. "Hector is in place with directions to watch for the girl. If able he will grab her, if not, he will monitor her position."

He kept his attention on Molina as he delivered the information, though in his periphery he could see Jasmine clench just slightly, a sure sign of just how new she still was.

Within six months, the idea of an abduction would cease to even register with her.

"Are you concerned about her at all?" Molina asked.

Thiago weighed the question a moment, his eyes narrowing as he considered it. "About her personally? No. About whether or not she saw anything? Nominally more."

Molina's eyebrows rose a quarter inch. "Only nominally?"

"Paulie called last night and said she was checked into the Marriott Hotel in Anaheim," Thiago said. "Which tells me she couldn't have seen much or the police would have her under guard right now."

For a moment Molina considered the data, his head slowly nodding. "She's scared, which means she knows she saw something. She just doesn't know what, or she would have acted on it already."

"That's what I'm thinking," Thiago agreed.

Reaching out, Molina wrapped his fingers around his drink, pulling it a few inches closer. "She'll still need to be eliminated once we return."

"Of course," Thiago replied. "Priority one as soon as we land."

Molina lifted his whiskey and took a long pull, smacking his lips as he returned it to the tabletop, placing it back on the same wet ring it had occupied before. "Let's wait and see what transpires this evening before assigning it top priority, but I agree, it should be swift."

Chapter Twenty

For the first time in ages, there was a smell dominating the cab of my truck that wasn't muddy boots or beef jerky. The source of it was two and a half feet, less than an arm's length, to my right. Still wearing the same clothes as yesterday, Lake sat with her arms folded across her chest, her multi-colored hair hanging in wet tendrils on either side of her face.

The scent of cheap soap and shampoo, the kind distributed in single serving sizes at hotels, clung to her, so strong it filled the entirety of the truck. Despite the foreign smell and the tiny fear that it would linger long after she was gone, I let it pass without a word.

The poor girl had to shower, and the only other option was the cheap dollar-a-bottle stuff I used.

We had waited until almost ten before getting a start on the day, using the late beginning to grab armloads of food from the continental breakfast. Squirreled away in our room we ate while she scrolled through television channels and I kept an eye on the cameras.

Despite my near obsessive watch over the images, nobody had been inside the room all night. Not once had the motion activation kicked on, never had the bottle I left propped on the door handle moved.

The lack of any intruder didn't necessarily mean they weren't aware of her or actively following. The odds were low that anybody at a hotel like the Marriott would just hand out her room number, and there was no way anybody was onsite in time to see us leaving.

Conversely, it showed that their reach was at least somewhat tethered. If they had police on the payroll they could have gotten the room number easily. Getting inside would have been a mere formality.

Whether that all meant Lake wasn't a priority or whoever she saw was still laying low for the time being, I wasn't quite sure.

Such thoughts bounced through my head as we cut a northwest path from Anaheim to Huntington Beach, avoiding the freeways and taking side streets as much as possible. The traffic was a little heavier, and we made much worse time, but it was far easier for me to watch the mirrors as we went.

So far nothing remotely suspicious had popped up behind us.

Besides, it wasn't like we had a schedule that necessitated efficiency.

"We're not going back to the Marriott?" Lake asked, the first conversation since leaving the hotel.

"No, not today, maybe not tomorrow either. We'll keep the cameras in place for a while longer, see if anybody turns up."

"Do you expect them to?"

I raised my eyebrows, shrugging one shoulder in unison. "It's possible. It would be a bold move, but people tend to do such things when they get desperate."

I didn't bother filling in the rest of the statement, that I hoped our side had them in hand before it came to that. Based on the conversation I'd had with Diaz a few hours earlier though, I was less than optimistic.

She glanced over at me, her wet hair swinging by her face. "I hope you realize there's no way my credit card can cover those expenses."

Turning to face her, I said, "I paid for four nights in cash. They just had to put your credit card on file for incidentals."

"Meaning?"

One corner of my mouth turned up just slightly before dropping back into place. "Meaning we wanted your name available to draw them out. Don't worry, you're not getting charged for your own protection."

If the words did anything to placate her, there was no outward sign. She turned her attention back to face forward, arms still folded in place.

Outside the familiar signs of urban sprawl began to thin out, local bank branches and minimarts giving way to residential neighborhoods. Grass became visible between structures, raggedy palm trees lining the streets.

In an odd sort of way, the scene reminded me of Montana. The sheer density of things was different in most every sense, but the appearance had a vague familiarity to it. Every car, every home, even most of the people, wore the effects of the elements plainly, what was snow and wind damage in the mountains having been replaced by an overabundance of sun here in California.

"Next left," Lake said, motioning with her chin.

I grunted in agreement, already knowing where I was going, having checked the directions many times over during our wait at the hotel. Ignoring her advice I went one black past and looped around, driving slow.

"Watch for anybody sitting behind the wheel," I said without looking over at her. "If somebody's watching we won't know what they're driving, but we might spot them camped out."

Her body visibly tensed as she nodded in silence, her arms sliding tighter around her torso.

Keeping my foot depressed just an inch on the gas, I pushed us to the end of the street and made a left, taking an immediate left back down the next one. Watching the house numbers tick by on mailboxes, I split my attention between them and the row of cars stacked tight along the curbs.

On purpose, I overshot her house by fifty yards before easing into a spot, the front foot or so of my truck bleeding into a yellow no-parking zone.

"Ten minutes," I said. "Grab only what you absolutely must have, nothing that you can't drop at a moment's notice if need be. No phones."

Twisting around in her seat, Lake turned to look at the house. "Why are we parked clear out here? Wouldn't it be easier if we pulled in the driveway?"

Keeping my attention on the mirrors, watching the street behind us, I gave my head one quick shake. "No. Remember what I said back at headquarters about us being walking caricatures? This is our chance to be seen. If anybody is out there, they'll report back to look out for ZZ Top and Lady Gaga."

Her attention snapped over to me, a look of surprise on her features. "You know Gaga?"

For a moment I considered asking if she knew who ZZ Top was, but decided against it. Right now I needed her focused, maybe even a little frightened.

"Ten minutes," I said, pushing the truck door open and stepping out onto the street.

The MK 3 was strapped to my left hip, the top half of it hidden beneath the tail of my t-shirt. The Glock was slid down against the small of my back, the handle pointed toward my right side, ready to be drawn in an instant.

Hidden behind sunglasses my gaze flicked over everything on the street, seeing, inventorying, and dismissing items in a steady stream of consciousness.

Nerves stretched taut, I circled around the bed of the truck and fell in beside Lake on the sidewalk. Her once proud figure had seemed to whither, her hands folded in front of her, her shoulders pinched inward. She walked quickly with her head aimed toward the ground, her mouth drawn into a tight line.

"I should pop in to the front house," she whispered. "I'm behind on my rent and don't want the landlord evicting me while I'm gone."

"It's been taken care of," I replied, not bothering to look her way. "And they've been told to stay away as well."

She accepted the information without a response, walking past the front of the two-story home. Made from yellow wooden siding trimmed in white, it vaguely reminded me of the house I grew up in, a lifetime and three thousand miles away. For just a moment I could almost see my young self and my father seated on the front step, the thought evaporating as my attention went back to the street.

Allowing Lake to take the lead, we turned down the driveway. Tucked away in the corner of the property was a smaller version of the main house, the same white on yellow motif employed. Feeling my pulse tick upward just slightly, I waited until we were a few feet away from the door before holding out a hand to stop her.

"Key."

She ceased moving forward without comment, jutting her chin toward the door. "Left flower pot."

"Any others?" I asked.

"Just the one on my key ring," she said, "which is still with my Jeep."

I paused a moment, expecting a crack about where her Jeep was or when she might get it back, but she remained silent. Instead she returned her arms to folded across her stomach, pulling them in tight.

"Stay here," I said. "I'll go in first. Turn and watch the street. If you see anything, don't be quiet about it."

She nodded a response as I stepped forward and fished a key out from the flower pot, fresh peat moss clinging to my fingers. Rubbing the brass against my jeans, I pushed it into the lock and drew the Glock, holding it at the ready as I stepped inside.

Every light in the cottage was off, the only illumination coming through the two small windows to either side of the front door. Weak sunlight streamed through them, spotlighting bits of dust and debris hanging in the air.

In one quick sweep I took in a kitchenette, dining area, and living area. Everything appeared to be in order, none of the items tossed since her last departure. Nowhere did I see any signs of life or any place large enough for somebody to hide.

Stepping forward I went straight for the short hallway leading to the back half of the building, ignoring the myriad of pictures on the wall. My boots echoed off of wooden floorboards as I moved into the bedroom area, a bed and dresser both appearing untouched.

Sweat coated my face as I extended my gun and inched forward to the closet, jerking the door back to find nothing but a dozen articles of clothes and twice as many empty hangars, a few pairs of running shoes on the floor.

Far and away the least amount of clothing I had ever seen a woman own in my life.

"It's clear," I said, lowering my weapon to my side and stepping into the hallway.

A moment later Lake appeared, blotting out much of the light entering the cottage. "We're good?"

Chapter Twenty-One

I sensed him long before I saw him.

With Lake blocking the doorway, I had no clear view to the driveway beyond her. Instead I saw a distortion in the shadows entering the cottage through the left window, a misshapen object moving across, altering the light filtering through. In one quick movement I snapped the Glock from my waist to shoulder level, my right hand wrapped around it, my left cupped under it for support.

"Down!" I yelled, the word coming out several syllables in length, leaving no room for interpretation.

In less than an instant the look on Lake's face passed from shocked to confused to frightened, her twisted up features the last thing I saw before she dropped straight down. One moment she was standing in front of me, blocking most of the doorway, the next she was in a puddle on the floor, melted from sight.

The new rush of sunlight lasted just a split second before a man appeared behind her. About the same height as her but much, much thicker, his width covered the entirety of the doorway. He stalked forward with both arms raised in front of him, a pair of elongated handguns outstretched, noise suppressors screwed into the ends.

The guns were the only thing to register in my mind as I squeezed the trigger, three quick bursts in a row, as fast as the muscles and tendons in my right index finger would move.

I knew from the gasp the man let out that at least one of the rounds had hit. I also knew from the sound of bullets smashing into wood, from the splinters and smell of fresh sawdust, that at least one had buried itself in the doorframe.

Pushing off my back foot I dove forward, sliding on my stomach across the floor, my face ending up just inches from Lake. Her entire body was pulled into a tight ball on her side, knees and arms locked in the fetal position, trembling uncontrollably.

Using the momentum of the dive I rolled upright and pushed her out of the way of the door, shoving it closed as a handful of bullets slammed into it, the entire thing shaking.

Setting the Glock on the floor beside us I grabbed Lake by the hips with both hands and hefted her over onto the rug between the futon and the television. Her form remained rigid as I did so, enough adrenaline pulsating through me to lift her entire body with ease.

"You alright?" I asked, dropping to a knee and peering straight into her face. She stared back at me with widened eyes, her pupils dilated like saucers, shock beginning to set in.

"Are you hit?!" I yelled, running my hands over her body, feeling no blood.

She stared back a moment before shaking her head, remaining in place, offering no assistance or resistance of any kind.

Three more bullets hit the front door before moving to the windows, starting in the kitchen. They passed through the plate glass as if it wasn't even there, large shards of it falling to the ground, shattering on contact.

The oversized Parabellums crashed into the front of the fridge and the stove, ripping holes into the aging appliances.

Lunging forward at the futon, I grabbed hold of the mattress draped over the frame and jerked it down toward me. The thick black cushion rolled forward without opposition, sending throw pillows and a blanket flying as it fell atop Lake, enveloping her body.

The pad would do nothing against a bullet fired directly into it, but would protect her from any glass or debris. I heard a slight wheeze as the weight of it came down upon her, still not a single word crossing her lips.

Keeping low to the floor, I grabbed up the Glock and inched back toward the door, inventorying what I knew.

Right now there was an injured, well-armed man firing bullets into a flimsy structure. There was no way of knowing where he was hit or how badly, though I had to assume he was well enough to stay outside as long as necessary.

Even given the hour and the fact that it was midweek, it was also safe to say that somebody had heard my first three gunshots. Waiting for them to call it in and for police to arrive was an option, though it would be a hassle trying to explain things and a potential embarrassment for Diaz to have to clean up.

It would be best to get this over with and get our people on the scene before anybody else.

More than anything though, this was somebody directly tied to whatever Lake had seen a few nights before. If I needed to put him down to protect her I would, but if at all possible it would be better to bring him in for questioning.

Either way, there was no way he was returning home tonight. It would just be infinitely better if we had some idea of who might be showing up in his wake.

The window above Lake exploded into broken fragments of glass as the gunman went to work on the opposite side of the house. The bullets passed through and slammed into the television and the opposite wall, gouging holes in the hanging pictures, ripping away chunks of sheetrock.

Kneeling there on the exposed wood inside the door, a plan slowly formed in my head. It went against every ingrained instinct I had, calling on me for maybe the first time ever not to be the aggressor but to stay right where I was and wait this guy out. More than once I had seen his type, the kind that wasn't afraid to open fire in broad daylight in a quiet neighborhood.

Knowing that, I also knew that he wasn't about to leave until he had gotten what he came for.

Doing so meant he had to come inside.

Remaining completely silent, I crouched low to the floor, staring up at the front door. I counted off the seconds in my head, listening to the stream of bullets from outside slow down, waiting for him to get impatient and make a move.

In total it took just three more minutes.

From the position I was in, I could have waited all morning. Not once had his line of fire dropped from eye level, fantastic for causing cosmetic damage but not nearly as effective for inflicting serious harm. With my hand wrapped around my weapon so tight the knuckles showed white beneath my skin, I sat and waited, my entire focus on the doorknob.

With my breath clenched tight in my chest I stared at it, waiting for it to move even a fraction of an inch. I knew it would be coming soon, his last pass with the guns a wild spray that went from left to right and back again, obvious suppression fire.

The moment it was done he went straight for the handle, the polished knob rotating in a quick twist.

I didn't bother waiting for it to finish its trajectory before launching myself forward with every bit of momentum I could muster. One instant I was crouched on the ground in a sprinter's stance, the next I was up and through the door, slamming into it with my shoulder. On impact I churned my feet and kept pushing, feeling the doorframe give way, the wooden barricade begin to move in the opposite direction of what it was designed for.

Given the sheer number of bullets that had already shredded the door, enormous chunks of it splintered off as I charged forward like a fullback hitting a hole.

"The hell?!" the man yelled as I felt his weight shift beneath me, his shoes fighting for purchase as he tried to free himself from the onslaught of the door crashing down.

Gaining momentum, I used the door to drive him back several more feet. His weight began to crumple as I pounded out the last steps, landing atop him in a twisted heap of limbs and chunks of wood. With my left hand I shoved two broken scraps to the side, getting a good look at the man beneath me for the first time.

Clearly Hispanic, his skin was dark brown, his hair shaved into a wide Mohawk. Jewelry glittered in the sunlight as I raised the Glock and smashed the butt of it into his right temple. The soft skin split easily, blood streaming down his face as his eyes blurred but somehow stayed open. Beside me I could hear his weapons fire, my weight pinning his arms down, directing the shots wide in either direction.

Raising the gun I again smashed it down into the exact same spot, the gash widening, blood spatter covering the side of my hand, dotting my entire forearm. This time his eyes rolled up in his head before fluttering shut, his body falling slack beneath me.

Fighting the urge to hit him one more time for good measure, I remained in place a moment before picking myself up off the remains of the door.

I had a lot of work to do and only a few minutes to do it.

Part Three

Chapter Twenty-Two

There was never any discussion as to where the meeting would take place. It was set for Mexico City, as close to a mid-point as existed between Ecuador and Los Angeles. Years before it had been decided that all business would be conducted on the neutral ground found there, both sides bringing in a limited party, neither flexing muscle of any sort.

Usually that meant each side was allotted a three person delegation – the leader, their assistant, and one person to handle security.

Seated on the right side of the table was the Guzman contingent, Daniel placed directly in the middle. Dressed in a white collarless shirt buttoned to the neck and a linen suit, his skin looked especially bronze under the harsh yellow light of the aging wrought iron fixtures on the wall.

On either side of him rested Rafa and Sanchez. The younger man had opted for a full suit, navy blue with a patterned tie, while the older Rafa had chosen an all-black affair, a two-piece suit with a matching shirt open at the throat.

All three sat with neutral expressions, none giving any indication of their true intentions as they waited for the meeting to begin.

Opposite them sat the Molina organization, Arturo seated directly across from his counterpart. Still dressed in the same suit and tie he had worn on the plane, he waited with his hands in his lap, the skin on either side of his face seeming to hang an extra half inch.

The reason for such was open to speculation.

On his right hand was Declan, the South African mercenary in slacks and a dark dress shirt buttoned at the throat and wrists. He sat ramrod straight in the high-backed wooden chair, the occasional twitch of striated muscle in his neck the only movement of any kind.

To the left rested Jasmine, the only woman in the room, a fact she seemed to be very aware of. Wearing a black cocktail dress and heavy makeup, she sat staring down at her hands that never stopped moving, clearly missing her usual notepad and pen.

She had been warned ahead of time that nothing at these meetings was to ever be put in writing.

Seated along the side wall, Thiago watched the posturing play out before him, fighting to keep the disdain from his face. As an unofficial part of the traveling party his position was to stay away from the main table until summoned, the same as Felipe opposite him. Doing so was just one of the many tedious rules the old men insisted on maintaining whenever the two came together, abiding by an antiquated code that had passed out of favor with the rest of the world long before.

Still, as Thiago had discovered on more than one occasion, it was such strict adherence that had allowed the operation to be as successful as it was.

Shifting his attention away from the table he allowed himself to inventory his surroundings, the site a new choice made through the assistance of a third party he knew to be standing right outside. Contracted specifically to oversee these meetings, they were tasked with getting both sides from the airfield to the meeting location.

Neither party could know beforehand where it was, would have no way to scout ahead of time.

Once onsite the contractors oversaw all security, ensuring that both factions abided by the truce, protecting them from anybody that might try to interfere.

Again, it was an expense Thiago didn't quite agree with, though he couldn't argue with the results.

It was only the second meeting he himself had ever been a part of, an even half of the four he knew to have taken place over the years. The last time he was present the clandestine affair had taken place at a renovated villa outside the city, the kickoff to the arrangement. The mood in that meeting had been jovial and optimistic, both sides eating and toasting until the wee hours of the morning.

This one was different in every way, from the medieval accommodations they found themselves in to the somber mood permeating the air.

Exactly ten minutes after arrival, Molina began the proceedings by motioning across the table.

Opposite him Guzman bowed his head forward a few inches, twisting it just slightly to the side, before sitting up straight. "Good evening, Arturo. I'm glad to see you and yours alive and well this evening."

"Goose," Molina replied, extending his hand again, this time to motion to Rafa and Sanchez. "I am glad we are able to come together like this and discuss matters in a civilized manner."

There was no direct mention of what had taken place a few nights before, though Thiago picked up on it immediately. Tonight would not be an instance for prolonged pleasantries, the two sides foregoing even breaking bread before cutting right to business.

"As am I," Guzman replied. "Would you like to begin?"

Raising a fist to his mouth, Molina coughed once to clear his throat. The sound of phlegm catching echoed through the room as he settled back and wiped his fist against the side of his thigh.

"Two nights ago, my men arrived at the Anza-Borrego National Park to receive our normal delivery. They were first to the rendezvous point, after which your team arrived. They waited a few moments to exit their vehicle though, stating later that they had seen something moving in the night."

He delivered the words with clinical precision, having listened to the story no less than a dozen times from Thiago. Only once he was certain he had every detail committed to memory did he refine them into his own monologue, using Thiago to fact check everything he said.

"At that point my team opted to hold off on the transaction, asking your men to use the spotlight mounted to their truck to ensure complete privacy before continuing. In the course of that search someone was spotted, at which point the exchange was called off and the two sides departed."

It was an extremely scrubbed down account of what occurred, though Thiago couldn't see where any greater detail was really needed. This version of the affair got the crux of the story across without insinuating blame of any kind, delivering the information and nothing more.

"Does this coincide with your version of events?" Molina asked, shifting the conversation back across the table.

From where he was seated, Thiago could see the faces of all three men on the opposite side, watching their reactions. The old man in the middle had been nothing short of stony since arrival, the men on either side flicking their gaze between him and Molina.

None gave away anything.

"Yes," Guzman said. He paused, arching an eyebrow. "From the report given by my team, it was their belief that no foul play was performed by your men."

Despite his dislike for Felipe personally, Thiago knew there was no way he would try to pin anything on he and Hector. The stakes were too high to allow some personal differences to submarine things.

"And I have been given the same information from my men regarding yours," Molina replied.

Three different times on the flight down Molina had asked that very question, pushing it to borderline annoyance, but each time Thiago had remained adamant.

"It is also my understanding that you were able to retain the entirety of your product," Molina said.

Rafa's face twitched just slightly, the only outward expression of any kind to the question.

"Yes," Guzman said. "All mules were taken to safety here in

Mexico. I trust that you received a full reimbursement for your payment?"

"I did," Molina said, nodding.

At that both sides fell silent, a tiny bit of tension bleeding from the air. The opening volley had been far less about establishing the basic parameters of what had happened than about either side ensuring the other knew they had nothing to do with it.

Now that each party had agreed that neither held the other responsible, that no drugs were lost or money squandered, they could move forward.

A moment passed as either side digested what had already taken place, preparing themselves to begin anew.

Guzman took the lead.

"Heat?"

"Nothing," Molina said. "Quite low key for us for some time."

"FBI? DEA?" Guzman asked.

"Not in over a year now," Molina replied. "In fact, things have been so quiet I was away on vacation with my wife when this occurred."

Thiago knew this was the ultimate stamp on Molina's assertions. Never would he risk leaving in the middle of a potential investigation, a fact every person in the room was intimately aware of.

"On your end?" Molina asked.

Light reflected off of Guzman's smooth pate as he shook his head to either side. "No, but that is not a surprise. Compared to the United States, Ecuador is essentially the Wild West. Rarely do we have much law enforcement looking into our affairs.

"What we do have is usually your organizations working internationally."

The last statement sounded just a tiny bit defensive, a fact Thiago was certain didn't go unnoticed by his boss.

"The mules have all been happy with the arrangement, keep arriving in a steady stream," Guzman said. "We are aware of increased presence from Federale's and border patrol, but have had no direct run-ins."

Three days had passed since the incident. In that time Thiago had riffled through every possible permutation in his mind of what happened. Thus far, he agreed with everything that had been stated by Molina and Guzman.

The effort was too random, too small, too uncoordinated to have been put together by any of the alphabet organizations. If it had been, they would have waited until an exchange was made. They never would have let the product leave the country, and they certainly wouldn't have allowed Thiago, Hector, and Dante to fire on them without response.

There was also the matter of the items they found in the sand, of searching the girl's house and the photos he had seen hanging on her wall. As much as he hated to ever allow anything to be attributed to pure bad luck, there didn't seem to be another viable answer.

"Your thoughts?" Guzman asked, leaning forward and resting his elbows on the table. He laced his fingers in front of him, staring back at Molina, ignoring every other person in the room.

Viewing only the back of his head, Thiago could see his employer nod twice. He knew the old man felt the same way he did about what they'd found, would not bother to share it unless he felt it absolutely necessary.

"After your men departed," Molina said, his slow cadence and low tenor making it clear he was about to venture into something he wasn't thrilled with, "some items were discovered."

Across from him Guzman leaned forward another inch, his gaze narrowing slightly.

"They were small, personal items," Molina said, "consistent with a hiker or some such person being out for the night."

The answer was not entirely truthful, the first time in years Thiago had heard Molina withhold even the slightest detail. It surprised him a tiny bit, though instantly he knew why his boss had chosen to do so.

If the girl was involved, he wanted the first chance to catch her. If she wasn't, he didn't want to present such a foolish unlikelihood as a solution.

"Meaning?" Guzman asked.

"Meaning as we speak, my men are tracking them down to determine how much of a risk they are," Molina said.

"And if they are?" Guzman pressed.

"We will eliminate them," Molina replied. He paused, waiting for some form of a response from Guzman, the tension in the room ratcheting upward a tiny bit.

"And we would even be happy to include a group of your men in doing so, if you would like," Molina added.

Chapter Twenty-Three

Diaz listened in silence as I relayed the entirety of the encounter with Hector Ortega to her. I had already done so when I first made the call to her right outside Lake's house, but this time was much more in-depth, covering everything in painstaking detail. I left nothing out as I recited the incident back to her, watching the folds of skin pile up along her jawline as she drew her chin back into her neck, frowning.

Twice throughout I tried to draw Lake into the conversation, more to get her talking, to take that first step out of shock, than to hear any input she had to add. Both times though she merely shook me off, offering nothing more than a near-inaudible murmur.

Once I was completely done, Diaz paced the opposite side of the room from us, her arms folded across her torso. The sleeves on her suit coat rode up her forearms as she did so, her hair piled high atop her head.

On first appearance, it looked like the last day and a half had been just as taxing on her as Lake and I. The dark crescents under each eye had grown a little more pronounced, her skin even more pale.

The heels of her shoes clicked against the tile as she paced back and forth, digesting the events of the day.

"Are you okay?" she asked me, glancing over as she continued to move.

I had washed away Ortega's blood from my hand and arms, though spots of it still speckled my t-shirt and the leg of my jeans. A few shards of wood had nested into my beard, my attention span far too short to pick them out one at a time.

"Yeah," I said, nodding. "This isn't my blood."

She nodded and flicked her glance to Lake, asking me how she was doing without saying as much.

In the six hours since everything happened, Lake hadn't said much at all. The young and defiant woman I had met the day before was gone, pulled back into herself, a hard shell put up in place.

I shrugged to Diaz, not sure how to respond.

To be honest, this was the girl I had expected to encounter when I first arrived. What she endured in the desert, being spotted and shot at, should have shaken her to near catatonia. Instead, due to any number of factors ranging from her escape to the belief that nobody knew who she was, it had only emboldened her.

Today, though, had shattered that false sense of security. She had gotten a clear look at what was out there, would now have to accept that she was on their radar.

A light flicked on in the adjoining room, shining through the one-way glass we were standing behind. It threw a bright white glow across all three of us, revealing an interrogation room. In the center of it was a metal table painted slate grey, a single wooden chair on either side of it.

"They must finally be done processing him," Diaz said, stopping her walk and turning to look into the room. The frown and the crossed arms both remained in place as the door on the far back wall opened.

The first person through was an oversized guard with mocha colored skin and arms that looked to be twice their normal size. His head was shaved clean and his natural facial expression was a glower as he went straight to the table and pulled back the closest chair.

Next to enter was Hector Ortega. Still wearing the same jeans and sleeveless Bob Seger t-shirt he had been at the house, the only difference in his appearance was a thick swath of bandages encasing his left arm, a result of the bullet I put into him, the round passing through and through without doing any major damage.

Had I even seen the man before pulling the trigger, I would have been quite proud of the placement.

As was, I was just glad I hadn't killed him, more for the opportunity he now presented than some moral ambiguity.

The third person in the procession was a second guard, a rail-thin man with buzzed hair and acne scars. He stopped flush with the threshold of the door and watched, an extendable baton in his hand.

Once Ortega was in his seat, his hands cuffed to the metal link rising from the center of the table, both guards retreated from the room.

Tomorrow he would be turned over to the federal penitentiary, brought up on charges of attempted murder and anything Diaz and her crew could get to stick. Until then he was property of the DEA, available for full questioning in an ongoing investigation.

Once the door behind him slammed shut, Ortega leaned forward, resting his forearms on the table. He raised his gaze just high enough to glare at us beneath bushy eyebrows, squeezing his right fist, his left dangling lank from the bullet wound.

"He knows he can't see us back here, right?" Diaz asked, watching the display the man was putting on.

The right corner of my mouth lifted itself upward, both in response to the comment and the candor with which it was delivered. "I bet he's having a great time mean mugging his own reflection though."

This time it was Diaz's turn to smirk, a tiny chuckle rolling out behind it. "Should I tell him his hairstyle went out of style in the eighties?"

I shrugged, not in a position to tell anybody how to cut their hair. "He's got good taste in music, at least."

Beside me I could see Diaz nod in agreement, though she said nothing.

We remained there a moment, sitting in silence, watching Ortega attempt to stare daggers through the glass, before she turned back to face me. "You going to stick around?"

"For a few minutes," I said. "I want to be sure to leave before you do, though."

"Why's that?"

I stuck my chin toward the window, motioning at Ortega. "In case anybody is casing him, hoping to draw us out. I was hoping maybe we could switch vehicles for a while, too."

My first thought was that a comment about driving my truck was coming, but to her credit none did. Instead she considered the request a moment before nodding. "Yeah. In the event they were working as a team, somebody might have seen your truck, maybe even followed the parade here."

She fished down into her right pants pocket and extracted a key ring, an automated locking fob and a single key on it. She tossed them my way and I snagged it with my left hand.

"Third row."

There was no need for her to point out the make and model. I had ridden in her car on more than one occasion the last time we worked together.

"Thanks," I said, sliding out my own keys and showing them to her before placing them down on the table beside me.

She nodded in understanding, but said nothing.

Once more she shifted back to the window and pushed out a long sigh. Her features hardened as she stared at the man, preparing herself for the battle ahead.

"That was good work today," she said without looking my direction. "We've been running down everything we can on Felipe Soto, but like I said before, so far the man has proven to be a ghost. This will give us another direction to run in, hopefully find something that ties them together."

I nodded, having thought the same thing all afternoon. There was no way Ortega's showing up at Lake's house had been random.

"Was he in the system?" I asked.

"Couple of misdemeanor carrying-without-a-permit charges,"

Diaz said. "First one got him some probation, second got him two nights in the clink before he was sent home due to overcrowding."

"Carrying twice and they couldn't tie him to anything heavier than a misdemeanor?" I asked.

"Apparently," Diaz said. "Both times the officers said there was no sign of intent to commit a felony."

I made no attempt to mask my snort as I again looked over the man staring back at us. "Somehow I have a hard time believing that."

"Me too," Diaz agreed, "but he's only been a naturalized citizen four years now, so take that for what it's worth."

She cast me a glance as she delivered the information, both of us knowing what it meant. More often than not somebody like Ortega worked across the border, putting in their time for an organization. If after a certain point they were deemed worthy, they were brought over and their immigration paperwork fast tracked, graduating up in the ranks.

Given the photos Lake had taken and everything this case seemed to be pointing toward, Ortega carried all the familiar earmarks.

"Check-in in the morning?" Diaz asked, looking in my direction.

"Eight o'clock," I said, nodding for emphasis.

We paused a moment before she matched the nod and dropped her hands by her side. "Alright, here I go."

"Turn the page," I added, drawing a smirk as she exited the room, the sound of her shoes echoing as she departed.

A full minute passed before she entered on the opposite side of the glass, her face a mask of acrimony as she strode into the room, a file in hand.

I watched the first few moments of the encounter, the drill playing out the same as it always did. For every pointed question Diaz lobbed, trying to strike flesh, Ortega had either a smart retort or total silence, his disdain for her rolling off him in undulating waves.

There was no doubt that eventually Diaz would get something she could use, but after five minutes I had had enough. Rotating in my chair I turned to regard Lake, her head raised, her focus on the interview taking place.

I waited a moment for her to acknowledge my gaze, but when it never came I prompted, "Doing okay?"

The sound of my voice caused her to flinch just slightly. She jerked her attention away from the interview and looked to me, her eyes a touch wider than usual.

"How did you know he was behind me?"

The question was one I wasn't expecting, the first complete sentence she had spoken in hours. The twang I had barely noticed in her voice before was now much more pronounced, all inhibitions beyond self-preservation falling by the wayside.

"I saw his shadow," I replied, opting for the truth.

Her eyes remained wide as she looked at me, a touch of shock still on her features. "That was pretty impressive, the way you handled things today."

I considered responding but decided against it, choosing to let her continue, saying whatever she needed to to help her through the moment.

"Sorry I was such a spaz."

Her choice of words brought a smile to my face, my head dropping toward my lap for a moment before I raised it to look at her. "You weren't a spaz, by any stretch of the imagination."

"But I kind of was," she countered, her voice still detached, though gaining a bit of steam. "I mean, I have wild hair and tattoos, I've been in major storms and some bad places for work before. I like to think I'm tough, but when it really mattered..."

I knew exactly what was she trying to say. I knew it better than she could possibly realize, had seen it from every angle before.

"Don't do that," I said. "I've been in the navy and the DEA with guys that reacted the same exact way you did their first time."

I paused, taking a quick breath, collecting my thoughts.

It was true, she had frozen up pretty stiff, but all things considered, there were worse ways she could have reacted. She didn't do anything foolish, getting one or both of us injured. She didn't scream and cry, hadn't thrashed about or thrown a tantrum in the aftermath.

Instead, she had allowed her body to do what it did best, which was protect her. Her hormones and neurotransmitters acted in concert to put her in the best situation possible.

"Being tough is one thing," I said. "Living alone, making a career as a photographer, those things are tough. What you went through today..." I let my voice drift off, hoping she followed what I was trying to say. "They can't be compared. You can't hold it against yourself."

She stared at me a moment, seemingly debating if I was serious or just putting her on. "But you seemed to do just fine."

Today, I did. But there were many times in the past, times such as the death of my family, when I hadn't, not by a long shot.

"It wasn't my first time," I said, leaving the explanation at that.

As if understanding what I was saying, perhaps even recalling the things she had overheard at headquarters, she decided not to press it and simply nodded. She shifted her attention back to the interview, her eyes glazing over as she stared at Ortega.

"You would have killed him if you had to, wouldn't you?"

Chapter Twenty-Four

The first call came in less than two minutes after the wheels touched down in Palmdale. Thiago had barely had a chance to turn his phone back on when it started vibrating, a local number that he didn't recognize popping up on screen. Ignoring it, he continued his conversation with his boss, setting out a course for the days ahead.

The meeting had been a success, both sides walking away safe in the belief that the other had nothing to do with the troubles their enterprise had encountered. Neither was especially happy about the outcome, or the loss of money and product that had been incurred, but both were pragmatic enough to realize that one isolated incident in years together was no reason to jeopardize a booming relationship.

Moving forward, Thiago had been tasked with finding the girl within thirty-six hours. At that time a call would be placed to Guzman, who would arrive either in person or via proxy for the interrogation, ensuring both sides were fully content there was no danger in recommencing activity.

Once that occurred, shipments would start again as usual. All told one aborted exchange and one that was cancelled due to the in-person rendezvous.

Not ideal, but far better than it could have been.

The second call arrived three minutes later, the plane just coming to a complete stop. This time Thiago killed it without even removing it from his pants pocket, merely squeezing the sides of it, feeling the buttons depress.

One last time Molina gave Thiago the directive to find the girl, out of sight if possible, but if special considerations had to be made, so be it. Once his orders were explicitly stated the old man released him, the same stewardess Thiago had slid past ten hours before dropping the stairs and motioning him out.

After being in the climate controlled cabin, the evening air felt cool as Thiago stepped down onto the tarmac. The grass was soft and spongy beneath his feet as he padded across it, seeing the small hangar two hundred yards away, a trio of security lights illuminating it.

Beside it he could make out his truck and the black Lexus, a small handful of other vehicles further back, nothing more than shadows.

Reaching into the inside pocket of the sport coat he'd been forced to wear for the evening, Thiago withdrew a Honduran cigar. Using a match from a booklet kept in the same pocket he lit it, filling his mouth to capacity with smoke and holding it, letting the flavor roll over his taste buds.

The phone rang a third time.

Shoving the smoke out in an angry huff, Thiago extracted his iPhone. He looked down to see the same number staring at him, the veins in his forearm bulging as he squeezed it.

"Who is this?" he snapped, bypassing any form of colloquial greeting.

"Where the hell have you been?" a male voice on the other end snapped back, bypassing both a salutation and Thiago's question.

The words only served to heighten the vitriol flowing through Thiago. He grabbed the cigar from his mouth and spit out a stray bit of tobacco, turning over his shoulder to ensure Molina and his staff were still inside the plane.

"Listen," he seethed, "I don't know who the hell this is or how you got this number, but I suggest you lose it, *now*."

"Thiago," the man said, "it's Paul."

For a moment Thiago fell silent, allowing the anger to flow away, waiting for his mind to compute what he was being told.

"Detective Paulo Gomez."

With the cigar cradled between his index and middle finger, Thiago raised his hand and scratched at the back his head. He muttered under his breath as he began walking again, cursing himself.

"Paulie," Thiago said. "Why the hell didn't your name come up on my phone?"

In the years Thiago had known him, never before could he remember Gomez actually calling him. He recalled their last encounter a day before, the detective almost sprinting to the meeting, wanting to run away the entire time he was there.

Whatever had caused him to be calling now couldn't be good.

"I'm at a payphone," Gomez replied. His voice was lower, his cadence faster than usual. Thiago could almost picture him hunkered down somewhere, turning over either shoulder, watching every person that walked by, twitching at every shadow.

The feeling of concern within him only grew.

"How bad?" Thiago asked, bypassing any question of why Gomez was using a payphone. He already knew the answer, figuring the detective was trying to leave as little trail between them as possible in the event somebody decided to go looking one day.

"As you know, I've got markers in the system for all you guys," Gomez said. "Somebody gets pinged, it comes up for me."

Thiago nodded as he reached his truck. Instead of climbing inside he merely leaned against it, the phone and cigar in either hand. "And?"

"And Hector got pinched," Gomez said, words so low they were barely discernible.

With everything that had happened in the preceding hours, Thiago had forgotten that his partner was still staked out on the girl's house. His being arrested meant that either someone had spotted him or that he had made a move and was taken down in the process.

"How bad?" he repeated.

"DEA," Gomez said. He added nothing more to the statement, allowing Thiago to take from it what he would.

Feeling his eyes slide closed, Thiago again raised his hand to his head and dug at his scalp. He could hear his fingernails moving over his course hair as he shoved the data in with what he already knew.

"Not LAPD?" he asked.

"Nope," Gomez said. "DEA, Santa Ana division."

This was much worse than he originally thought.

If Hector had been spotted or even picked up in the act of trying to grab Lake, it should have been LAPD to do it. For DEA to be booking him meant they were the ones that brought him in. For that to have occurred, they were either watching the house or were there with the girl, neither of which played well for the organization.

Santa Ana was just a few miles inland from her house, the closest station, making it even more likely they had been on him from the start.

"Alright," Thiago said, "thanks for the heads up, Paulie. You keep an ear out, let me know if anything else comes up, yeah?"

He could tell the thanks had come as a surprise to Gomez, the only response a sputtering promise to pass along anything before Thiago cut off the call. He shoved the cigar back into his mouth and used his hips to rise a few inches from the side of his truck, shrugging his jacket down off of his shoulders.

The breeze hit his skin, cooling him down, making him realize for the first time that he was sweating.

Resuming his position he shoved out a burst of smoke, watching as Declan began to exit the aircraft, Jasmine teetering on four inch heels behind him. At some point soon he would need to fill everyone in about what he had just learned, but not quite yet. There was still too much he didn't know to begin inciting any kind of panic.

Clearly the girl had seen something that night, enough to warrant seeking out protection. Whether she was now being used as bait or being protected didn't much matter. What did was that the DEA was sniffing around, and in his experience once they started it was damn near impossible to get rid of them.

That part of the equation he couldn't do much about at the moment, but he could still deal with the more pressing problem, and that was the girl.

Pulling his phone out again, he called up a recently installed app and worked his way through a series of commands, watching as the electronic device set to carry out his orders.

When it was done Thiago rose from the side of the truck and headed toward the driver's side door, a smile on his face for the first time all day.

Chapter Twenty-Five

The combined effects of consecutive nights without proper sleep and the enormous jolt of adrenaline supplied by the encounter with Hector Ortega had my system running on reserve energy. I could feel strength seeping out of me, my eyelids beginning to droop as I sat propped up in bed, the laptop perched atop my thighs.

Every other light in the room was extinguished, the pale white color illuminating my face and nothing more.

"Porn?" Lake asked, her voice emanating out of the darkness beside me. It sent a quick pang of trepidation through me, my muscles seizing momentarily before I relaxed, a weak smile crossing my face.

"That obvious?" I asked.

The heavy bedding she was buried under crinkled as she rolled over, a bit of ambient light catching her face, making it appear even more pale than usual. She glanced to me and then to the screen.

"Still watching that room at the Marriott?"

"Just making sure," I replied. "At this point I don't look for anybody to turn up there, but it doesn't hurt to keep an eye out."

For the second consecutive night we were squirreled away in a bland chain hotel room, under a different pseudonym. This time we had taken the extra step of driving a bit further away from Huntington Beach, going clear up into El Segundo to stay near the airport.

The traffic getting there was brutal, but it was worth it to have the extra density the location provided. It also made us one of thousands of rooms, just two more faces passing through, no matter how unique we might appear.

"You should sleep," she said. "I can tell you're tired."

I didn't bother to ask how she knew that, figuring the answer was pretty plain on my features. "As should you. Today was a big one, for all of us."

Her bedding ruffled again as she rolled over onto her back, staring up at the ceiling. After a moment I could hear her sniffle softly, see her hands rise to her cheeks, presumably to wipe away tears.

A hundred different thoughts came to mind, all some sort of placation I could pass her way. I could tell her that it was all going to be okay, that soon Diaz and her crew would have whoever this was pinned down. I could tell her that we got whoever wanted to hurt her, and everything would now be alright.

Truth was, I didn't know any of those things for a fact. So instead, I told her the one thing I did know.

"I'm not going to let anything happen to you," I said.

The breath caught in her chest as she heard the words, rolling over onto her shoulder to stare at me. She pulled the comforter up in front of her chest, using a corner of it to wipe her eyes, as I continued to watch the screen in front of me.

Nothing but an empty hotel room, bought and paid for at the bargain price of a hundred dollars a night.

"Tell me about yourself," she said.

The words pulled a short laugh from me, a purely reflexive noise that sounded extra loud in the quiet of the darkened room. I could feel blood flush my cheeks as I pressed my lips together and shook my head. "Afraid that's not really how this works."

"Why not?" she countered. "Aren't you supposed to build my trust?"

"Didn't I do that today?" I replied.

Instantly I regretted saying it, watching as she again rolled over onto her back, falling silent.

Since the moment I arrived two days before, I had made a point of maintaining a cordial, if not guarded relationship. It wasn't for fear of us becoming too close, this wasn't a bad romantic movie, she wasn't Whitney Houston and I damned sure wasn't Kevin Costner.

Rather, maintaining clearly defined roles made for better articulated spheres for us both to operate in. Keeping her at arm's length made it easier for me to observe, both her and our surroundings.

As much as I hated to admit it, I was approaching things like I was an active agent. I was keeping her safe, but I was also looking at things as if my primary objective was to work the case.

Nobody, Lake Pawlak especially, needed that from me.

"We'll go one for one," I said. "You go first."

"Okay," she said, not bothering to roll back over, snatching at the bait with surprising quickness. "Where are you from?"

Pushing a sigh out through my nose, I raised my hands to my face and rubbed vigorously, small white fireworks erupting behind my eyelids. "Here and there. Army brat."

By and large it was the truth, even if I did leave out enormous chunks, stories we didn't need to get into, not now and probably not ever.

"You?" I asked. "LA born and raised?"

Her lilt told me that wasn't the case, though her look seemed to indicate as much.

A derisive snort sounded out through the room, the intensity of it surprising me. "First fifteen in Plano, Texas. Next seven in Silver Spring, Maryland, of all places. You believe that?"

"No," I replied, the corners of my mouth curling up. "I've spent a fair bit of time in D.C. No offense, but I just can't see you playing the part there."

Again she snorted, this time with a bit more mirth. "I didn't, though most of what you see now happened once I got out here."

"Eighteen?"

"Twenty-two," she said. "Finished my degree and headed west."

"Ah," I replied. "UM?"

"Georgetown. You?"

"GW," I said.

"No shit?" she asked, her head rotating to look my direction. When no further explanation came she laid back and whispered, "Small world."

She paused, seemingly debating the information, before asking, "That how you ended up in the DEA?"

"No," I replied, "that wasn't until after the navy."

"Ah, a sailor," she said, no small amount of knowing in her voice. If she had spent her high school and college years in Silver Spring she had no doubt encountered thousands of young ensigns from Annapolis, the trace bit of disdain in her voice well earned. "Is that why the hair?"

Again my mouth turned upward in a smile, my head leaning back to rest against the wall behind me. "Naw, that's just something I do every winter. I go off the grid for a while, don't really care what I look like."

The smile grew larger. "That, and it's really damn cold up there in February."

I flicked my gaze over to her, for the first time seeing her teeth flash in the thin light. "And where is up there?"

For a moment I wondered if I should tell her, if her knowing might one day come back to haunt one or both of us. Fact was though, Diaz had already showed up to see me at my shop. If someone wanted to find me, I wasn't exactly hiding.

"Montana," I said. "I took all that tracking and survival training the government gave me and became a guide in Yellowstone."

"Yeah?" she asked, a bit of excitement creeping in. "I've always heard Yellowstone is incredible."

Keeping my head pressed back against the wall, I rolled it her direction. "Incredible doesn't begin to do the park justice. A photographer like you would love it."

"I bet I would," she agreed, her voice lowering itself a few decibels. "When this is over, you'll have to show me around sometime."

A moment passed as I considered the request. For anybody else, it would be seemingly simple, something I would be happy to oblige. For her though, there was no way of knowing what the coming days, or even weeks or months, might hold.

There was no way of knowing if she would ever be free to do things like take her camera to Old Faithful or set off on a hiking trail just to see where it took her.

Reaching out, I closed the top cover of my laptop, the only light in the room blinking out. I set the device on the table beside me and slid down a few inches into bed.

"We should probably both get some sleep. Tomorrow could be another long day."

Chapter Twenty-Six

Diaz recognized the scent long before it arrived. After twelve straight hours of chipping away at Hector Ortega she was beyond exhausted. There would be no time for sleep, not with so many unknowns still floating around, not with Hawk and Lake still exposed.

The coffee she smelled approaching fast would be a good start though.

Reclined in a hard plastic desk chair, Diaz remained with one elbow propped on the desk, her feet on an opposing seat, her thumb and forefinger pressed over her eyes. She stayed like that until the coffee was placed in front of her, the paper cup echoing off of the wooden desktop.

"Rough night?"

Diaz fought the urge to make a sarcastic retort, pulling her hand back to reveal Lefranc standing before her. She had known it would be him long before he arrived, he being the only person in the agency that didn't see the problem with drinking a vanilla soy macchiato.

"Like swinging a sledgehammer at a brick wall," Diaz said, watching as Lefranc shuffled from foot to foot before her, fidgeting slightly. He took a quick drink of his macchiato, fighting to avoid eye contact, until Diaz removed her feet from the opposing chair and used her heel to slide it in his direction.

The night before she had worked alone, not wanting to step on anybody's toes in the Santa Ana office by bringing in a large contingent. Even within the same agency pissing matches over turf issues were a common occurrence, something she could ill afford to bother with at the moment. Once it had become apparent that Ortega was going nowhere though, she had phoned headquarters and asked for somebody to join her in the morning.

Not once had she thought it would be Lefranc.

As soon as she was done with this investigation she would have to determine who she'd pissed off badly enough to warrant such a punishment.

"He didn't give up anything?" Lefranc asked.

Diaz shook her head, chancing to lift the lid from the cup of coffee he had brought her. Finding the liquid dark, she leaned forward and sniffed, finding no floral notes of any kind.

"Plain black," Lefranc said.

Nodding once, Diaz raised it and took a long drink, finishing a full third of the cup in one pull. The hot liquid burned down her throat and into her chest as it traveled to her stomach, the placebo effect of knowing liquid caffeine was in her system enough to raise her awareness a bit.

"Thanks," she said, taking a second, smaller drink before setting the cup down. She sat and watched him continue to fidget for a moment, seeing in an instant why Lake Pawlak had gotten the best of him.

The problem wasn't with his abilities as an agent. Twice she had done performance reviews on him herself, both times finding his skills more than adequate.

The problem was he was uncomfortable with women.

Under different circumstances she might have found the realization humorous, perhaps even used it for a bit of sport. On this morning she just found it annoying, one more hurdle she would have to deal with in the course of this investigation.

"Started by playing the *no habla anglais* card, I guess not noticing that I'm Hispanic as well," Diaz said. "Somewhere around midnight his attempts at broken Spanglish broke down and he just became angry. Couple hours after that he chose to take the *you-guys-have-no-idea-who-you're-messing-with* route."

Lefranc nodded, the knot of his tie bobbing beneath his throat. "So he admitted there is someone and that they're a heavy hitter."

"Pretty much," Diaz said, "but I don't think he realized it. By that point he was so high up on his moral soap box I don't even think he noticed I was still in the room."

Around them the office began to come alive for the morning. Handfuls of people started to filter through the door, the usual din of morning gossip and smells of coffee and bagels passing by. It was the exact same as every office Diaz had ever been in, ranging all sizes and functions.

Human nature was human nature.

As an extension of that she wasn't surprised when many of the employees cast her sideways glances as they passed, everybody curious who the new people using the loaner desk for the morning were.

"So what's the plan?" Lefranc asked. "Gearing up to make another run at him?"

"No," Diaz said, twisting her head to either side. "The prosecutors showed up a few minutes ago and are in there with him now."

She paused, taking another drink of the coffee. "Apparently since he was shot yesterday, keeping him up all night for questioning was already bordering on abuse. Any longer and we risked getting the case thrown out."

Dealing with the deep chasm that existed between what she could uncover and what it took to get a suspect through the court system was something she was fast coming to loathe. Day by day the requirements imposed on her grew, making it so that soon it would take up the lion's share of her time.

"He was shot?" Lefranc asked. "By you?"

"Hawk," Diaz said, her gaze fixed on a man approaching from down the hall. She could see Lefranc's eyes grow wide with surprise at the mention of Hawk shooting Ortega, but didn't bother to respond.

Instead she focused in as a man that looked to be no more than twenty-five grew closer. Dressed in a short-sleeve dress shirt and striped tie, a lanyard around his neck, it was plain at a glance that he was from the IT department.

Just the person she was waiting to see.

Leaving Lefranc with obvious questions on his face, Diaz stood and met the young man out in front of the desk. She thrust her hand out and said, "You must be Tobey."

"Tobey Plemons," he replied, returning the handshake. He had a weak grip and his palm felt sweaty, the top of his head barely reaching Diaz's chin. Short red hair was pushed to the side and his cheeks were blotchy, not the faintest whiff of facial hair present. "What can I do for you this morning?"

Extending a hand toward the chair she had just been sitting in, Diaz said, "Please, have a seat."

She waited as he did so, settling in behind him and folding her arms across her chest.

"As you can see here, this is the file for Hector Ortega, a suspect we have in custody at the moment."

Pulling a pair of horn-rimmed glasses from the chest pocket of his shirt, Tobey perched them on the tip of his nose. Behind them he squinted his eyes up tight and leaned in, his lips moving slightly as he read the screen.

"Okay," he said.

"At the bottom," Diaz said, resisting the urge to lean forward and take the mouse to speed things along, "it appears somebody has accessed Ortega's file recently."

It took a moment for Tobey to make his way to the bottom, finally spotting the marker. "Yes," he agreed.

Rolling her eyes behind him, Diaz made no effort to mask the growing disgust in her voice. "Can you find out who it was?"

In the reflection on the screen, she could see Plemons study the file another moment before a lopsided smile grew on his features. Using his foot he rotated around to face her and slid the glasses from his face.

"Give me an hour."

Chapter Twenty-Seven

The decision to use a hotel near LAX was deliberate. Not only did it provide us personal anonymity, just two more faces in a sea of tens of thousands passing through each day, but it gave us situational anonymity as well.

Unlike hotels further away, there was no parking lot for anybody to troll. The sedan Diaz had loaned us was tucked away in the valet-only parking garage beneath the building. There was no way anybody looking for it would just happen to stumble upon it, no chance that they could post up and wait for us to emerge.

Furthering our isolated position was the dense urban confines of the immediate airport area.

From where I sat, the computer chair pulled up alongside the window, the thin shade drawn closed, not a single blade of grass could be seen. Nowhere was there even a square of turf for a half mile in any direction, no place for the smallest of dogs to relieve themselves. Every last inch of available space was employed for some specific enterprise, whether it be a hotel, a dry cleaners, or a minimart.

What that meant for us was if there wasn't enough room for somebody to plant a single tree, there definitely wasn't the space to be wasted on parking. Anybody that somehow had an inkling we were nearby would have no choice but to keep circling, hoping they got lucky.

"Anything good out there?" Lake asked.

She was seated cross legged on the bed in a pair of running shorts and a tank top, her hair hanging wet and lank about her face. Spread on the bed before her were two small digital cameras, both with their visual display screens on, a series of images flashing by.

The combination of sleep and the passage of time had done wonders for her. The pale, shocked complexion she wore the night before had receded. She still wasn't quite back to the girl dressing Lefranc down at the DEA headquarters, but she was a lot closer to that than the shell-shocked figure I'd carried out of her cottage.

"Why people choose to live here is beyond me," I said, sitting and watching more folks pass in the span of an hour than I saw most weeks in Montana.

"Some would say the same about living up there in the boonies," she countered, glancing up from her work, a bit of a smile on her face.

"Actually, the preferred term is God's Country," I countered, matching the smile as I returned my attention to the street below.

To that she had no answer as she went back to the cameras, one of the few items we were able to grab and throw into a bag in the time between taking Ortega down and the DEA showing up.

"What did Diaz have to say this morning?" she asked, bypassing my comment entirely.

I smirked slightly, just enough to let her know I noticed, and said, "Ortega last night got them nowhere. Apparently somebody's been following him in the system though and they are looking into it right now. She seemed hopeful that it would lead them in the right direction."

I didn't bother to add that the right direction and the final destination were often far apart, or that Diaz sounded even more exhausted than the last time we had spoken.

She asked a follow up question that didn't register with me, all sound falling away. My focus pulled in on a red Chevy pickup truck, the paint faded from the sun. A trail of muddy spatter fanned upward from both the front and rear tires with a roll bar across the top.

The vehicle was easily recognizable anywhere, even more so in a place like Los Angeles. There were precious few reasons for a person in downtown to need that kind of horsepower, far fewer as to why they would have circled the same block outside the airport three times in under an hour.

On the bed Lake continued to prattle on as I stood and snatched up the phone from the desk. For the first time I ventured pulling back the curtain entirely, wanting an unobstructed view as the truck rolled by and pulled up to a stoplight at the end of the block.

It was less than a half hour since our regularly scheduled check-in, but still Diaz answered after a single ring.

"Run this plate," I said, not bothering with any opening comments. I issued the words not as a command, but with enough urgency she would know exactly what I was getting at.

"Shoot," she said, her voice exuding the same sense of urgency.

I rattled off the series of numerals and digits, allowing the curtain to fall back into place. Even still I remained in place and watched as the light turned green, the truck making a left and disappearing from sight.

"Tobey, get up," Diaz barked on the other end of the line, followed by the clatter of a chair rolling atop tile. A moment later I heard her plop down into a seat as her fingers danced over a keyboard.

I became aware that all other sound in the room had fallen away, Lake sitting up, her attention on me.

"Are you being followed?" Diaz asked, continuing to type.

"No, we're stationary right now," I said. "But the same truck has circled the place three times this morning."

"Shit," Diaz whispered, her voice trailing off, presumably as she read from a screen. "Hawk, give me five minutes."

The line cut out without another word, a simple click followed by silence. I pulled the phone away and stared down at it a moment before putting the ringer on as high as it would go and placing it back down on the desk.

"Get your stuff together, now," I said, shifting to Lake and making a circular motion with my hand.

On command she leapt up from the bed and began buzzing about the room, grabbing everything within reach and stuffing it into her duffel. The cameras she tucked into their bag before tossing them into the heap, piling more clothes above them before disappearing into the bathroom.

The sound of her bare feet shuffling on tile echoed through the room as I remained standing vigil at the window. For the first time all morning I became aware of the warm sun streaming through, of the heat starting to form beneath my beard and at the small of my back. My heart rate increased just slightly as I counted the seconds off in my head, willing Diaz to call back.

I made it to two hundred and ten before the phone erupted beside me, my hand snatching it up mid-ring and pressing it to my ear.

"Yeah."

"You're not going to believe this," Diaz said, pushing forward without giving me a chance to comment. "The truck is registered to a junkyard in East Los Angeles, the owner of which is listed as a Grace Peroux."

My brow furrowed as I tried to place the name, nothing coming to me. "Who is Grace Peroux?"

"I have no idea," Diaz said, "but she has the same history of somebody poking into her file as Ortega."

Chapter Twenty-Eight

"Shit," Paulo Gomez muttered, just loud enough that he could hear it but nobody else could. "Shit shit shit."

He rattled the curse out again and again, no other word feeling remotely applicable as he race walked away from the precinct. He kept his gaze averted, his body pitched forward as he made the corner and took a quick right, pausing just long enough to check his tail.

Content he wasn't being followed, he ducked into the back of Paddy's Bar, the place open no more than ten minutes. The front door was standing wide, a delivery man from Budweiser wheeling in stacks of long neck bottles, light streaming in around him.

Behind the beat up wooden bar running most of the length of the room Gomez could see the old bartender Sal leaning forward, his hands resting on the polished surface. A white towel was thrown over one shoulder as he conversed with the delivery man, both of them laughing at something that was said.

Gomez ignored them both, going straight for the payphone on the wall between the men's and women's restrooms. The combined scents of beer, urine, and smoke touched his nostrils as he lifted the receiver, bringing a sheen of moisture to his eyes as he pumped in a handful of coins and dialed the number from memory.

"Come on," he whispered, "pick up the damn phone this time, Thiago."

To his surprise, he did.

"Yeah?" Thiago asked, sounding distracted, annoyed.

"Thiago, it's Paul." He could hear clicking in the background, like a blinker ticking on a front dashboard. "Where are you?"

There was a long pause, nothing but the clicking sound followed by the roar of an engine. Once it leveled out, Thiago said, "I'm near the airport, following up on something. What's going on?"

"You've got to get out of there," Gomez said.

"Why?" Thiago asked, not a hint of concern in his voice.

"Because somebody's spotted you," Gomez said. "A hit just came up in the system on your truck."

A short rush of wind passed by, Gomez knowing that meant Thiago was blowing out a cloud of smoke, the byproduct of those damn cigars he was always working on.

"What does that mean?"

Turning to glance back, Gomez saw the delivery man had stopped working, he and Sal openly talking on either side of the bar. Both seemed to be enjoying the conversation, their laughter reverberating through the empty room.

"It means somebody with access to the law enforcement file system saw you and ran a search on your plates," Gomez said. "And five minutes later they ran Grace, too."

For the first time since placing the call, Thiago seemed to understand the urgency Gomez was feeling. He heard a loud burst of air pass through, followed by Thiago spitting, the one-two punch that signified he had gotten rid of the cigar.

That's how Gomez knew Thiago finally understood.

"Grace?" he said, his voice low, graveled.

"Yeah," Gomez said. "I don't know how or why, but it hit. You know as well as I do once they start digging there what happens next."

Another moment passed, long enough that Gomez wondered if the call had cut out. He pulled the phone from his ear and looked down at the receiver, before placing it back next to his head. "Thiago?"

"I've got to go," Thiago said, the line going dead for real a moment later.

Gomez opened his mouth to respond, refraining from doing so as he realized the call was already over. Once more he looked at the receiver in his hand before placing it back in its cradle. He ran a hand over his face, his palm coming back wet with sweat.

This was far beyond anything Molina had asked of him before. He had always willingly kept an eye on the business, but the last three days had seen more action than the previous year combined.

Pulling a handkerchief from his pocket, he ran it over the outside of the phone receiver and along the plate of numbers. He stuffed it away and glanced back to the front, slipping back out the same way he'd come in just a few minutes earlier.

As he left he could still hear the two men laughing up front, neither one having even noticed he was there.

Chapter Twenty-Nine

I had a choice to make, and neither option was particularly appealing.

Lake and I could stay right where we were. We could hope that being tucked away in the busiest part of one of the busiest cities in the country would be enough to deter whoever was circling the place in that red pickup.

Doing so though included the assumption that that person was alone, that there wasn't somebody on foot already inside the hotel and that they were merely the driver, there to ensure a hasty getaway.

On the flip side, we could grab what few items we had, hop the back stairwell into the parking garage, and hit the road. We could stay moving long enough to let Diaz finish running down the hits in the system, then have her meet us for another car swap.

That plan too was not without its drawbacks, chief among them the assumption that we would be able to lose whoever was following us long enough to pull it off.

If my entire career had taught me anything though, whether it be in the navy or later with the DEA, it was that erring on the side of being proactive was never a bad idea. It was always better to react and change course when already in motion, maintaining control easier done when not sitting and waiting for whatever might come next.

Knowing that, I tucked away my laptop and drew the bag to my shoulder. Tossing the strap of my duffel atop it, I shoved the Glock into the rear waistband of my jeans.

Beside me Lake loaded up her gear as well, not having to be told that we were about to go on the move. More than once I could tell she wanted to ask where we were off to, but to her credit she remained silent.

Truth was, I had no idea where we were headed next. The LAX area had served its purpose, allowing us both to bank some much needed rest, though staying any longer would only enable the opposition to bring in reinforcements.

We needed to stay on the move, but it was imperative we remained in heavily populated areas. We had to make sure there were always ample witnesses around, plenty of obstacles to interrupt sightlines.

The actions of Hector Ortega the day before told me that whoever it was didn't have a great deal of fear of being seen, though I had always found people had a much higher tendency to get trigger happy in remote areas.

Besides, right now my job was to ensure Lake stayed safe, not to engage in open warfare.

Starting with the peep hole, I checked to make sure the hallway was clear before stepping out and peering in both directions. Seeing nothing unusual, I moved just a few feet away from the wall, placing Lake between myself and the smooth beige surface. From there I set the pace, moving fast, pulling her along without saying a word.

Thirty seconds after leaving the room I passed through the pressure release on the stairwell door, checking our tail as I motioned Lake past.

Aside from a pair of maids at the opposite end unloading supplies from their cart, there was no sign of anybody in the corridor.

The décor around us switched from carpet and painted walls to bare concrete and grey block, the sounds of our feet slapping against the stairs echoing through the empty space. It reverberated around us, intensifying the sound as we moved fast, dropping from the fifth floor to the first.

Every part of me wanted to tell Lake to wait right there, that I would go for the keys. I knew I could move faster without her, wanting her to stay shielded as long as possible.

At the same time, whoever was watching us had most likely already seen us together. If they now noticed me moving alone, they would know she was nearby and unprotected.

It was a risk I couldn't take.

Staying close to the wall, I kept a hand on the door to the stairwell as I peered out and scanned our surroundings, ready to pull us both back inside in an instant if necessary. In front of us a single car rolled by, a valet in a white shirt and red vest behind the wheel, heading up the ramp onto the second level. The man turned and glanced once our direction as he went, dismissing us just as fast as he rolled past.

If it was my truck in the lot, I would have taken us straight to it. I would have pulled the hide-a-key from the undercarriage and driven us directly out, bypassing the valet stand altogether.

As it stood though, we were stuck with the sedan, the only keys in the place tucked inside the booth at the mouth of the parking garage.

"Stay close," I whispered, feeling Lake's hands slide around my forearm, her shoulder pressing into my bicep as we walked forward. Each step pulled us further from the shadows of the concrete structure, the bright California sun visible outside, giving everything an unnaturally bright glow.

I could feel Lake's palms grow sweaty against my skin, my own heart rate rising as we approached the valet stand. Less than ten minutes had passed since the truck's last appearance, though that didn't necessarily mean anything. No larger than the city blocks were in this part of town, he could make a revolution and be back in half that if the lights were cooperating.

As we approached, a valet stepped out. Dressed in the same combo as his cohort, he had a head shaved bald and a thin goatee encasing his mouth, a gold chain around his neck. Despite the early hour he already looked bored, not the least bit surprised to see us approaching on foot.

"Claim ticket, please," he said, holding out a hand expectantly.

Reaching into my back pocket, I allowed my hand to graze the Glock tucked away, feeling the reassurance it provided. In most instances I didn't need a weapon to feel safe, but no part of me liked being this exposed, knowing somebody with ill intentions was circling nearby.

"We only need the keys," I said, forcing a smile into place as I extended the ticket to him. "I can drive us out."

"Can't do it," the man said, snatching the ticket away and checking the number. Ducking back inside the stand he selected our keys from the rack on the wall and said, "Against company policy. I'd lose my job."

Twenty different arguments sprang to mind as I watched him head out in the opposite direction, his gait in no particular hurry as he headed for the ramp and began to ascend.

Right now, his job was the least of my concerns. If not for the fact that it would have only gotten the police called on us, I would have pulled the Glock and made him hand the keys over.

Doing anything of the sort though would have only drawn more attention to us, something I could not abide right now. Instead I bit my tongue and watched as he sauntered off, wanting to yell for him to hurry his ass up, but keeping quiet.

"Get inside the stand," I whispered, pulling my arm across my body, helping Lake take the first few steps.

"What? No," she said, clinging tighter, her nails digging into my skin. "You're not leaving me here."

"I'm not," I said, looking past her, my attention on the road outside. "I'm just getting you out of sight."

Her grip remained a moment before loosening on my arm. The soles of her running shoes scraped against the concrete as she stepped up into the booth, settling herself down on one of the two stools inside.

Turning my body sideways, I rested my shoulder against the frame of the structure, making myself a small target, staring at the traffic rolling by.

By any approximation, the truck would continue in the same

counter-clockwise pattern it had adopted earlier. Circling around and coming in from the opposite direction would be tough, requiring multiple turns across the oncoming flow.

Seconds ticked by as the fingers on my right hand twitched just slightly, tapping at the thigh of my jeans, ready to draw if necessary.

"Where the hell did they park it?" Lake asked, strain apparent in her voice. "Bakersfield?"

I didn't bother responding, my entire focus intent on the traffic moving by.

So intent that I didn't give my opponent his due, my first real mistake since taking over with Lake.

I heard the squeal of tires long before I saw the truck, feeling the simultaneous surge of adrenaline and stab of dread in realizing my blunder. I had been so assured that he wouldn't change up his pattern that I hadn't been watching both directions, allowing him to spot me long before I saw him.

"Out, now!" I yelled, stepping away from the booth. Both bags slid from my shoulder as I stepped away, drawing the Glock and extending it in front of me.

Behind me Lake came flailing out of the booth, her feet slapping hard as she stumbled along, fighting to catch her balance and stay hidden behind my body.

For the first time I got a clear look at our pursuer through the front windshield, the rest of the windows tinted too dark to see a thing. Bunched up and riding high behind the wheel, he was wearing a white ribbed tank top, his skin dark brown, hair shorn tight to his skull.

His right hand was clenched into a fist at the top of the wheel, his left snaking out of the driver's side window. I couldn't see his hand for the thick frame of his truck blocking it, but knew beyond a shadow that a serious handgun was about to be pointed our way.

The first two shots I fired went straight into the windshield, hitting less than four inches apart. Both of them should have taken him center mass, passing just above the steering wheel and penetrating his chest, but instead the reinforced glass kept either from punching through, a simple star pattern appearing on the exterior and nothing more.

"Move!" I yelled, shoving Lake to our left, out of the path of the oncoming truck. More importantly it put the body of the enormous vehicle between us and his gun as I sighted in again, aiming at the passenger side tire.

The smell of burning rubber and the shriek of tires fighting for purchase against slick concrete attacked my senses simultaneously, the truck fishtailing as it slid to a stop.

"Run! Run, run!" I yelled, shoving Lake forward, propelling her body out through the mouth of the garage.

Turning my back to her I squeezed off three more shots, each one slamming into the side of the truck, doing no damage. Smoke began to pour from the rear tires as the man put the truck in reverse and attempted to change direction, moving fast.

Spinning on the ball of my foot, I sprinted out through the opening of the driveway, turning left up the sidewalk, following Lake in front of me. The flat bottoms of my boots slapped against the brushed concrete as I pounded forward, catching Lake in a matter of seconds and grabbing her by the hand.

"This way!" I yelled, jerking her off the sidewalk and out into the street, a trio of horns erupting as cars slid to a stop around us, drivers fighting to keep from smashing into us and each other.

Keeping Lake's hand in mine, I pulled her across three lanes of traffic as gunshots erupted in our wake. In quick succession six shots rang out, paired with a woman's scream and more honking.

A searing heat tore through my right arm, the entire appendage clenching tight in excruciating pain before the nerve endings became overloaded, numbness setting in. The sleeve of my blue t-shirt turned darker as blood stained it, saturating the cotton before running toward my elbow in a trio of uneven tendrils.

Gritting my teeth, a loud grunt escaping between them, I kept a firm grip on Lake's hand and darted through an alleyway. Sweat poured from my body as lactic acid began to burn in my thighs, my every muscle tense as we kept moving. Behind us I could hear the continued sounds of traffic, a large engine rumbling.

"Through the garage," I managed to push out between breaths, releasing Lake's hand as we made our way straight through the lower level of an LAX parking structure. Plunged into darkness I could barely see anything, going straight ahead, hoping that nothing stood in our path.

Thirty seconds later we emerged on the other side, the bright sun again appearing overhead. My pupils contracted, fighting to keep out the glaring light as we caught a walk signal on the corner intersection, darting across without breaking stride.

People streamed by on either side of us, many turning and openly staring as we continued running. My right hand swung heavy from my shoulder, more blood seeping downward as we kept moving, not once slowing until we were inside the massive steel cage that was LAX.

Chapter Thirty

The first stop Diaz made upon entering the Northeast Precinct of the East Hollywood Police Department was on the fifth floor. Using her badge, and the voice she normally reserved for interrogations, she explained to the captain that she needed to speak with one of his detectives immediately.

The captain, a ruddy, overweight man with a bulbous nose and watery blue eyes, at first bristled at the directive. His response was so intense, so instantaneous, that Diaz figured it had more to do with trying to adhere to a decades old jurisdictional pissing match between the LAPD and her agency than it did with what she was actually asking.

The decision to start with him wasn't one she was overly fond of, though she didn't have much choice in the matter. Despite her clearance as a federal agent she was still a visiting law enforcement officer that owed the ranking command the respect of informing him of her presence and the reason for it.

Apparently the captain was not of the same opinion about such pleasantries.

Not until she turned and closed the door did he stop objecting long enough to hear what she was telling him. As a federal agent she had full authority to speak with whomever she wanted. Given that the nature of her questions were related to why a member of his precinct was keeping tabs on multiple suspects in connection with a major investigation, any further obstruction he presented would reflect on him personally and every other employee inside the building, making them all susceptible to a visit from Internal Affairs.

Under different circumstances, if there wasn't a witness right now in hiding, if she hadn't called in an enormous favor to keep her safe, if she had been to bed in the previous two days, she might have considered playing nice. She would have made the man think that they were partners, perhaps even made him believe that the DEA might be impressed enough with his cooperation to give him a look.

That day was not today.

Once the full litany of her not-so-thinly veiled threats were laid out, she laced her fingers atop her stomach and leaned back in her chair. She watched the color drain from the captain's face, saw his mouth work up and down a few times in hopes of stringing together a retort that never materialized, felt Lefranc take a similar posture beside her, his attention aimed at the floor.

In the end, the entire encounter concluded with nothing more than a weak, "Detective Gomez is on the second floor."

"Thank you," Diaz replied, standing and letting herself out, Lefranc following her as she bypassed the elevator and took the stairs. Bounding down two at a time, she felt her stomach begin to churn a tiny bit, thinking of what lay ahead.

She had had more than an hour to devise the best way to approach the ensuing conversation, though she still wasn't entirely certain what that was. There existed no doubt that Paulo Gomez had flagged multiple people in the system. From what she could tell there was no reason for him to be doing so, most of his cases of the white collar variety, the addresses for Ortega and Peroux both well outside his purview.

The only thing that did seem to match so far was the personnel record for Gomez, revealing a connection she would not be afraid to exploit if necessary.

Her breathing a touch labored from the three story sprint, Diaz emerged onto the second floor, moving fast. Behind her she heard the door swing completely shut, echoing through the corridor, before it opened again, Lefranc jogging to catch up. Reading off the titles stenciled on the nameplates of the doors as she passed, Diaz strode nearly the entire length of the hallway, her shoes clicking against the hardwood floor.

Most of the offices were empty as she passed, their windows darkened. It reminded her of the DEA headquarters a hundred miles south, the majority of units largely empty, their occupants out in the field.

Coming as no surprise at all however was the fact that a light was on inside the office of Detective Paulo Gomez.

The door was shut as Diaz stopped, a glow visible through the frosted glass that covered most of it. Curling her fingers back toward herself she knocked three times, the flimsy structure rattling on its frame, reverberating much louder than intended.

Not that Diaz especially cared.

She paused just a moment before pounding again, this time seeing the glass vibrate as the door shook. Through the opaque window she could see a shape take form, hear the approach of footsteps.

The door burst open a moment later, a man standing with his finger raised, his mouth open, appearing as if he might unleash fury, on the other side. The sight of Diaz and Lefranc before him seemed to derail his thoughts though, no sound escaping him as his features twisted up, his head shifting an inch to the side.

"Detective Paulo Gomez?" Diaz asked, her tone the same she had used on the captain upstairs, on Ortega the night before.

"Yes," he replied, the same quizzical look in place.

Best estimate, Diaz figured him to be a handful of years younger than her. Most of his hair was already gone, a fact he was trying in vain to hide with a comb over. Despite that fact his skin still looked relatively taut, only a few fine lines around his eyes hidden by a pair of glasses.

What jumped out more than anything to Diaz though was the discolored patch on the left side of his neck, most of it hidden by the collar of his dress shirt. To someone that wasn't as attuned to such things it might have slid by unnoticed, perhaps even been written off as a birthmark.

To someone as adept with the southern California scene as Diaz, it stood out as the mark of the Toros, removed years before.

Everything so far fit exactly with his personnel file.

"Special Agent in Charge Mia Diaz, DEA," she said, unclipping her badge and waving it at him. "This is Special Agent Andrew Lefranc. We need to speak with you."

It was a move her past supervisor had taught her, not giving the opposition an inch of wiggle room, making sure there was no way they could lean on what Diaz knew was coming next.

"I'm sorry, but right now really isn't a good time," Gomez replied.

"It wasn't a question," Diaz said. She took a half step forward, making sure the toe of her shoe was across the threshold of the door to block it from being closed if she needed to.

Both the response and the move seemed to put Gomez on his heels, his mouth dropping open as he looked at her. After a moment he stepped back, extending a hand to the side. "Sure, I have a few minutes."

Diaz gave no response as she followed him inside an office that appeared to be the handiwork of someone with severe Obsessive-Compulsive Disorder.

The bookshelf on the wall was broken into two sections. The bottom half was lined with volumes, all arranged precisely by height. Above them were a pair of shelves with assorted mementos from his time on the force, each framed meticulously and lined up in a uniform pattern.

They were the only signs of personality at all in the entire room.

The remainder of the space was filled by a wooden desk. Behind it was a desk chair pushed in tight, a window serving as a backdrop with the shade drawn even with the wooden frame dividing it in half. A computer monitor rested in the exact center of the desk, the keyboard and CPU tower both hidden from view. Opposite it sat two matching chairs, both equidistant from the edge of the desk and each other.

With the exception of a couple of photos on the bookshelf, there was no indication at all that Gomez was a member of law enforcement. Not a single thing posted on the walls, not a stray document anywhere in sight.

It was Diaz's experience that most detectives, even those landing in posh settings such as East Hollywood, were often up to their eyes in work. The state of things in Gomez's office seemed to indicate he was either dead weight or highly secretive about his affairs.

Deciding which was not a difficult prospect.

"So, what's this about?" Gomez asked, pulling his chair out and settling down into it. He rested his elbows on the arms of his chair and pulled himself forward until his stomach was just a few inches from the polished wood, sitting with perfect posture.

Forcing herself not to wince, Diaz made a point to move her chair a few inches to the side, angling it so she could see him directly without interference from the computer monitor. She watched as his eyes tracked the movement, already calculating putting it back into position once she was gone.

"Last night we brought in Hector Ortega for questioning," she began.

Seeing the state of the man and now his office, there was little doubt to Diaz that he knew something. Instead of going right after him, starting with the fire and venom routine, she decided to start a little bit further out, seeing how much he would divulge on his own.

Gomez remained silent, waiting for her to continue.

"He was brought in for attempted murder," Diaz said, watching as Gomez's face remained completely neutral.

"In our jurisdiction?" Gomez asked, his visage making it apparent he already knew the answer to the question.

Just watching him brought the taste of bile to the back of Diaz's throat. "No, down near Huntington Beach."

"Hmm," Gomez said, his features still having failed to move an iota since he sat down. "The DEA is now investigating attempted murders?"

The taste of bile rose a little higher. "Mr. Ortega was also placed at the scene of an attempted drug deal a few nights earlier," Diaz said, leaving out everything about Lake Pawlak, "hence our involvement."

Across from her Gomez flicked his gaze to Lefranc before

returning it to her. "Agent Diaz, if what I'm hearing is correct, I'm not sure how I can be of much assistance. I deal largely with the proverbial white collar crimes - fraud, embezzlement - things that you tend to see more of in an area like East Hollywood."

He attempted a smile to signify the comment had been a joke, the gesture looking odd and disjointed.

"But I'm afraid I don't really deal with drugs or murders, haven't even been to Huntington Beach in probably five years."

For just a moment, Diaz met the smile. She watched as something moved behind his eyes, just the slightest flicker that he might have pulled it off.

"How about Maywood?" Diaz said. "Been there recently?"

The smile fell away as Gomez stared at her. All remaining color faded from his features, his olive skin becoming pasty.

"I mean, that is home, right?" Diaz said. "Just the same as Hector Ortega?"

"I, uh," Gomez stammered, the overhead light starting to shine off the perspiration coating his forehead. "What are you trying to imply, Agent?"

It was obvious the man was reeling. Whatever sway he felt he had over the situation just a moment before was gone, replaced by the type of deep rooted fear Diaz loved to prey on.

The situation, the location, might be different, but it was very apparent that this was an interrogation just like any other. The man across from her might have had the protection of being employed as a detective, he might even have years of experience on her side of the table to help guide him, but he was guilty of something.

She just had to determine exactly what.

"And what about Grace Peroux?" Diaz pressed. "She lives out that way too, right?"

Again his mouth dropped open, his chin twisting to the side. "I, I don't know. I can't recall having ever heard that name before."

At this, Diaz paused. She leaned back, allowing her disbelief to play across her face. She glanced to Lefranc, seeing the same look on his features, matching her beat for beat.

"Then why the hell do you seem to be spending so much time in their files these days?" Diaz asked.

At once, his mouth and eyes all three formed into congruent circles. He looked straight at her, all trepidation he once held retreating to full-on fear.

"What?" he asked.

"Yeah," Diaz continued, forcing herself not to show the amusement she had at his reaction, the first bit of a positive feeling she had felt all day. "If you don't know either one of them, don't work that beat, haven't been to the area, then why are you keeping tabs on them?"

Gomez failed to respond in any way.

"I mean, what could possibly have you do something so stupid as to use your name and serial number to check on them and have you sitting here sweating bullets right now?"

Diaz leaned forward, resting her elbows on her knees. She peered across at Gomez, waiting, practically baiting him into responding.

He never got the chance though.

Instead the conversation was cut short by Diaz's cellphone erupting on her hip.

Chapter Thirty-One

Terminal 1 at LAX housed Southwest Airlines, the perfect place for Lake and I to wait for reinforcements to arrive. The sedan was still back at the hotel, the valet presumably scratching his head trying to figure out why there were fresh skids marks on the ground, the smell of charred rubber in the air, and neither one of us to be seen.

Going back for it wasn't an option, if not for the simple fact it would mean possibly crossing paths with the man in the red truck, then because our car was marked. Somebody had seen us the day before and followed us to the hotel.

There was no other explanation for how they knew to start circling first thing this morning.

Choosing a short row of connected seats backing right up to the outside windows, I placed Lake in the chair on the end, her shoulder bag on the cushion beside her. Nobody inside glanced our way as they went about their business, working the self-serve kiosks, turning over their baggage in exchange for boarding passes. People of every age and ethnicity passed by as we waited, tucked away in the corner.

Keeping my shoulder shielded behind a steel support post in the center of the window glass, I let my hands hang by my side. I could smell the metallic scent of blood as it seeped from the trench carved in the meat of my upper arm, the handful of paper towels pressed tight keeping it from running free. A light tingling had settled in over most of my upper body, a natural reaction to the wound, my system trying in vain to protect me, to staunch the flow of blood and preserve as much as possible.

The overall exertion caused sweat to drip down my forehead and off my nose, beading up along my forearms.

"You alright?" I asked, keeping my attention on the flow of traffic outside. Every few seconds a new car pulled up to the curb, depositing a passenger. Those with family spent a few minutes hugging before moving on, taxis wasting no time at all as they went in search of another customer.

The thought of using a taxi had occurred to me, though I had decided against it for the same reason I had chosen the location the night before. There was protection in highly visible places. Right now, standing in a place rife with TSA and Homeland Security agents was our best option for safety.

The second reason I had chosen not to employ a cab was the fact that I wasn't prepared to relinquish control. Sitting in the backseat of a car operated by someone else, especially in heavy traffic, made us an easy target.

After all that had happened so far, there was no way we would succumb to something so foolish.

"Yeah," Lake said, nodding. She looked up at me, her eyes clear, already doing better than she had the day before. She was adjusting to life on the run, which wasn't necessarily a good thing. "How about you? How's your arm?"

"I'm okay," I replied, my stock response, out before she was even done asking the question. "Just a ricochet, stripped away a little skin."

"You sure?"

The corner of my mouth turned upward as I glanced away from the street, letting her see my face. "I'm good. And I'm the one that's supposed to be worrying about you, remember?"

A matching smile crossed her face as she looked down at her lap, her fingers twisted together atop her shorts. "Yeah, and who worries about you?"

I let the question pass without comment, seeing a sedan much like the one we just left at the hotel approaching. It slowed as it grew closer and pulled up alongside the curb, but nobody emerged.

"Come on," I said. "Our ride's here."

Jerking her bag up from the seat, Lake followed me out through the double doors, the air having grown warmer during our time inside. It wrapped around us, intensifying the sweat on my body, exacerbating the smells of oil and car exhaust in the air. Coupled with the injury, it caused my head to spin for a moment, my legs feeling numb before full feeling came back, my gait leveling.

The passenger side door opened as we approached, Lefranc climbing out. Without a word he started for the backseat but I waved him off, telling him to stay where he was.

There was no way I was riding in the backseat with him. I was reasonably certain Lake felt the same way.

My gaze traced over our surroundings as Lake climbed in through the rear passenger side door and slid across. No automobiles matching the truck jumped out, no people even close to the man I'd seen driving caught my eye.

In one fluid movement I dropped down into the seat, Diaz pulling away before the door was even closed.

"What happened?" she asked, adjusting her rearview mirror to see me in the backseat. Dark sunglasses covered most of her face, though I could tell she was working on the back end of a very long night.

"Bad luck," I said. "Whole helluva lot of bad luck."

She alternated her attention between me and the road, Lefranc and Lake both content to let us do the talking.

"What happened?" she repeated.

In quick, bullet-point fashion I ran through our encounter, starting with the valet's refusal to let us drive out to the truck happening to circle by in the five minutes we were exposed.

Throughout the narrative Diaz kept her attention on the road, a frown on her face. It grew deeper as we described the man trying to run us over with his truck, even more so as we told of him opening fire on a crowded roadway.

When I was done, I fell silent, allowing her to process.

The situation was ugly, there was no way of denying that. She had gone out on a bit of limb bringing me in, not that she had much choice. I wasn't exactly playing things by the book, not that there existed one for me to follow anyway.

Both of us were pushing forward on a mix of mutual faith and adrenaline, hoping first to keep the girl beside me safe, second to find whoever was chasing her. If ever there was a question about what she had seen it was now gone, the actions of the previous twenty-four hours making it obvious that somebody was quite concerned with whatever they thought she might have witnessed.

"Why do I smell blood?" Diaz asked.

"Round trenched me," I said, referring to the wound left behind by a bullet just grazing the skin.

The sunglasses slid down her nose a half inch as she glanced back at me, showing her eyes for the first time. "You alright?"

I matched the gaze. "Good. Quick covering and it'll be fine."

She held the gaze a moment, long enough to allow me to signal if things were any worse than indicated.

Through it I matched the look, offering nothing further as she eventually looked away, putting the sunglasses back into place.

"The car is still at the hotel?" she asked.

"Our bags, too," I said. "The clothes I could care less about, but the other has the laptop and cellphones."

I didn't bother to elaborate further. There was no need to.

Turning to face Lefranc, Diaz said, "Email Santa Ana right now, tell them to get somebody over to retrieve everything."

In front of me his head moved straight down as he went about following her command. A moment later I could hear his mobile device as his thumbs beat out a steady message.

"How'd it go on your end?" I asked, seeing her attention again move in my direction.

Pulling up to a red light, Diaz pushed her sunglasses up onto her head, the curly hair holding them in place as she rubbed her eyes. "Paulo Gomez is dirty as hell."

"Fact or opinion?" I asked.

"Opinion," she replied, "which hopefully will soon become fact."

I knew exactly what she was getting at, having had the same premonitions many times over myself.

A person doesn't last long in the life, doesn't ascend to the position she was in, without having spot-on instincts. If her first impression of Paulo Gomez said something wasn't right, it was only a matter of time before she was proven correct.

"Where is he now?" I asked.

A long, heavy sigh rolled out of her, forceful enough to lift her shoulders a few inches before dropping back into place. "East Hollywood."

"Was he able to account for his interest in every single person we've come across so far?" I asked.

"No," Diaz said, "but we didn't quite get that far."

Heat flushed my cheeks as I glanced to the mirror. I waited for her gaze to move my direction before mouthing the word *sorry*, her only response a quick shake of the head.

I knew she would never point out that coming to get us had pulled her away before she had a chance to nail him down, but she didn't have to.

"Not that it would have mattered," she added. "The guy was nervous and fidgety, couldn't play poker for shit, but he knew enough to keep his mouth shut. He wasn't going to say anything incriminating unless we hauled him in."

"Which would have been a nightmare," I said.

"For a ton of reasons," she said, nodding in agreement, "not the least of which was the fact that all we have are some very circumstantial threads connecting him to our guys."

For a moment I considered the statement. Right now we had one guy locked up, another riding us hard. Both had Paulo Gomez keeping tabs on them, a detective that reeked of suspicion.

To our side of the table, it was enough to keep pushing.

For a court room, it would be just right to get us laughed at and told to come back when we had some evidence.

"So where to now?" I asked.

"Now we take a drive out into the desert," Diaz replied. "We collect ourselves and figure out how to nail Gomez to the wall."

Chapter Thirty-Two

Anger permeated every cell of Thiago. It vibrated through his body, rolled out of him in undulating waves, his corporeal form unable to contain it all.

He was pissed at Hector for overstepping, for disobeying what he'd been told, doing something foolish and getting caught. He was angry that in doing so his hand had been forced, causing him to do something stupid as well.

More than anything though, he was pissed at the motley pair that had somehow evaded him.

Replaying the events of the morning in his mind, he couldn't help but get even angrier as he squeezed the wheel. Clenching with both hands he kept the grip as long as he could stand it, veins popping in his forearms, his knuckles flashing white, lights erupting behind his eyelids.

Only then did he release it, drawing in deep breaths of air.

Seeing them in the guard stand had been a stroke of luck. It signified that they were about to move. The tracking device ensured he knew where they were going, but this gave him something more. It provided him with a vehicle to monitor, allowed him to follow at a distance, get a feel for who he was up against.

Instead of taking the opportunity though, he had gotten impatient. He had allowed the situation with Hector, the prodding from Molina, to cause him to be rash.

In doing so he had let them slip away. He had given them a good look at himself. He had allowed the furry one to put two bullets in his windshield.

As he watched the pair sprint away through traffic, disappearing into the parking garage, he had considered pursuing them. Doing so though would have meant abandoning his truck, leaving it to be recovered by police, scoured for evidence that would eventually point back to him and Molina.

Too many witnesses had seen the encounter, had watched him fire his gun at the fleeing duo. His best bet was to let them go. So long as the girl clung to her bag he had a way to find them again.

It had taken a couple minutes for the logjam of cars on the street to clear enough for him to get through, cutting straight across town. He stayed away from the freeways and other major arteries that the cops were known to patrol the heaviest, staying in Inglewood and Compton before making his way back to Maywood.

Along the way he made three phone calls. The first was to Paul, leaving a message to let him know an incident had taken place and chatter would probably soon be popping up over the police bands.

He knew there was nothing the detective could do to make it disappear. Even attempting to do so would only bring more attention to the organization. Perhaps if he knew it was coming though he might be able to position himself accordingly to catch wind of anything that could be of help in the future.

It was a long shot, and put far more faith in Paul than the man deserved, but it was worth the fifteen seconds invested to try.

The second call was to the junkyard, one of the many front organizations owned by Molina that were semi-legit. The phone was answered on the second ring by a man he knew only as Theo who listened to every word Thiago said, commenting only at the very end to confirm everything was understood.

The truck was now a liability. Some traffic camera had seen the plates. Soon a BOLO – be on the lookout - would go out over the line for him, which would be a disaster for he and his employer.

In the slim event that nobody had gotten his number down, it was only a matter of time before somebody noticed the twin puckers in the front glass and began asking questions. He had to get off the road and into something less conspicuous, especially before he went to see Molina.

The old man himself was the third call, the one Thiago was least enthused to make.

Everything, from his decision to flee to his swapping cars, took just over an hour. Despite the passage of time, the feeling of dread remained in the pit of his stomach as he pulled up outside the home of Molina and eased his way into the driveway.

A mirrored match of his philosophy on cars, the house was built to be recognizable, command respect, but not draw attention. Standing two stories tall, the exterior was white stucco, the roof red Spanish tile. Several tiers provided texture to the front face, each window complete with a short balcony and curled wrought iron railings.

The front lawn was replaced each spring, the new turf just beginning to take hold. The various shades of green stood out against the white exterior of the house, the strips of grass uniform in length and width.

Allowing the engine to idle, Thiago rolled around to the side of the house and pulled to a stop behind the black Lexus SUV. The brakes on the loaner were a bit touchy as he came to a stop, lurching him forward before rocking back into place.

The sudden jolt did nothing to improve his mood.

Stepping away from the vehicle, Thiago slammed the door shut. There was no need to announce his presence before going up to the side entrance, the sensor at the end of the drive having done that, alerting everyone inside that someone was on the grounds.

The feelings of dread and acrimony battled for top position as Thiago grabbed the doorknob and pushed inside. The rubber stripping wheezed in protest as a puff of cool air passed over his skin, polished red brick flooring leading a path into the kitchen.

At the end of it stood Declan, a bored expression on his face. He cocked an eyebrow at Thiago as the two made eye contact, gesturing with the top of his head to the left before disappearing from sight.

Shaking his head in disgust, Thiago did as instructed. He passed through the kitchen, everything sitting silent, and out into the patio to find Molina, Declan, and Jasmine waiting for him.

The space was exactly as Thiago remembered it, the floor the same heavily glazed brick as the kitchen and hallway. In lieu of walls there were only screens, stretched from floor to ceiling, allowing a steady breeze to flow through while keeping insects at bay. Scattered about was a handful of wrought iron furniture, their seating surfaces padded with thick cushions, colored cream with red and green plant life strewn about.

Seated in his customary position on the couch was Molina. His body was leaned back against the rear support, the position twisting his open collar to the side. On an armchair to his left was Jasmine, a notepad balanced on her knee, her exposed legs tucked up close to her body.

In the far corner was Declan, his body rigid, judgment on his features.

It took everything Thiago had not to draw his weapon and empty his clip into the man, bringing at least some bit of good from the day.

"Thank you for coming so soon, *mijo*," Molina opened, his graveled voice not matching the words coming from it.

Thiago knew it was a classic ploy the old man liked to use, attempting to put someone at ease before lashing into them.

He also knew there was nothing he could do to stop it.

"Of course, Mr. Molina."

Molina nodded. "I appreciate it. I'd also appreciate you telling me what the hell you were thinking."

Remaining rooted in position, Thiago was careful not to give a single outward reaction, whether it be a clench of his fist or a narrowing of his eyes. He knew that anything he did would probably be spotted by the old man, most certainly by Declan.

"I was thinking of the clock," Thiago said. "Hector is in jail,

Paulie called this morning to inform me that Grace had been pinged in the system."

At the mention of the name, some of the accusatory nature bled from Molina. He paused, working the information over in his mind, before saying, "They found Grace?"

Thiago had a rough idea in his mind, though nothing concrete enough to share. "I don't know."

"When did Paulie call?"

"Couple hours ago," Thiago said. "Right before the incident happened."

Mentioning Grace was something Thiago knew would be his best approach before entering the house. It was the only thing that would truly set Molina back, forcing him to be more careful, seeing past any initial anger.

The discovery of Grace had not been anywhere near the top of Thiago's priority list when he moved on the girl, but if he could use it now to his advantage he wouldn't hesitate to do so.

"The girl got away?" Molina asked, moving past any further explanation and cutting right to the matter.

"She did," Thiago said, "but she wasn't alone. Had a guy with her, clearly trained, knew how to work a gun."

The remark drew a sharp intake of breath from Declan, no doubt a stifled smirk.

Thiago ignored it, watching Molina as he arched an eyebrow. "You ever see him before?"

"No," Thiago said, "but there won't be any way of missing him again."

"That good?"

"No," Thiago said, "that unique. He had long hair and a crazy beard, even for Los Angeles."

At that Molina simply nodded, falling silent. He shifted his gaze out through the screens, staring straight ahead, his focus bisecting the gap between Thiago and Declan. He stayed that way for several minutes, nobody else in the room moving as he thought.

"You know tomorrow is supposed to be the next exchange," Molina said.

"I do."

"And that if we don't make it, this will be the third one missed in a row," Molina said.

For a moment Thiago considered saying that they could still hold the next drop off. They would choose a new location, somewhere there was no chance of a random passerby seeing anything.

Just as fast he stifled the notion, knowing the old man would never go for it.

"People are beginning to talk," Molina said. "Our distributors are running low on product. If we can't provide it, they will look elsewhere."

Thiago had been in the game long enough to know how the cocaine business worked. If somebody smelled a competitor's weakness, they would not hesitate to act on it.

More than once their own organization had done that very thing, allowing them to amass the network they had.

"Guzman?" Thiago asked.

Molina flicked his gaze up at him before shifting it back into position. "No, but it won't take long for him to get restless either. He has product to move, mules to carry it. If we're not ready, he can easily find someone who is."

Several thoughts, both in agreement and refutation, sprang to Thiago's mind. Each one he let pass without comment, knowing his employer was building toward something.

"I think it's time we call him in," Molina said. He delivered the decision with no small amount of weariness in his tone, letting it be known that it was not his preferred choice. "It's the only way we show good faith, ensure that our relationship endures."

Anger, embarrassment, shame, flooded into Thiago. He felt his body seize and color flush his face as he stood, praying that the meeting would end.

"It is very clear that she saw something that night," Molina said, stating aloud what everybody already knew. "The number of hits Paulie's catching in the system, the fact that she has armed protection with her, the way she was able to elude Hector, it's all too much to be coincidence."

He paused, looking at Jasmine, Declan, and Thiago in turn. "Until we snuff this out and get the heat off our back, finding her gets top billing. As soon as Guzman's guys arrive I want you to take them all to the streets and make sure this gets taken care of."

Chapter Thirty-Three

I t was still early afternoon, but already it felt like I'd been awake for days. The effect of having adrenaline spike every bodily function before dissipating had left me feeling like a deflated balloon. Coupled with blood loss, my energy reserves were depleting quickly.

I didn't dare give off a single sign intimating as much though, looking across at Diaz, who clearly hadn't been to bed yet and had no sign of doing so anytime soon.

"These are the pictures we collected from Lake's camera," Diaz said. She spun around a pair of glossy 8x10's in front of her and pushed them across the conference room table toward us.

The images were almost identical, taken just a few seconds apart. They were in color, though given the time of night and the low amount of light coming from the trucks, that didn't help a great deal. They had been digitally enhanced and blown up, though that still didn't provide us with any real level of detail.

"Is the man that tried to run you down in them?"

In each one of them, four men were clearly visible. Two of them were facing toward the camera, Felipe Soto and his partner. His cohort I discounted at a glance, his skin tone too dark, his look too unique to be the man behind the wheel.

Standing opposite them was a pair of men, both with dark tan skin. The one on the left had his hair shaved into the thick wedge of a Mohawk, a sleeveless t-shirt covering his upper half.

"Hector Ortega," I said, pointing to him and raising an eyebrow to Diaz.

"We believe so," she agreed, nodding once.

That pulled my attention to the fourth man in the image, the closest to the camera as it was taken. Of the four he was the most obscured, nothing more visible than the white ribbed tank top and jeans he was wearing, the uniform length of his haircut, and the oversized weapon in his hand.

Guns weren't really my thing, but if I had to guess I would ballpark it as a German assault rifle.

"Definitely *could* be," I said, examining the photo before looking back up. "But, without sounding like a bigot, that could also be a lot of other people in Southern California."

A flicker of mirth passed over Diaz's face at the comment, though it didn't grow into a full smile. She knew what I was getting at, and that I hadn't intended it to be a joke.

Given the situation, I didn't have a long time to sight in and get a clear read on the man behind the wheel. All I had noticed were the general characteristics of this man - short hair, tan skin, tank top, big weapon.

Beyond that, there was no way of knowing for sure. The Hispanic population in the greater Los Angeles area was enormous, as was the heavily-tanned Anglo crowd.

Without a clear look at the man in the photo or the man driving, trying to say it was the same person would be guess work, spurred on by wishful thinking.

"How about you?" I asked, shifting my attention to Lake beside me. She had not said a word since we sat down in the conference room, now seeming to be completely absorbed in the photos.

For a moment I felt like I could almost read her thoughts as she looked down at them, putting herself in the moment. More than likely she was trying to piece backward the string of events that had occurred, wishing she could alter any one of them and not be sitting at DEA headquarters.

Reaching out a hand, I slid the photos away from her, pushing them over to Diaz.

Trying to recreate the past, or even worse blaming herself for it, would only lead to self-pity. I knew, because after the death of my family I had spent five years doing the same.

Lake's lips parted a fraction of an inch as she watched the images slide away, staring after them with a look that bordered on longing. Once they were out of sight she glanced to each of us and said, "I didn't really see anything today. You said run, so I ran."

The door at the head of the room opened, pulling our collective attention toward it. A moment later Lefranc appeared, his gaze aimed down at a single printout in either hand. He glanced alternatingly between the two as he circled around to the opposite side of the table, extending both to Diaz before slouching into the chair beside her.

Nobody said anything as she read them over, the lines around her mouth and eyes growing deeper as she scanned whatever was found there. I had a pretty good idea what she was reading, and could tell the results were not what she was looking for, though remained silent.

She would fill us in when she was ready.

In total it took her just three minutes to read and digest both pages, the expression on her face even more severe than when she started.

"Phone records?" I asked.

She nodded. "And financials."

I gave her a moment before prodding, "That bad?"

"Worse," she said, tossing the pages down on the desk in front of her. She leaned back and rubbed at her eyes, sighing loudly through her nose. "There is absolutely no clear financial trail between Paulo Gomez and anybody. The only money coming into his accounts is from the LAPD, his 401(K) and IRA's both commensurate with his rank and compensation patterns."

The news was certainly bad, but it wasn't final, there being no less than a dozen ways to easily hide money. "Phone records?"

"In the past couple of days there have been a few calls come in from an unidentified number. Research shows it to be a burn phone, bought anywhere..."

"Paid in cash," I finished, already knowing where it was going. My old boss had often said that the development of cellphones, or more aptly cheap disposable cellphones, had made the work of the DEA exponentially more difficult.

By the time I had joined though every person in the world had one in their pocket, my only choice to take his word for it.

If the last few days were any indicator, even our own agency was now using them to keep our tails clean.

"So, unknown number, just in the last couple of days," I said, letting her pick up my train of thought.

"Right," she agreed, "once all this started."

"Nothing before that?" I asked.

"Not in the previous four months we pulled," Diaz said. "But yet again, heavily circumstantial, nothing concrete."

Sliding my left hand back through my hair, I scratched at my scalp, chewing on what I knew. From the account Diaz had given of their encounter with Gomez, he was nervous to the point of jittery. That seemed to indicate he was hiding something, though he was far too careful to ever divulge anything or do something to incriminate himself.

"You said he was OCD, right?" I asked, my gaze fogging over as I thought.

"Painfully so," Diaz replied.

"Which means he's meticulous," I said, my voice a bit removed as I thought out loud.

Across from me I noticed Diaz's hand fall away from her face, nothing but a blur in my periphery.

"And would never leave behind something so obvious," she said.

"Which is why the calls were coming in, but never going out," I said. I blinked twice, clearing my vision as Diaz picked up one of the printouts and glanced over it.

"We've got his desk phone records here too," she said. "They're clean."

"No," I said, shaking my head, "he wouldn't use a phone he thought anybody could ever pull the records on."

"Burner?" Lefranc asked, his sudden appearance in the conversation surprising me, drawing a scowl from Diaz.

"No," I said again. "If he had a phone they could call into, they wouldn't have used his personal cellphone."

Falling silent, he retreated back into himself again, Diaz glaring him into submission before looking back at me. "Payphones?" she asked.

I raised my eyebrows and said, "They're a dying breed, but there's still a few around. Should make it easy for us to run a check."

Repositioning herself in her chair, Diaz sat up straighter. She looked over to Lefranc and said, "Get the analysts to run a check for all payphones surrounding Gomez's home and office."

"Tell them to put a one mile radius on it," I said. "Average walking pace, that would allow him to be there and back without arousing suspicion."

Lefranc's mouth dropped open, all color bleeding away.

"And tell them to go back three days," Diaz added. "Anything before that probably won't help us anyway."

Again Lefranc remained silent, glancing between the two of us. It was clear he had bad news to deliver, but wanted no part of actually doing so.

"What?" I asked, feeling my own disdain for the man beginning to match Diaz's.

"Well," Lefranc managed before drawing in a deep breath, "I think they already tried that. Said they would keep digging, but they weren't having much luck."

I flicked my gaze to Diaz, watching as her hands balled into fists and her mouth drew itself into a tight line. A less strong-willed person would have exploded on the spot, but she swallowed it down, forcing a loud exhalation out through her nose.

"Just go tell them to keep digging," she said. "Give them our parameters. Anything they can find helps."

A look of surprise passed over Lefranc's face as he rose and almost sprinted from the room, slamming the door behind him. In the wake of it Diaz turned to face me, shaking her head in disgust.

"Unbelievable."

"Actually," I said, "we're good. Let me make a call."

Chapter Thirty-Four

D aniel Guzman had been expecting the call for the better part of
a day. As such, it made mobilizing once it did arrive that much
easier, his bag already packed, Rafa and Sanchez told to do the same.

Less than two hours after getting the word from Molina that
things were beginning to unravel in Los Angeles, all three were seated
in the back of a Gulfstream aircraft, the Pacific Ocean visible under
the afternoon sun thousands of feet below.

The plane was a rental, something Guzman kept on standby in
the rare event he needed to travel internationally. For the most part his
business interests remained inside the borders of Ecuador, the cargo
plane piloted by Morris more than ample to fill the needs of the
operation.

It was the second consecutive day that they had needed to employ
the craft, though there was no sign of their previous passing. Every
last surface had been scrubbed clean and buffed to a mirrored shine,
the faint scent of disinfectant in the air masked by a heavy misting of
lavender and vanilla.

Originally designed to accommodate more than a dozen passen-
gers, the rows of seats on the inside had been removed, replaced with
a design that was equal parts mobile business center and leisure.

On one side was a pair of overstuffed reclining chairs, each secured to the floor through a single steel post, both capable of lying completely prone for easy sleeping. Behind them was a full mini bar and fridge, libations of every sort readily accessible.

Opposite the spread was a wraparound bench, a desk in the center of it, the entire affair resembling a corner booth in a diner. Beneath the glass surface of the desk was a pair of flat screen monitors, each hooked directly to the tower of electronics tucked away in the back corner. Fully remote accessible, the layout allowed for functional capability while in the air without worrying about the clutter of wires and loose pieces of equipment.

Rafa and Sanchez had taken up posts on either end of the wraparound, both dressed down in slacks and shirtsleeves. To one end Sanchez sat with perfect posture, a notepad on the table as he stared at Guzman in one of the recliners. Opposite him Rafa lounged, his oversized frame splashed across the leather seat, his feet stretched out before him, crossed at the ankles.

"What do we know for sure?" Rafa asked, his features screwed up tighter than usual, his demeanor the most irascible Guzman had seen it in ages.

"The girl has disappeared," Guzman said, spreading his hands wide before returning them, his fingertips steepled in front of him. "Multiple attempts at apprehension have now failed."

The first part didn't seem to surprise Rafa or Sanchez. No details had been given to them when told to report to the airfield, but it wasn't difficult to piece things together.

The real shock for both seemed to come at the second half of the statement, their eyes growing a bit wider at the disclosure.

"Thiago?" Rafa asked. "Twice?"

Guzman sniffed once, the same thought having entered his mind upon receiving the news. "No. Apparently the first one was conducted by Hector, a real mess that landed him in prison. Thiago tried a cover-up operation that also ended badly before calling in for support."

Thiago Ruiz was one of the few people in Arturo Molina's operation that Guzman trusted implicitly. Never had he seen the man flustered or acting brash. The fact that he had been wise enough to call in support when it was needed proved that.

"Still..." Rafa said, shaking his head slightly.

Guzman agreed with the sentiment, but remained silent.

"Who's doing the protecting?" Sanchez asked.

"They're not sure," Guzman said, "but mention of the DEA was made."

Hearing the name of the agency, Rafa winced just slightly. As an organization with international reach, the fact that Ecuador and the United States shared an ironclad extradition treaty was mildly concerning.

All three men fell into silence as they thought on the new information, adding it to what they already knew.

This trip was their last attempt at saving the relationship. Thus far only a couple of deliveries had been missed, but the problem was much larger than just financial concerns.

Working with Molina had provided them with a way into the North American market, giving them the umbrella of protection they needed to form a presence without being shoved aside by the larger groups from Columbia and Peru.

For every kilo of uncut product they sent north, a flat fee was remanded to them of twenty thousand dollars. This also included the cost of providing all refuges, the proverbial mules to carry it across the border. Once it was there the Molina clan was free to do with it as they pleased.

Guzman knew that the quality of the product they supplied could be sold on the street for three or four times what he was getting in return, but that was far from the point. The partnership had allowed him to develop a reputation, to form a following in the largest market in the world.

That alone was worth his loyalty.

The fact was though, the time had long since come for a new monetary balance to be struck. No longer was he a fresh player in the game, content to accept peanuts for the privilege of being included.

As much as he hated the idea of using the current situation as leverage, he couldn't help but wonder if perhaps the trip would double as an opportunity to make acquaintances with some other distributors in the Los Angeles area.

"Just the three of us?" Sanchez asked.

The question was rhetorical, Guzman knew. There would be no point in making the journey with just three men, especially given that two of them were decidedly not combatants and the third carried a good deal of silver in his mane.

"I contacted Felipe and Dante," Guzman said. "They will meet us at the airport."

Sanchez nodded, but remained silent.

"Obviously Molina will have men on hand, too," Rafa said.

This time it was Guzman's turn to nod without comment. He knew Molina could have as many men as he wanted available at a moment's notice. Los Angeles was teeming with young people ready to fight for a few dollars or a bump up their nose.

It wasn't truly help his counterpart needed, he had some of the best available at his right hand that he barely used, it was to make a show of good faith. For that reason, and that reason alone, he had culled his crew together to make the trip.

Across from him, Rafa reclined even further into his seat. He laced his fingers together and balanced them across his stomach, staring up at the ceiling.

"All this because of one lost girl in the desert..."

Chapter Thirty-Five

The visage of Mike Palinksy filled the back wall of the conference room, nothing but the upper third of his body stretched to almost five feet in height staring back at us. Sitting three across, Diaz on one side of me, Lake on the other, we waited as his attention was shifted away from the screen, his hands moving in a flurry just out of sight, the sound making it painfully clear what he was doing.

"Did you guys work together in the seventies or something?" Lake asked, glancing from the screen to me.

Behind me I could hear a muffled snort from Diaz, my own mouth turning downward a bit.

"You realize I'm only like five years older than you, right?" I asked.

"Okay, then the eighties?" she clarified. "I mean, were you guys DEA agents or rockers during the glam band days? Just you, Poison, Motley Crue, all sitting around, hanging out?"

I knew what she meant the first time, though I still had to feign indignant. This time I didn't bother trying, letting her see a smile form on my face.

While pointy, I had to admit she had good taste in music.

"Young lady," a voice said, the face on the screen moving in sync as he looked up at us, "I hardly think you're in a position to be making fun of anybody's hair."

All three of us smiled as Pally leaned back in his seat, lacing his hands behind his head. As he did so the sleeves of a baggy grey sweater fell down around his elbows, revealing thin forearms striated with veins, the skin the same ghostly pallor as his face.

By and large he looked the same as he had the last time I saw him six months earlier, only nominally different from the best IT and logistical support expert in the DEA I had worked with five years before.

His hair - like mine - was longer than before, now pulled back into a ponytail. His narrow frame had somehow managed to strip away even a few more pounds, his jaw line sharp and defined, a series of pockmarks standing out on his cheeks.

The moment Lefranc left the room an hour before, I had a feeling he and his team weren't going to be of much use. He had basically confirmed that they had tried and struck out on the payphone angle. Already they had spent the better part of the afternoon on it. If they hadn't turned up anything yet, I wasn't holding out hope that they would suddenly put together everything they needed.

Instead I called in a favor of my own, compounding the one Diaz now claimed to owe me by adding Pally on to her tally as well. The two had worked together tangentially through me in the past, providing them with some familiarity already.

It had made convincing Diaz to go along with it much easier, though she still wasn't overly enthused about the possibility of more marginal spending on the case.

Only once I pointed out the alternative was to sit and wait for Lefranc did she come around on the notion, claiming she would pay whatever it took.

Five minutes later we had Pally on the line.

After another five minutes of explaining the situation and asking if what we were looking for was even possible, he was off and running.

Now just an hour later he was up on the screen before us, claiming to have what we were looking for and a whole lot more.

If that was the case, I was really going to owe him big.

"Pally, good to see you," I said, taking lead in the conversation. I raised a hand in a wave as I did so, all five fingers spread wide, held high overhead.

"You as well," Pally said, bringing his right hand forward and offering a small salute. "Agent Diaz, nice to see you again."

"You as well, Mr. Palinsky," she replied, nodding at the camera installed on the wall above the screen. "Thank you for doing this. We wouldn't be asking if it wasn't important."

"Don't mention it," Pally replied. "We've all lived the life. I know how these things go."

He didn't bother delving into further detail, but I knew exactly what he was getting at. Hundreds of times in the years we worked together, even several times in the one unofficial case we handled last fall, instances would arrive where help was needed. In those times we would call on him, sometimes with seemingly impossible requests, and stand back as he worked his magic.

In a weird sort of way, I think he craved the challenge. There were of course the underlying wanting-to-serve-his-country and do-right-by-those-affected-by-the-drug-trade factors, but more than anything I think he liked being able to apply his craft to something that made a difference. He could have made a fortune designing video games or troubleshooting IT systems, but that wasn't his style.

Even now, as I had no idea what he did with his time, I highly doubted it was anything that could be construed as being a corporate sellout.

"And this brightly colored young lady here with us is Lake Pawlak," I said.

"Ah, the damsel in distress," Pally said, giving her a salute as well. "Mike Palinksy, call me Pally."

"Hey," Lake said, offering a quick wave, a smile on her face.

Introductions conducted, the congenial nature bled away from both sides.

"Were you able to find anything?" I opened, knowing already that he had, but giving him as much latitude as possible to begin wherever he chose.

"Did I ever?" he replied, his gaze shifting, presumably to look at an adjacent screen. His pale face took on a shade of white normally reserved for those with Gothic tendencies as he leaned forward, his eyes squinting slightly.

"There are three payphones within easy walking distance of the Northeast Precinct. Of those, one has not had a single call to or from it for the past eight days, my guess being that somebody ripped the cord out of the thing and the city has no interest in replacing it."

The reasoning made sense, though none of us bothered to comment on it.

"Door number two is located in a small Irish bar called Paddy's less than a half mile from the police station. In the last three days a total of thirteen calls have been placed from it, two have come in."

He glanced up to us as he read, all three staring intently back at him.

"Of those thirteen calls, three matched the number you gave me."

He paused for a moment and leaned back, the white reflection of the screen falling away from his features. A loud breath passed through his nose, his nostrils flaring just slightly.

"Unfortunately, your initial assessment on the number was correct. Burn phone, impossible to do much with."

I cast a quick glance over to Diaz, who only nodded in response. We both knew it was a long shot, though just knowing that Gomez was using a payphone to place outgoing calls told us plenty. It meant he was having discussions he didn't want showing up anywhere. It also lent itself to the supposition that he was funneling information where he shouldn't have been.

Not enough to get a warrant yet, but definitely sufficient to make him sweat under questioning.

"You mentioned a third phone?" Diaz asked.

"Ah, yes," Pally said, springing forward, giving us a profile shot of his face as he went back to reading the screen. "Bachelor number three is at a bus stop eight blocks from the precinct, a pretty good hike for a detective in tasseled loafers. If he was making the trek up to this place, it was with good reason."

He paused a moment, his lips twitching slightly as he read from the screen. It was a move I had seen him use countless times before, pretending to be checking something while really just building antici-pation on our side.

Again, I let him have his moment.

"Somebody near this bus stop really likes their pizza," Pally said. "Twelve different phone calls to Domino's in just three days. Seems a bit extreme if you ask me, but who am I to judge?"

Once more I didn't bother to comment.

"Aside from those, a couple others stick out," Pally said, his voice a bit detached as he worked. "Again we have the burner number showing up, three calls in a fifteen minute window last night."

Holding a finger for Pally to stop, I shifted my head to the side, remembering the previous evening. Hour by hour I rifled through the day before realizing what had precipitated the calls. "We had Hector Ortega in custody."

The look on Diaz's face seemed to indicate she had reached a matching conclusion at the same time. "He was calling to let them know what happened."

A quick flash of venom passed through me, my teeth clenching as I thought about what this meant. Somebody in the inside, someone sworn to protect others, was funneling information to those bent on causing harm.

"Bastard," Diaz hissed, her face twisting into a glower.

"But wait, there's more," Pally said, drawing our attention back to him. "Just this afternoon another call was placed to the number, total length just twenty seconds. Immediately thereafter a second call was placed, this one to a landline in East LA."

The venom inside shifted, a familiar surge passing through me as I computed the words. "Landline. As in, with an address?"

"Can you see who it belongs to?" Diaz asked.

Retreating back into position in front of his camera, Pally pointed to the screen beside him. "The home is registered to a Grace Peroux, though as far as I can tell the only place she exists is on paper."

My heart rate ticked a bit higher, the name Grace Peroux clicking in the back of my mind. She, like Hector Ortega, had been flagged by Paulo Gomez.

"Meaning?" I asked.

"Meaning she has a shitload of property holdings," Pally said. "And has a social security number, even a police file, but nothing else."

"Nothing else, such as..." Diaz said, motioning with her hand in front of her for him to continue.

"Such as, no history of her ever having a driver's license, graduating high school, getting married, becoming a legal citizen," Pally said. "Nothing."

It was the second person in the short time we'd been on this case to have absolutely everything cleansed from their history. As I had found out all too well over the previous half decade, nobody, no matter how much they wanted to be out of sight, ever truly was anymore. Not with the way the world worked, with connectivity making every movement accounted for.

"So you think somebody's scrubbed her history?" I asked.

"Honestly," Pally said, "I'm thinking more like a false front. Best guess, this is a shell person put up to protect someone else."

Leaning back a few inches, I let my chin rise toward the ceiling. I hadn't considered that at first, so focused on the phone calls and police records, but what Pally was suggested made infinitely more sense. Whoever was employing Ortega, and the man that tried to run us down, was no doubt a major player in the drug trade. They wouldn't just want their own name attached to things, so they would create someone to serve as their proxy.

It was a modern day take on what Andy Dufresne did in *The Shawshank Redemption*. Anybody that came sniffing after Grace Peroux would find real records, but not much else.

"What's in the police file?" I asked.

"Some small stuff," Pally said. "Parking ticket, moving violation. Nothing real, just enough to have a file."

My eyes narrowed a bit, considering the data. "Who entered them?"

A bit of a smile crossed Pally's face, almost as if he was proud of me for putting things together so quickly. "Every last item listed by one Paulo Gomez."

"Bastard," Diaz hissed beside me again, receiving a nod in agreement.

"Can you crack it?" I asked.

A look that bordered on hurt passed over Pally's face, a low scoff passing his lips. "You forget that just last fall I followed a money trail through Grand Cayman *and* Switzerland for you? This will be nothing, it will just take me a few more minutes."

I glanced over to Diaz, a look of renewed vigor on her face, a bit more color on her cheeks. Like me she was already putting together what Pally had told us, adding it to what she knew we needed to make things stick for a warrant and an arrest. Right now we still had a long way to go on Grace Peroux and whoever she represented, but we had more than enough to make a move on Paulo Gomez.

"Alright, Pally, keep us posted," I said, excitement, anticipation, beginning to roil within me. "That's damn good work, we appreciate it."

Chapter Thirty-Six

B eing summoned twice in one day had never happened before. Very few were the items that required personal briefings, Thiago not sure what to make of things as he pulled back into the house nestled in the center of Maywood.

Logistically, the call could not have come at a worse time. Late afternoon traffic in Los Angeles was even worse than most media sources made it out to be, the fight back across town taking over an hour. Once business was concluded it would take even longer for him to return to position, the entire affair lasting the better part of three hours.

Whatever it was Molina needed to say, Thiago knew it had to be important.

Working to keep his features free of any annoyance, Thiago passed through the side door without knocking. He didn't bother pausing to wipe his feet or even acknowledge Declan standing in the same spot in the kitchen, regarding him as if his sudden appearance was completely expected.

Making a hard right past the island of kitchen appliances sitting silent, Thiago went straight onto the patio to find Molina sitting in the same spot on the couch. In a matter of a few hours he had managed to move himself just six inches, perching himself on the front edge of the cushion to take his afternoon coffee, a cup and saucer sitting before him.

For a moment Jasmine looked startled as she stared up at Thiago, her features retreating back to neutral as recognition set in.

Ignoring the girl entirely, Thiago presented himself directly in front of the old man, his knees just a few inches back from the edge of the coffee table. He clasped his hands together before him and parted his lips just a bit, enough so his breath wouldn't be heard pushing out through his nose in angry bursts.

There he waited, watching as Molina sipped at his *cafecito*, the scent so strong it filled the space, despite a light breeze pushing through the screens around them.

The thought that Hector was lucky to only have to smell his cigars passed through Thiago's mind, though he remained silent, waiting for whatever information was so important to have pulled him back.

In total his wait lasted over two minutes, Molina finishing the light tan liquid from his cup and replacing it on the table. He retreated back to his traditional place on the couch, wiping his mouth with a cloth napkin before tossing it away.

Only then did he look up to directly address Thiago.

"There's been a new development," he said, "with Paulie."

With everything that had occurred in the past few hours, Thiago had almost completely forgotten about the sniveling detective tucked away in Hollywood. He quickly ran the scenarios in his head, figuring that someone had finally put together the connection between him and the organization.

"How much do they know?" Thiago asked.

Molina regarded him a moment, a look bordering on impressed crossing his features before fading away. "He didn't think much, seemed to believe it was more of a fishing expedition than anything."

Many times over the years Thiago had seen the results of a supposed fishing expedition. Just like with Hector, once law enforcement got a bead on somebody, rarely, if ever, did they willingly let it go.

This was all information that could be readily inferred.

The bigger concern was how Molina knew this and he did not.

"Please tell me he didn't make direct contact," Thiago said, all previous agitation gone, replaced now by dread that finally their inside man had done something foolish enough to classify him as a liability.

The somber look on Molina's face told him he had done just that.

"Said he couldn't get through on anybody's cell, so he called the house," Molina said.

Thiago raised his gaze toward the ceiling, his eyes sliding shut.

"Seemed to believe his being shook down was important enough to risk it," Molina said.

Dropping his gaze back to face forward, Thiago felt renewed venom rise within him. It burned hot just beneath the surface, his face contorting itself slightly as he bit back a string of curse words.

Even so, Molina seemed to know exactly what he was going to say.

"You know what this means," Molina said.

He made no further explanation, but Thiago didn't need him to. It was the very reason he had been called back in person, the kind of order that could never be issued over the phone, especially once it was known that the authorities were sniffing around.

Paulo Gomez, longtime associate, had officially lost all value to the organization. Replacing him would be burdensome and take some time, but it paled in comparison to whatever trouble lay in keeping the relationship active.

"Any special requests?" Thiago asked, slipping right into the short-hand code they used when discussing such matters, especially in the presence of someone like Jasmine.

"No," Molina said, shaking his head, his jowls quivering from the movement. "Just be fast and quiet. After that, get back here as quick as you can, preferably before our guests arrive."

There was no way to know exactly what hour it was, though Thiago didn't especially care for his odds of making it back anytime soon. Already it was well into the afternoon and would soon be marching on toward evening, the newest task he'd just been charged with promising to take a few hours minimum.

"Where?" Thiago asked.

"I told him to hole up at the All-Niter," Molina said. "Take the bus, wear a hat, keep his head down."

Thiago nodded. The ruse was one they had used before, the All-Niter a rundown joint on the outskirts of Pasadena that Molina kept on the payroll. Once a year they received a hefty contribution from the organization for looking the other way whenever something went down on their premises.

For their investment, Molina received a ready-made place to lure unsuspecting people that had outgrown their usefulness and the guarantee that no cameras would ever be installed on the premises.

"He's a cop," Thiago said. "They'll have to phone it in eventually."

"True," Molina conceded, "but not until tomorrow at check-out at least. That should keep the DEA or whoever else tied up for a while, give you guys plenty of time to get rid of the girl."

Once more, Thiago nodded. It was messy, but it would work.

As things stood right now, she was the only thing that could truly bring down the organization. Hector was in prison, but that was an isolated incident, easily explained as a home invasion gone awry. He would serve a few months and when the time was right, Molina would devise a way to spring him.

Everybody knew Hector would keep his mouth shut, even despite his deep-rooted hatred for life behind bars.

Gomez was a potential problem, though at the moment all anybody had was maybe some phone calls between the two sides. As his last breaths were just moments away, there would be no way he could testify, nothing that could hold up beyond being circumstantial.

Given the fact that he was from the neighborhood, it could even be spun as a feel good story, Molina the father figure he still kept in touch with out of gratitude for helping him get turned around.

That left only the girl. Without her testimony the DEA, FBI, even GOD, would have nothing to pin a case on.

Business as usual could begin anew by the first of the week.

Chapter Thirty-Seven

Though it ran counter to my every instinct, I stayed behind. A small part of me yearned to be riding shotgun with Diaz as she pulled away from the headquarters, making her second trip up to Hollywood for the day.

Judging by the look on her face as she watched Lefranc climb into the passenger seat, she wanted nothing more as well.

We both knew that my place, the reason I had been brought on to begin with, was there with Lake. Enormous pieces were beginning to fit together, providing us with a rough outline of how everything worked. Just a few more were needed to bring the picture into complete clarity, allowing us to make the arrests that were needed, to get Lake into witness protection until she could testify.

Until then, she was my responsibility. No matter how much my instincts, and even my ego, burned to be there when Diaz walked in and put Gomez into custody, I couldn't do that.

"Eating you alive, isn't it?" Lake asked, her body curled onto a cot in the back of the DEA headquarters. One of a handful kept on hand for agents to grab a few hours while working cases, it was just smaller than a twin mattress. A brown fleece blanket covered the body of it, edges tucked in tight, a pillow in a white pillowcase on the end.

"What's that?" I asked, glancing over at her from the chair I was sitting in, my feet propped on the edge of the adjoining bed.

"Being here instead of out there."

I made a non-committal gesture with my face I hoped she bought before pulling my feet up under me. Pressing my palms down onto my thighs I rose to a standing position and stretched my hands up overhead.

"Naw," I said. "Just different, being on this side, that's all."

She glanced up at me before looking down and staring at her fingernails. "Sorry."

"For?" I asked.

"For you being stuck here guarding me instead of out there."

"If not for you, I would be in Montana," I said, dropping my hands by my side. "Still wouldn't be out there arresting anybody."

Once more she looked up at me, pressing her lips together tight, before dropping her gaze again.

"And if not for you," I added, "Diaz would be working something else, another criminal would be free to do his thing. No need for you to apologize either way."

I walked to the opposite end of the room, the entire space no more than twenty feet in length. The beds took up the bulk of the area, each one dressed in the exact same way. On either end was a series of wooden lockers, none of them having doors, nothing more than cubby holes for agents to store personal effects. A couple of posters with the DEA logo hung on the wall, though for the most part the place was completely Spartan.

A space intended to be functional, not necessarily concerned with aesthetics.

In my experience, a pretty accurate microcosm for the administration as a whole.

"I bet you were good, weren't you?" Lake asked, again looking up at me.

I could see her pink hair in my periphery as I thumbed down a stack of magazines piled in one of the cubbies at eye level, scanning their titles. "Meh, I was alright I guess. No different than anybody else."

"Bullshit," she said, almost spitting the word out.

The intensity of the statement surprised me, pulling my attention over toward her, half-smile on my face. I let my fingers fall away from the shelf and walked back toward her, shoving my hands into the front of my jeans.

"Enough about me," I said. "Tell me about the hair, the tattoos, all that."

An exaggerated eye roll lifted her face toward the ceiling, a low groan sliding out. "Oh, Lord. You're not going to try and go all *dad* on me now are you?"

The smile receded from my face as I lowered myself back into the chair, my hands still in my pockets. For a moment I thought of my own daughter, long since deceased, both she and my wife casualties of my career, in more ways than one.

"Again, only like five years older than you," I said, my voice a bit distant, even in my own ears. "Just curious is all. I mean, it is a unique look, I'm guessing there must be a story behind it."

"Says the guy who looks like-"

"Jesus Christ, the guy from *Duck Dynasty*, a grizzly bear," I said, rattling off in order the monikers she'd given me. "My excuse is I live miles from the closest neighbor and its really damn cold in Montana. Your turn."

An amused expression crossed her face as she studied me a moment, her mouth fixed at an angle that hinted there was some retort ready to be lobbed my way. Deciding against vocalizing it, she pressed her lips together and said, "Like you said, it's unique. There's no way anybody ever looks at me and sees someone else."

She left it at that, though it wasn't hard to pick up the insinuation, Psychology 101 kicking up in the back of my mind.

"Siblings?"

"Twin sister."

"Ah," I replied, rocking my head back as my phone began to vibrate on my hip. Pulling it out I checked the caller ID, recognizing the string of digits straightaway.

"Pally," I said, putting the call on speakerphone.

"Hawk," he said, his voice low and even. "Dude."

I glanced over to Lake, my pulse rising just a bit. "Who is Grace Peroux?"

"Dude," he repeated. "Your girl is either the luckiest or the most screwed person on the planet."

I wasn't sure if we was referring to Diaz or Lake so I remained silent, allowing him to continue.

"Ever heard the name Arturo Molina?" he asked.

"No," I said, "should I?"

"Not really," he said. "He was small time during our tenure, really starting expanding in the last few years."

"How big?"

"Say that name to Diaz and I guarantee you get a different response," Pally replied. "The guy is a major provider in the cocaine business for everywhere east of the 110, and we're talking clear out to Riverside and San Bernardino."

Visualizing the greater LA area in my mind, I superimposed the freeway he was alluding to. A long, shrill whistle slid through my lips as I thought about what he was telling me, the area he described representing three-quarters of the entire region, if not a little more.

"Yeah," Pally said, barely a whisper.

"So Grace Peroux..." I began.

"Just a false front," Pally said. "One of many, from what I can tell. This lovely lady in particular though owns two homes, two junk yards, and a recycling plant."

"Means for obtaining and destroying cars, and assorted other evidence," I said, thinking out loud.

"And I'm guessing his other aliases hold a number of other like-kind enterprises, all equipped for aiding in the real money maker of the empire."

I nodded in agreement, remaining silent, putting things together in my mind.

If what he was telling me was true, this would be a real coup for the DEA. To fall backwards into a score that big would win the administration untold amounts of good favor on the national scene, as well as push Diaz's wattage through the roof.

It also meant that on the opposite side, there was no length that would be too far in eliminating Lake if they needed to.

"Hey, thanks a lot, Pally," I said. "I'll trust you to forward this to Diaz. If more is needed on our end I'll be sure to be in touch."

"Always a pleasure, my friend," Pally said, the line cutting out. For a moment I stared down at the screen, the frozen timer blinking in place, before clearing it away.

I considered calling Diaz straightaway, if for nothing else than to hear her take on Molina, but knew she was in the middle of bringing in Gomez. Already I had interrupted her once on the day as she tried to interrogate him, so I stowed the phone, opting to let her reach out when the time was right. The new information held no bearing on bringing him in, but would be a real hammer when the time came to begin questioning.

Even though I had no clue who Arturo Molina was, I trusted Pally enough to know he wouldn't exaggerate. If the man controlled near the breadth of what was being described, or was even capable of being active on that large a scale, he had untold resources available to him. Not once would he pause to employ them if need be, the impending arrest of one of his informants most likely being the push he needed to get to that level.

It also meant he would be smart enough to keep an eye on DEA headquarters in looking for her.

"We need to go," I said, my gaze shifting over the polished wood laminate floor. "Soon, within the next few minutes."

If Lake was surprised in any way, she did nothing to show it. "Where to?"

Three separate times while I was an agent we had attempts made on the very building we now sat in. Many more times than that we heard stories of attacks on the precincts in San Diego and Los Angeles, the locations posted online, easily found through a simple Google search.

People like Molina abided by certain rules, none of which coincided with ours. When it came to matters of legality, most often they chose to ignore any even existed. If they had an issue to deal with, whether it be the holding of key personnel or the possession of a vital witness, they would not hesitate to act.

In a matter of minutes, it would circulate that the DEA had Paulo Gomez in custody. When it did, Molina would either go underground, or he would act immediately.

The optimal decision for Lake and I would be for him to disappear, but in the event he decided to be proactive, we needed to be far away from anything affiliated with the DEA.

"Out," I said, "away from the city."

Across from me she remained silent, watching me.

I continued running the possibilities in my head, thinking of the parameters Diaz had given me just a couple days before. One by one I considered and dismissed the options, drawing on my knowledge of the cityscape, pulling up images I hadn't used in years.

"Ever been to Big Bear Lake?"

Chapter Thirty-Eight

There was no talking, no discussion of any kind.

The moment Thiago passed through the painted green door to room number 211 he drew his weapon, the noise suppressor screwed down on the end of it. With a flick of his left wrist he swung the door closed behind him, waiting until he heard it slam shut before raising the gun and firing three times.

Not once in the five seconds it took for Thiago to enter and fire did Paulo Gomez make a sound, let alone move. He had been pacing at the foot of the bed as Thiago entered, stopping to stare as outside light washed over him, the bright onslaught keeping him from seeing the weapon pressed against Thiago's thigh.

After the door was shut, his vision was ill-equipped to see much of anything, a quick blossom of the muzzle flash illuminating the darkened space.

The first bullet struck him in the chest, piercing his left chest plate. Crimson blood spurted down onto his white dress shirt, a second matching wound appearing a moment later.

The final blow was a bullet to the head, the round cleaving a clean hole through his cheek, equidistant between his nose and right eye.

The force of it jerked his head backward, his body hanging suspended in the air, before dropping onto the mattress.

The springs of the aging bed wheezed as he bounced once, dust motes rising around him as he came to rest on the multi-colored bedspread, never to move again.

Thiago waited a full minute, watching as the blood drained from Gomez's body, before tucking away his weapon and turning back to the door. The smells of gunpowder and blood were heavy as he flipped the lock on the door and pulled it shut behind him.

Forcing himself to move in slow and careful steps, he took the side stairwell down to the parking lot and climbed into his truck, waiting until he was behind the wheel and the engine started before peeling off the black driving gloves on his hands. Not a single other person populated the parking lot as he turned away from the All-Niter and headed toward the freeway, careful to keep his speed in check, to obey all traffic signs.

The hit itself was something he was completely ambivalent about. He had never really much cared for Gomez, though his distaste for him usually fell much closer to irritation than outright hatred. More than anything he had tolerated the man, recognizing the role he played and the loyalty he had to Molina.

Despite everything else the guy had working against him, that much could never be questioned.

Just as certainly, the call had to be made. As a police officer, there was only so far he would be able to go in protecting the operation. Now that a clear connection between him and Molina had been made, he needed to be eliminated.

He simply knew too much to ever be allowed to speak freely.

Angling his truck toward the 210, the evening traffic was heavy, per usual. Easing to a stop behind a line of brake lights, he pulled his iPhone over onto his thigh.

"Call Art," Thiago said, reciting the abbreviated name he used in the event he ever lost his phone. The number was a private one that only four people had, a phone that stayed in the inside pocket of Molina's jacket.

It was that fact that first told Thiago that Gomez had messed up a few hours before.

A moment later a shrill ringing sounded through the truck, followed by the graveled voice of the old man. "Is it done?"

"It is done," Thiago said, both sides skipping pleasantries of any kind.

"Any problems?"

"Less than two minutes total," Thiago said.

Silence fell for a moment, followed by Molina saying, "It was a shame."

"But necessary," Thiago said, finishing the sentence. More than once he had heard his employer make similar statements, intimating that he felt the tiniest bit of remorse without allowing himself to ever get all the way there. "I agree."

A low grunt came back to him in response, but nothing more.

"Have you heard from our guests?" Thiago asked.

"They should be arriving soon," Molina replied, his voice returning to its usual pitch, the moment for Gomez already passed. "Where are you?"

Leaning down a few inches, Thiago glanced up at the green road sign passing overhead. "Waiting to get on the freeway."

"Good," Molina said, ending the call there. He didn't bother stating that Thiago should now make his way back, the fact already known.

With a swipe of his thumb Thiago cleared the screen, his truck moving forward just a few feet before coming to a stop again. In front of him a red Geo filled with teenage girls shook from their coordinated dance moves, the sound of kitschy pop music pouring from the speakers.

Ahead in the distance the sun sat just a few inches above the horizon, orange light blazing straight at him, forcing his eyes to squint as he sat and waited. To avoid staring straight into it he again lowered his gaze, his focus settling on the phone. An idea formed in the back of his mind as he looked out at the cars lined up nose-to-tail, all of them fighting to get on the freeway, anxious to trade in one concrete parking lot for another.

With a few movements of his thumb, he pulled up the tracking app on his phone and activated it. A moment later a digital map appeared on the screen, a blinking red pin appearing in the middle of it.

All saliva fled from Thiago's mouth as he stared down at it, watching a blue circle pulsate out around it, indicating the marker was in transit. His pulse picked up slightly as he watched it move, his mind racing to compute what it represented.

From where he now sat, he had two options. He could fight his way south through evening traffic, hoping to arrive at Molina's just in time to meet the Guzman crew. From there they would load up and use the app to track down the girl, possibly finding her holed up somewhere, having to do battle with a detachment of DEA agents in the process.

On the other hand, he could turn due west and intercept her while moving. He could move fast in the opposite direction of traffic, fall in behind her, at the very least have some concrete information to hand over about her position when he made it back to Molina's.

For a moment his fingers twitched above the phone as he stared at the image onscreen. In front of him the Geo moved forward, the music fading away as he sat and thought, trying to make a decision.

Chapter Thirty-Nine

The evening sun was positioned directly out through the driver's side window as I pushed north on the outskirts of Los Angeles. It bathed the entire side of the truck in a tangerine hue, so bright it forced my left eye almost completely closed, feeling warm against my skin. Propping my elbow up on the window sill, I formed my hand into a makeshift visor, using it to shade some of my face.

Around us the traffic was beginning to thin out, still heavy, but moving. Small gaps were finally starting to appear before us, only the occasional brake light flaring as we drove in the middle lane, holding a steady pace.

"You a skier?" Lake asked, her voice garbled by food, the smell of it filling the interior of the truck. With her legs folded up onto the seat, the source of the smell was nestled between her calves, an In-n-Out wrapper hosting the remains of a burger and a small squirrel's nest of fries.

"What?" I asked, glancing over in her direction.

"You know, skiing. Sliding down a mountain with boards on your feet," she said, moving her hand in a gliding motion to illustrate the sport.

"Naw, not really," I said. "Do a lot of snowshoeing back home, but never was much into skiing."

"Oh," she said, pushing the straw from her milkshake into the corner of her mouth. "So then how'd you come across Big Bear?"

The question was innocent enough, though I didn't much feel like getting into the answer. My wife, years before, had been a skier. Growing up in New England, she had spent considerable time on the slopes there, the Adirondacks practically her backyard.

After I joined the DEA and was sent to the desert, twice a year she demanded we make the trip up to hit the slopes, wanting our daughter to experience some small part of the joy she had as a child. The excuse was of course a front for her own amusement, Alice too young to do much more than play in the snow, leaving me with her on the bunny slopes as she carved up the larger runs above.

Dutifully I had made the trips, though the sport never really stuck with me. As someone that spent so much of my career careening into dangerous situations, the thought of doing it for sport seemed too perverse to ever really wrap my head around.

In the time since, her memory was just too attached to the entire activity to even consider.

"Fishing," I lied. "Damn good fishing up that way."

"Ah," she replied, her voice telling me she didn't entirely buy the response, though she wasn't going to press it.

Around us the traffic thinned down even more, a bevy of signs announcing we would soon be entering San Bernardino, a whole host of food and lodging options presenting themselves.

The decision to move wasn't one that had been made easily, though I didn't see many other options. Staying at headquarters might have provided us the most structural security, but it was also an obvious target for anybody that might find themselves acting under sudden desperation.

If Diaz was successful in apprehending Gomez, that would soon certainly describe the Molina cartel.

We could have moved back into the city. The room at the Marriot was still being held, my cameras tucked away inside. I'd checked them a couple of times in the previous days, the bottle balanced on the doorknob still in position, nobody having entered.

That too presented problems though, namely the fact that Lake's name was on the account. What had started as a means of drawing out anybody that wished her ill could be her undoing if we were foolish enough to return.

Tens of thousands of other options were available, but the encounter by the airport proved how foolish that could potentially be. Most urban hotels limited our exit points, made evasive maneuvering nearly impossible.

The combined sum of this information led me to one incontrovertible fact - I was relatively new at this. Never before had I been assigned on a protection detail, and the one thing I had found over the years was that when doing something outside of a comfort zone, rely on as many known skills as possible.

For me, that meant the mountains. It meant getting outside, where I had freedom of movement and a clear advantage over ninety-nine percent of the people walking the globe.

In order to do that, and still be within any kind of reasonable distance of Los Angeles, meant Big Bear Lake.

The decision, and the roundabout reasoning I had used in getting there, was still bouncing around in my head as I glanced in the rearview mirror. My heart rate increased instantly, my pulse pounding through my temples as I stared at the mirror, only glancing intermittingly at the road ahead.

The first time, and an unknown number of times before, I had missed it.

This time, it was too obvious to ignore.

Pressing my foot a little harder on the gas, I pushed in front of a DHL shipping truck and changed lanes, opening up a small gap between us. Easing off of the accelerator a tiny bit, I maintained a steady pace, my entire focus on the traffic behind me.

Less than thirty seconds after making the move, the same black truck I had first noticed appeared. It increased its speed to match mine, pulling up alongside the shipping vessel and staying there, in plain sight of us without drawing any closer.

Cursing myself for not paying more attention, again I pushed on the accelerator. A larger gap opened between me and the container, a small sedan easing between us.

Again the truck pulled forward, falling in beside the sedan, keeping us in plain sight, but no more.

Dropping my left arm away from the window, I took the wheel in both hands. A quick glance over showed Lake to still be working on her food, her attention aimed out the window, watching a steady stream of restaurants and strip malls fly by.

The truck was too far away to draw any definitive conclusions. From where it sat I had no way of seeing its license plate number, nothing to do with it even if I could.

The late day sun splashed across much of the front windshield, obscuring any view of the driver.

Around us the cityscape grew thicker as we came upon the heart of San Bernardino, my mind racing. At this point pushing on toward Big Bear Lake was out, the only road in that direction a two-lane that wound up through the mountains. Alone and with a sufficient head start it would provide perfect cover for us, but knowing someone was following closely, it would only bottle us in.

That left me with only two options, neither of which was particularly appealing. The first was to make a quick exit somewhere, hoping that the sudden change would occur before he could get off the freeway. From there we could shake him through the labyrinth of city streets, popping up somewhere else and heading in the opposite direction.

The second was to keep going and catch the 210 back toward the downtown area, hoping it might still leave the possibility of the mountains open in the future, throwing them off of our true intentions. It also could provide us space and time, allowing me to call on Diaz, perhaps even have someone intercept the truck.

Weighing the two a moment longer, I leaned heavy on the gas, pushing the truck just north of seventy miles an hour as the signs above announced the freeway split approaching. On them was a visual depiction of how the roads would veer in different directions, two thick tendrils of white twisted in a heap, their ends pointed away from each other.

The wrapper crinkled loudly as Lake finished the last of her meal and wadded it up, depositing everything into the sack at her feet. She wiped her mouth with a napkin and resumed staring out the windshield, a single finger extending outward.

"I think you missed your turn."

I said nothing as I kept the pace steady, merging back into the center lane and swinging in a lazy arc toward town. Around us most of the traffic fell away, the work crowd headed toward home for the night, having no interest in returning to the city.

With my attention focused on the mirrors, I shoved my foot down another half inch toward the floorboard, the V-6 grunting in response as our speed continued to climb.

"What's going on?" Lake asked, unfolding her legs and dropping her feet down. She reached out to grab the dashboard and started to turn, my hand shooting out, stopping her halfway.

"Don't," I said. "I think someone is following us, but I don't want them to see you looking."

Color bled from her face as she stared at me before easing herself back against the seat. She folded her arms over her stomach, her body rigid, her face aimed straight out through the windshield.

Completing the loop, the nose of the truck aimed due west, the late day sun streamed straight in on us. It painted us both bright orange, raising the temperature a few degrees, my back beginning to sweat beneath my t-shirt.

Behind us a handful of vehicles made the same trek, arriving in a misshapen pattern strewn across four lanes of traffic.

Among them was the black truck, pushing hard.

"Shit," I muttered. "He knows he's been seen. Hold on."

Abandoning any concern for traffic laws or posted speed limits, I mashed the gas pedal down, using so much force it nearly lifted my backside from the seat.

The front end of the truck bucked slightly, an angry gnashing of gears finding my ears as it lurched forward, adding another ten miles per hour and climbing fast. In the passenger seat Lake spread herself out wide, a grip on the handle above the window, another on the seat cushion beside her, like an oversized spider.

Behind us the truck matched our increase in speed, growing a bit closer in the rearview. Much larger than my rig, it no doubt had at least a V-8 under the hood, if not one of those diesel monstrosities capable of reaching triple digits without breaking a sweat. Little by little it drew even tighter as we sped past neighboring traffic, nothing more than wisps of color in our periphery.

For all of my training, my years of experiences, defensive driving was not a specialty. Handling a weapon, physical confrontation, even tracking someone through the wild, there were few people better.

Behind the wheel of a car though, I was strictly a Point-A-to-Point-B man.

The reality of that left me with precious few real options. There was no way I could just hope to outrun him. He had more under the hood than I did, and at some point the traffic would get too thick to allow it.

I could try to draw him in closer, hoping maybe to shoot out a tire and disable him. That too came with a whole host of problems, among them the fact that I would be firing on a crowded freeway at a moving target.

Sounded more like an opening to a bad movie than a legit plan.

It also presented with it the high likelihood of my getting arrested, which would leave Lake alone and susceptible.

Of everything, I could least allow that to happen.

Easing back on the gas just a fraction of an inch, I leveled off our speed at ninety-two. With my heart pounding I watched as the truck came ever closer, drawing to within just a few car lengths. Gaze flitting over the traffic ahead, I spotted what I was looking for, willing my truck to stay the course until getting there.

Little by little the black truck came upon us, less than twenty feet separating the two. It held there for just a moment before switching lanes to the left and punching the gas again, his front bumper drawing even with my rear tire and closing fast.

"Oh, shit," Lake said, abandoning my earlier directive and openly staring over my shoulder at our encroaching attacker. "Oh, shit. Oh, shit."

The same thought pushed through my mind as I held position for another moment before jerking the wheel to the right, swinging us across two lanes of traffic.

The tires on the driver's side bit into the asphalt, an angry screech erupting, followed by the smell of scorched rubber. A cacophony of car horns erupted in our wake as Lake's body slammed into my shoulder, her thin frame tossed about by the sudden movement. She remained there, pressed against me as I maintained a diagonal angle, shooting off the freeway and down an exit, never once dropping below sixty miles an hour.

Balanced on edge, my truck wobbled precariously before the passenger tires slammed down, the vehicle bouncing once before leveling out. Lifting my foot from the gas, our speed dropped as traffic continued whipping by behind us.

Waiting as long as I could while approaching the end of the ramp, I smashed my foot down on the brake, our back end fishtailing as we slid to a stop, the smell of cooked rubber again rising around us. A puff of white smoke formed in our wake as the truck quivered to a stop, my heart pounding as I turned behind the wheel and stared out at the freeway behind us.

Nowhere was there any sign of the black truck.

Chapter Forty

Twin billboards welcomed us to the San Manuel Amphitheater on the northern edge of San Bernardino. The first one was there to tout the prestige of the venue itself, exclaiming to all that the place could hold sixty-five thousand concert goers, making it the largest outdoor amphitheater in the country. Beside it was a listing of some of the bigger names set to appear in the coming months, ranging from Van Halen to Toby Keith to Kid Rock.

Built large enough to be seen by drivers passing by on the freeway more than a mile away, they towered high above as I pulled up to the closed gate outside the place and put the truck in park.

More than an hour had passed since exiting the 210, though my nerves were still pulled taut. Sweat clung to my exposed forearms and matted the beard along my jaw line, my lower back soaked through. It stuck to the cloth seat, tugging a bit as I turned off the ignition and stepped out, an evening breeze hitting the perspiration and cooling me a few degrees.

The gravel of the parking lot outside the concert venue crunched beneath my feet as I strode around to the bed of the truck. In the distance I could hear the faintest sounds of freeway traffic flying by, the evening sun dipping below the San Gabriel Mountains to the west of us.

In its wake a purple, pink, and orange glow rose up from the horizon, the first stars begin to peek out overhead.

The passenger door let out a low groan as it wrenched itself open, Lake appearing a moment later. She had yet to say a word since the incident on the freeway, her face still pale as she kept her arms folded before her and walked toward the rear of the truck.

Neither of us said anything as I grabbed her duffel bag from the corner, unhooking the bungee cords holding it in place. Clutched in my left hand, I walked to the tailgate and lowered it down, putting the bag in front of me.

"What are you doing?" Lake asked, her voice a broken whisper.

I had only gotten a glimpse of the man on the 210, but at a glance it looked to be the same one that had chased us eight hours earlier. At the very least the two were connected, the coincidence just too great for them not to be.

Taken together, that meant somebody had to have a way of keeping tabs on us. The possibility existed that they might have followed us to the hotel the night before, but there was no way for somebody to have found us on the outskirts of San Bernardino many hours later.

They were tracking us, and I needed to know how. Doing so would dictate my next move, could make all the difference between Lake Pawlak living or dying.

"I think they've planted a tracking device on us," I said, unzipping her bag. Moving as slow as I could force myself to, I pulled out each item inside one at a time, examining them carefully for anything that might emit a signal.

My original thought was that they had tagged my truck in some way, though that was before remembering that this morning we were using a loaner from the DEA. It had been a completely random thing, Diaz switching us on the fly.

Lake's phone had been confiscated days before, leaving only her bag.

Starting with two t-shirts, I checked each over, flipping them inside out just to be certain. Once complete, I set them off to the side, doing my best not to get them dirty or damage them, moving fast. Next came out a pair of jeans, followed by the cargo pants she had been wearing the day before. Each item took a little longer than the shirts, checking the zippers and rivets, doing a close examination of the heavy seams.

As far as I could tell, there was nothing in those either.

"There's Diaz," Lake said, her tone the same quiet and detached it had been a moment before. She remained rooted along the passenger side of the truck bed, watching me go through her things, not objecting in any way.

The headlights on Diaz's sedan illuminated us both for a moment before blinking out, the sound of her tires biting into gravel finding my ears. She pulled up to within a dozen feet before easing to a stop with a small squeal of the brakes, the engine cutting out.

The front end hissed in the cool night air as a pair of doors opened behind me, followed soon thereafter by feet approaching.

"In the mood for a show?" Diaz asked, walking up alongside me as I went to work on Lake's toiletry bag, emptying the items one at a time. Somewhere behind me I could hear the second set of footsteps stop as well, presumably Lefranc, choosing to remain far back and out of sight.

"You just missed it," I said, glancing up to her.

The expression on her face, her appearance in general, told me her afternoon had been no better than ours. Operating on her second full day without rest, her cheeks were beginning to look hollow, her face drawn and gaunt. Dark circles enveloped her eyes like a raccoon's, frown lines even more pronounced than usual.

"What happened?" she asked.

I relayed the story to her in quick order, almost ashamedly admitting that I hadn't gotten a clear look at the driver or his plates. As I spoke I checked through the last few items in the kit before putting them all back inside, finding nothing.

"How about you?" I asked, already knowing what she was about to tell me just by reading her expression.

"Paulo Gomez is gone," she said, turning and leaning back against the edge of the tailgate. "We went to his office and his residence, found no sign of him."

I cocked an eyebrow over at her, waiting for her to continue.

"Car is still in the driveway, nothing to indicate he packed in a hurry."

The last sentence confirmed my initial suspicion at her use of the word *gone*. Paulo Gomez wasn't running, he was most likely eliminated.

It wasn't the first time either of us had seen business handled in such a manner, someone removed the moment they ceased to be of value.

"Who is Arturo Molina?" I asked, placing the pants and shirts back in the bag and zipping it up. I pushed the bag away and turned around, Lefranc coming into view as I assumed the same pose as Diaz.

"So you talked to Pally?" Diaz asked, obviously having done the same.

"That's why we were relocating," I said. "If this guy is as bad as Pally seemed inclined to believe, we weren't necessarily safe there at headquarters."

Diaz looked to me in her periphery, her head nodding just slightly. "I don't know how bad he is, but he's extensive."

There were likely stacks of files somewhere in storage, hundreds more saved on computers someplace, full of data she could give me about the man. The particulars didn't as much interest me at the moment though. If she seemed to think he was someone to be reckoned with, that was sufficient for my purposes.

My goal, again, was to protect Lake, not to solve a case.

I respected Diaz enough to handle that part on her own.

"What's your plan?" I asked.

She pushed out a long, slow sigh, unfolding her arms and raising both hands to her brow, rubbing her face in slow, concentric circles. "Well, this is a game changer for sure. Arturo Molina isn't the kind of guy you roll up on with a stack of circumstantial evidence and some strong suspicions."

I nodded, already figuring as much. My old boss had always called guys like Molina Keyser Soze's after the villain from *The Usual Suspects*, the kind you got one shot at. After that, they would never lower their guard enough for you to ever get close again.

"We'll go back to headquarters and start building an airtight case."

Again I nodded. For her end, that made perfect sense. Things like tracking down Paulo Gomez would pale compared to the prize of Arturo Molina. That was where her entire focus would be, as it should be.

That just didn't provide a lot of solace for me and Lake.

"Her?" I asked, not bothering to clarify, but knowing I didn't need to.

At this point, with the promise of someone as big as Molina in the mix, Diaz would probably be able to swing entering her in the witness protection program. Bare minimum she would be able to assign DEA agents to her full-time, her own personal entourage wherever she went.

"You out?" Diaz asked, raising an eyebrow in my direction.

"No," I said, shaking my head. "Just wasn't sure if this changed things."

"It does," Diaz said, "but I see no reason why that aspect should adjust, so long as you're good with it."

Asking if I was good with it was a loaded question. I was more than willing to continue offering my skills in any way I possibly could. Lake Pawlak had done nothing wrong beyond needing to pay her bills and driving to the unluckiest place in California to try and do so. She deserved far better than to be dogged by Molina and his team of henchmen.

At the same time, I was self-aware enough to know whatever shortcomings I might have. I was not a trained bodyguard, had cut my teeth in the DEA, not the secret service.

"Okay," I said, "provided we can leave Los Angeles."

The timeframe on this operation had just gotten longer. So far we had been fortunate, but we couldn't ride that forever, especially as the heat intensified on our opposition. We needed to get somewhere that I was better suited for.

"How far we talking?" Diaz asked.

"Far," I replied, the single word letting her know exactly what I was thinking, not wanting to say it in front of Lefranc.

On the freeway nearby an eighteen wheeler rolled past, its oversized engine pushing out a low rumble. A soft breeze flitted by as Diaz studied me, her features giving away nothing.

There were a hundred reasons why she could or even should turn me down. She had overextended bringing me in to begin with. Granting me this courtesy would put her directly in the crosshairs of the Justice Department if it fell apart.

This was an ultimate all-or-nothing scenario for both of us, and we each knew it.

After a moment she tilted her head upward, just a few inches in total, nothing more.

It was all the confirmation I needed.

We were headed to Montana.

Chapter Forty-One

Thiago hadn't bothered to mention the encounter on the freeway upon arriving back at Molina's. Instead he acted as if nothing at all happened, parking in the driveway behind the black Lexus SUV and entering through the side door per usual. From there it was easy to simply blend in, the house very much alive, a stark contrast to his previous visits.

The kitchen, quiet and empty just hours before, was now teeming with people. Many of them he had never seen before, a pair of chefs in white togs working the stove, a bevy of servers in white shirts and bowties preparing trays and drinks. A myriad of smells washed over him as he passed through, bringing an involuntary murmur from his stomach, his mouth watering at the aromas.

Fighting every urge his stomach sent his way, Thiago walked on past, earning nothing more than a few curious glances from the servers as he went. Finding the patio empty, he circled back through and headed for the main dining hall, discovering it already prepared for a dozen people, China place settings and cloth napkins before each seat.

Extra inserts had been placed inside the table, extending the length from its normal six feet to more than twice that. Chairs that normally rested at either end of the table had been removed, allowing all twelve guests to sit across from each other, nobody considered any more important than the others.

Seeing the excessive, and unnecessary, insistence on ceremony brought a sour taste to his mouth.

The encounter on the freeway had been just short of a total disaster, an opportunity to sidestep all of this lost. In an ideal world, he would have found the girl, alone and on the run, and brought her in. At the very least he would have tailed them to wherever they were set to hole up next, having onsite intel to provide around the table. From there things would have been easy, using the combined forces to show up and steamroll one single man with a beard.

Instead he had allowed himself to be pulled into a high speed chase on the freeway. The move was nothing short of foolish, the kind of thing he had often chastised Hector for doing. Once he had been spotted he should have fallen back entirely, allowing them to move on, content with the knowledge that he was only a few strokes on his iPhone away from finding them again.

Somehow they had managed to elude him twice in a single day. The fact grated on him in a way that went well past bruising his ego, threatening his status in the company and the esteem Molina held him in.

Just thinking of it again caused him to pull his phone out, activating the app. He waited for it come alive, watching as the red pin was now a good piece above of the city, moving north on I-15.

"Where have you been?" the old man asked, appearing at the opposite end of the room.

Thiago ignored the question a moment as he looked down at his screen, the blue pulsating circle around it indicating his target was on the move. Already it was closing in on Barstow, nothing beyond that until Las Vegas.

The thought brought a stab of anxiety to his stomach, mixing with the acrimony already flooding through. If she made it there his job would become infinitely more difficult, especially as he was about to be hamstrung with a crew of Guzman's thugs at any moment.

"Thiago?" Molina asked, jerking Thiago's attention upward.

Already dressed for entertaining, a tie was back in place at his neck, a silver-tipped cane in his hand. Behind him Jasmine stood in a sheath dress that ended a full six inches above her knees, not daring to move atop the stilettos she was wearing.

Declan, the usual third leg in their trio, was nowhere to be seen. Most likely he was securing the grounds, Thiago knowing he was never more than fifty yards from their employer at any given time.

"Traffic," Thiago said, not a blatant lie, but far from the truth.

"Any problems with Paulie?" Molina asked, reiterating what he had asked hours before.

"No," Thiago said, shaking his head as he stared down at the phone in his hand. The pin seemed to indicate they were now exiting Barstow, heading further north on the highway, the state line now just an hour or so away. "Nobody saw or heard a thing."

Seeming to sense his hesitation, Molina took a step forward. "Any problems with anything else?"

Glancing up at him, Thiago started to reply. He cut himself short and instead held his phone up, wagging it at his employer. "She's running."

Taking another step forward, Molina reclined his head, peering down the length of his nose at the phone. "She's running? Now?"

A flush of heat rose to Thiago's cheeks, not wanting to get into the events of the afternoon. "Apparently."

"Hmm," Molina said, considering the screen, a deep frown accentuating the lines on either side of his face. He regarded it a moment before waving a hand at it, shoving the issue aside. "So let her run. We'll find her."

Feeling his lips part, his jaw sag open a bit, Thiago stared at his boss in silence.

"You have her marked," Molina said, motioning to the device. "And the further she is from Los Angeles, the less harm she can do."

The flippant nature of Molina surprised him, a bit of agitation rising within. "But I thought you said she was priority number one?"

"She is," Molina said, "starting in the morning. Tonight we must welcome our guests, eat and drink like civilized people. Tomorrow you will lead a party out after her, and you will not return until she is gone."

Stunned into silence, Thiago stood and waited, unsure how to respond. The implication of the last statement was clear, though he couldn't quite agree with the logic in giving them a twelve hour head start.

On that highway alone was Las Vegas and Salt Lake City, both with airports capable of sending her bouncing all over the country, even the world. By tomorrow morning she could be virtually anywhere.

As if watching the internal monologue playing out inside Thiago, Molina stopped in place, both hands resting atop his cane. "You forget, *mijo*, this is not the first possible witness I have had stand against me. While to you her running seems a catastrophe, to me it proves quite the opposite.

"If ever anybody was moving in on us, the disappearance of Paulie has stalled that. They've sent her away so they can circle up and try to figure out something else."

There he paused, allowing Thiago to process the simple logic of the statement.

"In the meantime you find her, eliminating the only two possible witnesses they could have," Molina said. "They have no product, they have no way of finding the money."

A thin smile grew on his face. "They have nothing."

From the rear opening to the room Declan passed through, appearing alongside Jasmine, her body tensing in his presence. He walked straight forward, his arms held rigid by his side, and said, "Our guests have arrived."

Molina turned and nodded at the information before shifting his attention back to Thiago, a thin smile on his lips. "In the morning, you may take the plane wherever you need to find her. Until then, it is imperative we be gracious hosts and ensure that by this time next week everything is back in order as it should be."

Chapter Forty-Two

The grocery sack sat on the counter, its contents spilled out around us in a wide half arc. Among them were a pair of scissors, a box of hair dye, and an electric shaver, all grabbed in a quick dash through a 24-hour Wal-Mart.

I had expected more of a fight from Lake, but to her credit she let it go without comment. Whatever bit of defiance was still inside her seemed to have faded away, pushed aside by multiple vehicular encounters and armed attempts on her life within the previous couple of days.

The light fixture above the sink flickered as we stood side by side in the cramped bathroom. The floors were dirty and the towels stacked above the toilet threadbare, not that the condition of the place mattered in the slightest. Located eighteen miles north of Las Vegas, it had been chosen because it was out of the way and accepted cash payments.

Neither one of us would be sleeping here, our total stay no more than the time it took to alter our appearances and be on the road again.

"Remind me why we're doing this here?" Lake asked, taking up the box of hair dye and tearing back the top flap.

"As opposed to?" I asked, grabbing for the shaver and pulling apart the plastic casing housing it. Tucked away beneath the object was a black charger cord, the length of it coiled up and wrapped tight with a drawstring. Unspooling it, I jammed the plug into the wall, watching as the red light appeared as it began to charge.

"As opposed to wherever we're going," Lake asked, pulling each item out of the box and aligning them one at a time on the sink.

"Like I said the first time we met, right now whoever is after us is looking for Rainbow Brite and Jesus Christ. Once we alter that, if they ever show up and start asking around, whoever they speak to will have no idea what they're talking about."

She rocked her head back an inch in understanding, though said nothing.

"Besides," I added, "where we're going, you would be way, way too obvious."

I didn't bother filling her in any further, though I'm guessing she understood what I was getting at. Shaggy hair and a beard would never be glanced at twice in Montana, but pink locks and colorful tattoos would stand out in the mind of every single person she encountered. The cold would ensure her arms were covered enough to render the ink on her arm moot, but the hair was something we had to be more proactive about.

"You want to go first?" I asked, slide stepping into the doorway. There wasn't enough room in there for the both of us to do what we needed to simultaneously, the space cramped as we simply stood beside one another.

"Sure," she whispered, her voice relaying zero enthusiasm for the upcoming project.

Without asking if she needed help, her current state proving she was more than adept at working with hair dye, I stepped out into the room. A moment later the door clicked shut behind me as the sink came on, pushing water out full blast.

Leaving the light in the room off, I walked past the single king bed with the floral bedspread made of some material that looked to be approaching vinyl, and stood just to the side of the window. Staying far enough back to ensure I didn't disturb the paper thin curtain or allow for a shadow to be seen, I stared out at the parking lot, the late hour rendering the place silent.

A uniform single story tall, the place had two dozen units, half of the doors facing out on our side of the building, the other half on the opposite side facing the highway. Despite being less than two hundred yards from I-15, only two other cars could be seen, the front half just as barren when I checked us in.

The young kid behind the cash register, in his mid-twenties with heavy acne and a bad haircut, had barely glanced up as I filled out the registration slip and laid two twenties on the table, using names and addresses from *Friday Night Lights* as my alias.

In total, Lake spent over twenty minutes in the bathroom, the water intermittingly coming on and off. Otherwise there was no sound until the door cracked open, a sliver of light spilling out onto the wall opposite the bathroom. The sight of it turned my attention toward her, entire body stiff, obvious she was not pleased with the curtain of chestnut brown hair hanging damp around her face.

"Look at you," I said, stepping away from the window.

"Shut up," she said, just barely above a whisper.

"It looks good," I said, passing the bed and heading to take my turn.

"But it doesn't look like me," she said, standing off to the side as I slid past her and into the bathroom.

I didn't bother pointing out that was the idea as I shut the door behind me, pulling my shirt off over my head and taking the shaver up from the counter. I set the adjustment for the blade length to level three, the highest it would go, and started at my right ear.

There was no hesitation at all, no examination of what had taken months to grow out, not the slightest bit of melancholy as I scraped the razor down along my jaw line. Thick swaths of hair fell away as I worked, piling up on the sink in front of me, my full face becoming visible for the first time in months.

Once the beard was gone I started in on the top half, beginning in the center of my forehead, cutting a wide trench through the shaggy hair. As if mowing a lawn, I worked side to side one stripe at a time until the top of my scalp was clean before moving my way around the edges.

The cheap item became bogged in some place, tugging at the tangle of hair as it tried to chew its way through. It yanked and ripped until finally everything was buzzed clean, a uniform half inch all the way around.

Clicking it off for just a moment, I ran my palm over my head to ensure I hadn't missed any bits before dropping the blade to the shortest setting and once more going over my beard, buzzing it down to just stubble.

The entire process took me no more than ten minutes, a small woodland creature's worth of hair on the counter by the time I was done. Raking it into a pile with my fingers, I stuffed it and Lake's trash back into the plastic bag, tying it at the top. I ran a bit of cool water into my hands and rubbed it over my freshly exposed face and scalp, finishing by pulling my shirt back on and stepping out.

In the time I was inside, Lake had moved a total of two feet, standing in front of a cracked mirror above the dresser. She twisted a damp tendril of hair between her thumb and forefinger, her head tilted to the side as she studied it.

"Remind me why it had to be brown again?" she asked.

For a brief instant, a shot of annoyance passed through me. The idea that anybody would have to be convinced to do something that could save their life, especially something as innocuous as dying their hair, seemed foreign to me.

Just as fast, it passed. Lake had been through a lot in the previous days, and as I knew better than most, you couldn't tell a person how to handle emotion, whether it was shock or fear or grief.

"Because three quarters of the Caucasian people in the world have brown hair," I said.

She nodded, accepting the information, before turning to look at me. Her eyes widened as she saw me for the first time, her lips parting just a bit.

"Don't look like a grizzly any more, huh?" I asked, the corner of my mouth turning up just slightly.

"No," she said, a small smirk lifting her face, "now you look like a Hawk."

Part Four

Chapter Forty-Three

The truck appeared seemingly from thin air. Rounding a curve at well over seventy miles an hour, it was on me before I even realized it. Eyes half glazed, my body powered down into a low energy state, it materialized from nowhere, jolting me alert.

An eighteen wheeler pulling a full trailer, the big metal beast showed up from around the curve, running lights outlining a body twenty feet in length. On the front end of it was a pair of oversized headlights, enormous yellow lamps throwing out a wide cone of light, illuminating the path before it.

The two of us passed by in opposite directions without a second glance, just two more lonely automobiles in the dead of night. With so few others out on the road, the sudden emergence of each other had been surprising, but nothing to be of concern.

Blinking three times, I sat up higher in my seat. I rubbed at my eyes, still seeing the lights behind my eyelids as we continued moving through the night. Like twin flashbulbs they remained visible each time I blinked, small distorted twists of color seared into my retinas.

Flashbulbs.

All thought of the truck fell away as I focused on the single word, the mere mention of it setting off an alarm deep in the recesses of my brain. It remained there, festering, growing larger until it was too big to ignore.

"Lake," I said, my voice sounding louder than usual inside the silent confines of the truck. "Lake."

She was curled up on the seat beside me, her lower half twisted onto the faded canvas seat, her torso leaning against the truck door. Her right arm was curled into a ball resting on the window sill, her head pressed down atop it.

Reaching out, I placed a hand on her knee and shook it softly.

She shifted slightly, readjusting herself, but her eyes remained closed.

"Lake," I said, shaking her a bit harder, this time pulling her from her slumber. She pushed out a loud breath and sat up in her seat, blinking rapidly as she looked at me, squinting in the darkness.

"Lake, where are your cameras?" I asked. There was more edge in my voice than I intended, but the realization I had just made needed to be acted on immediately.

I had been on the right track the night before, checking Lake's bag. I just hadn't been thorough enough. Anybody that was looking to plant a tracking device wouldn't do it someplace as obvious as a t-shirt, they would look for something that would never be noticed but always with her.

For anybody that spent even a nanosecond in Lake's cottage, they would know that to be her cameras.

"Where are we?" she asked, confusion on her face.

"Lake, your cameras," I repeated, bypassing her inquiry.

She pressed both hands to her forehead for a moment and exhaled through her nose before lowering them into her lap. She opened her eyes wide and looked at me before saying, "Um, it's in evidence at the DEA."

"No, not that camera, the ones you grabbed at your place, that you had at the hotel yesterday."

Pushing herself up to the edge of the seat, she turned and extended an arm into the space between us and the rear window. Draping my left wrist over the wheel I split my attention between her and the road, watching as she grabbed the same small shoulder bag she'd had the day before and pulled it over, dropping it on the seat beside me.

Easing off the gas, I slowed down and drifted to the side of the road, rumble strips vibrating loudly, shaking the truck as it came to a stop on the shoulder. The dense forest of northern Utah butted up to us on either side, blotting out everything but a narrow strip of the night sky above.

No traffic of any kind could be seen in either direction, our headlights flashing off a few reflector strips the only signs of civilization to be seen.

"What's going on?" she repeated.

Once more I ignored the question as I unclipped the bag, folding the top flap back. Inside were two small cameras, near identical copies of each other, their lenses facing out in opposite directions to avoid scratching.

All moisture bled away from my mouth as I lifted them both out, a small handheld model not much different than the trail cameras that were still set up at the Marriot in Anaheim. Dropping both down into my lap, I ran my hands down inside the bottom of the bag, feeling a metal bulge tucked away in the corner.

My stomach dropped out on me as I pulled back the padded interior of the bag, revealing what looked like a small Zippo lighter wedged in the corner.

"Son of a bitch," I muttered, lowering the case and looking over to Lake.

She glanced from me to the bag and back again. "What?"

"I knew there was no way that guy showing up twice yesterday was coincidence," I said. "That's why I searched your duffel, but I completely forgot about this bag."

Staring down at it, seeing it right there, so obvious once I figured out to look in the right place, brought a well of wrath up within me. It roiled through my core in an angry knot, threatening to burst out of any opening it could find.

Tightening my hand into a tight ball, I lowered the side of my fist down to the dashboard, wanting nothing more than to hammer it into oblivion, smashing the fiberglass into hundreds of tiny pieces. I kept it there a moment, willing myself not to act on it, reminding myself that my error was not what was most important.

"So they know where we are?" Lake asked, a renewed fear, stronger than anything I'd heard since we met, in her voice.

Releasing my fist, I pulled in a long breath through my nose, thinking on what I knew.

The tracking device was simply a relay point. It would tell someone where it was, but it couldn't record video or audio of any kind. To whoever was watching this, we were nothing more than a blinking dot on a map.

Most likely, somebody had been watching as we drove through the night out of LA. They probably figured us for Vegas or even Salt Lake, but now that we were well past both they had to figure we were either going to hide in the mountains or make a run for Canada.

That meant they would likely react one of two ways. They might decide that Lake wasn't worth that kind of effort and just let her go. More likely though, they would do whatever they had to to ensure her silence.

Already they had shown a willingness to commit murder in broad daylight and conduct a high speed chase on a busy highway. Whatever Lake had seen, they were clearly deeming a worthy business venture that needed to go on. The fact that Arturo Molina, whoever he may be, was involved only confirmed it was most likely quite lucrative.

Sum total, there was no way anybody was ever going to stop looking for her. Even if they didn't come today, they would keep an eye out, they would find another Paulo Gomez to keep a watch on the records, and some day they would get Lake Pawlak.

"No," I said, shaking my head, "they have no idea where we are. They know where this transmitter is."

I glanced up to see her jaw hanging open, her face twisted to the side. "What does that even mean?"

Replacing the device into the bag, I put back both cameras and clipped the top shut. I pulled my phone from where it rested in the cup holder in the middle console and thumbed through my call list, finding the one I was looking for and hitting send.

The clock on the dashboard told me it was just after three in the morning, though I had a feeling the man I was phoning would be awake just the same.

Two rings later my assumption was confirmed.

"Hawk," Pally said, his voice clear, not a hint of weariness or agitation.

"Apologies for the hour," I said, "need another favor."

I paused, waiting for him to make a crack about that being the usual reason for my calls, but he said nothing.

"I need a hotel room," I said. "At least one night, with the possibility to extend it to as many as necessary."

Over the line I could hear bare feet shuffling over the floor, a desk chair being pulled out. "Okay. Where and when?"

The last town we had passed through with any size was Ogden, less than an hour north of Salt Lake. That still put us a little ways from Idaho Falls, the last real town before I-15 got to Montana.

"Idaho Falls," I said. "Arriving here shortly."

The clatter of fingers pounding on a keyboard found my ears. "Done."

"Also, I need you to use the alias," I said. "You know the one. And put it on a card that can't be traced to anybody."

Once more Pally remained silent. I figured that was because he already knew exactly what I was telling him, though I needed to say the words as much so I could hear them as anything.

"How visible?" he asked.

"Very," I said. "Lots of foot traffic. Cameras if possible."

"I'll send you the details," Pally said. "It'll be ready when you arrive"

"Thanks," I said, cutting off the call without further discussion from either side. I left the phone perched on my thigh and stared out at the empty road, my mind forcing everything I knew into place.

"We're going to Idaho Falls?" Lake asked. Her entire demeanor had a stoic, distant quality to it that told me she could sense my tension. Seeing the tracking device had made everything even more real for her.

Again I disregarded one of her questions.

Keeping the phone in place, I pulled the phone menu back up and scrolled through it. I bypassed Pally's number and went to the next in the recent call history and dialed.

This one I hated to make even more for the simple reason that I knew she needed sleep, but I couldn't afford to hold off on making it.

"Diaz," she replied, picking up after four rings. Her weary tone sounded like she hadn't been asleep, but that she was fast drifting toward it.

"I found the tracking device," I said, pushing right in without preamble.

A moment passed, presumably as she tried to piece together who this was and what I was saying, before recognition clicked into place. "Hawk."

"It was in the camera bag," I said. "Tucked away in the bottom."

Now I could tell I had her attention, her voice gaining a bit of steam. "So yesterday, at her place..."

"That's what I'm figuring too," I said. "They got there before your team did, planted it and waited for us to come by. For whatever reason, the guy got jumpy, went off script."

"Shit," Diaz whispered. "I've got all the manpower we have here digging at Arturo Molina. The man is careful and insulated as hell."

Her last sentence told me everything I needed to know. Right now, as with all else on the case thus far, they had a mountain load of circumstantial evidence and nothing they could credibly pin him down on.

"Gomez show up yet?"

"Nothing," Diaz said.

I thought on that a moment, considering every angle that still existed, before abandoning it. That was her job to complete. Right now mine was to handle the task at hand.

"The reason I'm calling," I said, "is I need you to have a couple agents sent to Idaho Falls."

"Okay," she said, no pause, no consideration. "What's in Idaho Falls?"

"A hotel," I said. "Pally is setting it up now. I'll let you know the minute I do."

A moment passed, a few mouse clicks just barely audible. "We don't have a presence there, but I can have somebody sent over from Boise. Be there in a couple hours."

"That's perfect," I said. "We're about the same distance out."

"Okay," she said, "and what am I going to have them do there?"

I glanced over to my side and said, "Have them watch Lake for a day or two."

Lake's eyes grew three sizes and her mouth dropped open, her head swinging itself from side to side. She remained silent as she began to wave her left hand in front of her, taking her right and repeatedly making a slashing gesture along her neck.

"And where are you going?" Diaz asked.

I heard the trepidation in her voice, saw the theatrics of Lake beside me, and pushed them both aside. I thought back on the man at Lake's cottage I had fought with, on the guy that tried to run us down in his truck multiple times, and felt the same anger rise within.

"I'm going to take the camera bag up to Montana and see what happens."

Chapter Forty-Four

Every last mile from the side of the road to Idaho Falls was spent with Lake protesting. Loudly. Vehemently. Angrily. Not a single thought or argument against what I was proposing was left unused, ranging all the way from saying the new agents would be repeats of Lefranc and she couldn't trust them to questioning my own sanity and safety in the decision.

The first few comments I responded to before giving up and retreating into myself, allowing her to keep going. At times she yelled, at times she cried, but through almost all of it I remained silent, preparing myself for what waited ahead.

There were only two places that I knew well enough to go. One was Yellowstone, which was federal jurisdiction, and almost completely snowed in this time of year. The other was my personal cabin, which was far from ideal, but did have its advantages.

I had no idea if whoever was on the other end would even follow, or how long I might have to wait for them to arrive.

In the meantime, I would need to prepare and assume they would bring at least a handful of people with them.

The closer we got to Idaho Falls, the louder Lake's protests became, reaching a crescendo as I pulled off the highway and followed the road signs to the Holiday Inn. Pally had secured us a corner room on the top floor there, providing as optimal a vantage point as a hotel could provide.

Pulling up out front, I parked under the awning leading to the front door, twin glass models on a sliding track that allowed us to see into the lobby. Standing there by the continental breakfast, paper cups of coffee in hand, were two men in dark suits. They seemed to be deep in conversation, each with one hand shoved into the pocket of their slacks, the other used to take intermittent hits from their drink.

Being inconspicuous was clearly not their forte.

Just the sight of them brought a disgusted moan from Lake, did very little to calm my nerves about the entire endeavor.

The plan, as a whole, had a great many holes. I was fully aware of it, knowing that for the first time since meeting her I was leaving Lake's side. If anything happened to her between now and my return, it wasn't on the pair of men standing a few feet away.

It was on me.

At the same time, what I was about to do, she couldn't be a part of.

"Have you heard a word I said?" Lake asked, glaring at the men before turning to look at me.

"Every last one," I said, glancing past her to the agents before settling back in my seat. "And I agree with you entirely. Finding the tracking device changed things, though."

Hot tears again appeared along the bottom of her eyes as she turned and stared at me. They hung there a moment, threatening to streak down her cheeks, until she reached up and wiped them away, saying nothing.

"I know," I said. "You won't believe me, but I feel the same exact way."

She held her pose a moment before looking out the front windshield. "Somehow, I doubt that," she whispered.

Truth was, she was right.

There was no way she could feel the amount of guilt I felt.

In reality, she was much closer to my age than my daughter's, but that didn't stop it from carrying a similar weight. She was a young woman, not helpless in the general sense, but completely without recourse in the situation she had found herself in. She had been brought to me for protection, to be looked after.

For me, doing that had nothing to do with her providing testimony in some trial. It was another chance for me to do what I should have done before and didn't, an error I would spend the rest of my life trying to atone for.

All of that I wanted to tell her, to make her understand why I had to leave her now, no matter how much I didn't want to. I wasn't abandoning her, I was shielding her. I was making sure she didn't see not only who was coming, but what I was going to do to them.

Instead, I said nothing.

The temperature outside had dropped more than thirty degrees since leaving LA. It ran over my freshly shaved skin as I pushed the door open and walked to the rear of the truck. I unstrapped her bag and grabbed it by the handles, walking to the passenger side as Lake climbed out.

She shoved her door closed, walked forward, and said, "I wish you weren't doing this."

"So do I."

"You don't have to," she said, a puff of morning air twisting her now-brown hair behind her.

I turned toward the door, seeing the men approaching, their dark shapes stopping just inside the entry without stepping out. Thrusting my head upward a few inches, I nodded at them, Diaz having provided our new descriptions, the only two people arriving at such an unusual hour.

"Yes, I do," I said, extending her bag, holding it at shoulder height.

Lake moved past it and wrapped her arms around my waist, her hands sliding along my t-shirt and squeezing tight. After a moment, I allowed my arms to envelope her shoulders as well, the two of us holding the position for several seconds before pulling away.

Fresh moisture underscored each of her eyes as she took the bag and looped the strap over her shoulder. She sniffed deeply, the cold already turning the rims of her nostrils red.

"You be careful," she whispered.

"You too," I said. "Try not to give those two too much grief."

She stifled a smile, looking down at the ground between her feet. She nudged a rock with the toe of her shoe before casting it aside with a flick of her ankle, sending it skittering across the pavement.

"You'll be back, right?"

I nodded, looking up past her to the mountains rising on the edge of town. In the distance I could hear the falls in the city center, could feel the icy breath of the air filling my lungs.

After five years in the Rockies, the mountains were my home. They provided me with a strength, a confidence, that no outside party could ever hope to understand.

In that moment, I practically dared the man in the black pickup to come again, to try and harm someone I cared about.

"The second I am done."

Chapter Forty-Five

A gentle, pervasive spring breeze passed through the floor-to-ceiling screen encompassing the patio. It was just strong enough to offset the afternoon sun streaming in, the golden orb still high over-head, shining straight down. In a few hours it would be at an angle, pushing light and heat into the room, but for the time being Arturo Molina and Daniel Guzman both sat comfortably in the shade.

Bypassing his traditional place on the couch, Molina was in an armchair on one end of the coffee table. Done to ensure he and his guest were on equal footing, he sat with his body cocked to the side, one ankle raised to his opposite thigh. Balanced across his leg were a saucer and a cup of coffee, fresh from the French press he had brought in for the occasion.

Four feet away Guzman sat in a matching chair, both feet planted on the ground. In his left hand he held his own saucer just six inches below his chin, using his right to raise the cup and drink deeply.

Between them on the sofa sat Jasmine and Sanchez, each staring intently down at their laps and the blank notepads balanced atop them. Somewhere nearby were Declan and Rafa, the only two men left behind to watch over the home.

Both Molina and Guzman had agreed they would be more than sufficient for whatever might arise before the others returned.

"This is quite impressive," Guzman lied, taking another swallow and replacing the cup to the saucer, lowering them both to his lap. He did his best to display a look of pleasure, feeling the swill slide down the back of his throat.

Molina had commented upon making it that the beans were freshly picked nearby just days before, a fact that hardly seemed worth boasting about. Compared to what Guzman grabbed from his back-yard in Ecuador each day, they were no more than a half step up from what could be purchased at the local fast food joint for ninety-five cents.

"Thank you," Molina said, dipping the top of his head an inch. "I am glad you like it."

He himself was strictly a *cafecito* man, in the rare event he even drank coffee past breakfast. To him, any time later in the day should be celebrated with libations, not something hot and caffeinated.

"I appreciate you making such an effort to open your home to us," Guzman said. "And for involving us in the apprehension of the girl."

The line was thinly veiled, and both men knew it. If the previous night's awkward dinner was any indicator, the two sides were not friends, were barely even acquaintances.

They were business associates at most, two men making a tremendous amount of money and buttressing their reputations in one of the richest drug cultures in the world. Alone, neither would be able to flourish, but together they were building an empire.

The standing of that empire, and all the potential it had for expansion moving forward, was the only reason any of this was occurring. If the returns on investment for either side were middling, if there was an easy way to cut losses and start anew, they would both do so.

The fact was though, Arturo Molina's star had been fading badly before he went into business with Guzman. The producers he worked with out of Columbia were taking larger cuts for inferior products, goods that were not worth nearly as much on the street as they once had been.

Through blind luck and good timing he had been introduced to the man across from him, a neophyte on the scene with quality yields and a hunger to make a name for himself.

Being so new to the scene, none of the other major players in California had so much as shown the respect to take a meeting with him. They had gotten as far as hearing he was based in Ecuador and scoffed at him, never once even providing the opportunity to sample what he was offering. When the chance to meet with Molina, a player if more in reputation than substance, arose, he had taken the opening and made them both into stars.

It was no secret that at this point, he held more sway over the partnership. His product had proven itself, just as he knew it would. There was a distinct outcry for it, one that might soon force them to reexamine the way they were bringing it into the country, using mules to swallow a kilo at a time no longer being sufficient.

Still, Molina had brought him into the fold when he didn't have to. He had provided the mechanism for getting it into the country without having to deal with airports or custom agents, miles of paperwork and millions of prying eyes.

"This is very important to both of us," Molina replied. "I trust that if trouble had occurred on your side of the line, you would have done the same."

The words were made as a statement, though no small amount of a question was present.

"Of course," Guzman said, bowing the top of his head. "The American justice system, it is a very peculiar thing."

Molina nodded in agreement, leaning forward and placing his cup and saucer on the table, having managed to drink it down to the last dregs. "I know, all too well. I have been fighting with it for decades now."

Guzman considered the statement, adding a thoughtful shake of his head. "In Ecuador, things are much more straightforward. One individual, no matter what she saw, would never present such a problem."

"That is the way it used to be here," Molina lamented. "There was nothing that couldn't be done through a discreet payment or a well-placed bullet. In the early years, I had so many cops on the payroll I had to have a special assistant just for keeping track of all the intel they were bringing us."

Guzman nodded, the situation sounding similar to what he could possess in Ecuador if he so chose. Given that most of his business occurred thousands of miles away, it had not been deemed a prudent expenditure on the local level, but there was comfort in knowing the possibility existed.

"Times changed," Molina said. "In the eighties, cocaine was the hottest thing around. People couldn't get enough of it. Then a few actors, a couple of athletes, some people in the public eye, had to take it too far. Started turning up dead in hotel rooms, getting their pictures on the evening news.

"Suddenly, the general public, even the casual users, swung sharply in the other direction. They started heading to the polls, replaced the old guard politicians with new people, young blood that promised to clean up what was going on."

"Mm," Guzman said, nodding. "Just like that?"

"Not entirely," Molina said. "Obviously, our side didn't go down without a fight, but it got tougher. Law enforcement starting targeting us, federal agencies exploded in size and scope. New designer drugs started shifting the customer base."

He let his voice drift for a moment, staring at the table, his vision blurring as he thought back.

"For a while, we fought the changes. Took it to the streets, made things bloody. In the end though, that turned out a foolish business model."

He stopped there, letting everyone in the room infer that the losses were too great to be sustainable. Any small victories he might have garnered were offset in men and money, a poor way to build a network.

"So that's why the girl?" Guzman asked, arching an eyebrow.

The question drew Molina from his thoughts, causing him to blink several times. He dropped his foot to the floor and ran his hands down the front of his thighs, straightening his tie before him.

"So to speak," he said. "The combined effect of all those experiences was that the best way to handle business in the new America was to be invisible. Whereas before it was beneficial to be a figurehead, to provide customers with someone they could point to, nowadays being that well known is a burden. It paints a target on you, both from competitors and from law enforcement."

He didn't bother to explain that that was why everything he owned was put under a pseudonym. There was no need to point out that many of his ground distributors didn't even know they worked for him, the network a series of middle managers.

"In this instance, all other strings that can be traced back to our relationship have been snipped clean. Once she is gone, her testimony silenced, there will be absolutely nothing anybody can pin on us. They'll know that, which will keep them from even bothering to try and bring a suit."

Guzman's gaze tracked over him as he considered the words, mulling over what was being said. "And without a suit..."

"We get back to business," Molina said. "New locations, maybe a change in our approach, but at the end of the day, our product continues to flood the streets.

"In the end, isn't that the most important thing?"

A moment passed before the corners of Daniel Guzman's mouth turned up in a small smile. A myriad of thoughts played through his mind, ranging from the fallacies in Molina's thinking to his own standing in the operation.

Still, he let them pass without comment, stating only, "Indeed it is."

Chapter Forty-Six

Armed with just four hours of sleep in the preceding two and a half days, Mia Diaz felt like she was drifting through a state of semi-consciousness. Enough adrenaline had ebbed and flowed through her system in the previous sixty hours to keep her afloat, but it had also eroded most of her nerve endings, leaving her feeling a degree or two below total alertness. That feeling of borderline numbness permeated her body as she pulled up outside the All-Niter, Lefranc in the passenger seat, his mouth hanging agape at what he saw.

A full crime scene workup was already in effect as they parked on the edge of the lot and climbed out, yellow police tape stretched across most of the structure. A handful of black-and-whites were parked at odd angles in front of it, doing their best to shield all comers.

For their part, a crowd of curious onlookers stood just beyond the artificial barricade, held at bay more by the half dozen men in uniform standing in front of them. None appearing to be more than twenty-five years old, they hid behind mirrored sunglasses, ignoring questions lobbed their way.

Behind them rose a two-story structure painted brick red, a series of green doors spaced evenly across each floor. Cheap brass fixtures displayed numbers on each of them, thin curtains hanging over most of the windows.

Rusting iron pillars supported the second story walkway, a sign stretched between two of them announcing the place to be the All-Niter. Faded, with yellow lettering on a black background, it fit with the general décor of the place, all of it screaming 1970's.

Off to the right was a small standalone structure measuring no more than a dozen feet square, the word *office* emblazoned on the window in red neon. Below it in matching script was the word *vacancy*.

"Great," Diaz muttered, grabbing up her badge from the middle console and stepping out of the car. She left the badge out and in her hand, flashing it at the pair of cops closest to her. On either end they lifted the caution tape and allowed her to pass through, kneeling just slightly to get beneath it.

The call had come in two hours before.

That morning, a maid at the All-Niter had entered room 211 for basic turndown service. Upon entering, she found a middle-aged man lying face-up on the bed, two shots at close range to his chest, a third to the face.

The room had been rented to a Walter White the afternoon before, a man who had not been seen by anybody since. Nobody had been noticed entering or exiting the room, and no cameras were on the premises.

The first responding officers had checked the man for identification, finding his driver's license and detective's badge, both naming him as Paulo Gomez. Once the name entered the system, it hit on the bulletin Diaz had posted, filtering its way to her within an hour.

At the time, Diaz was up to her elbows in information on Arturo Molina, working with every tech wonk she had available to find something they could pin on the man. Short on time and growing frustrated, she had grabbed Lefranc and got on the road once the call came in, heading straight to Pasadena, early afternoon traffic be damned.

The concrete stairs running along the edge of the building were beginning to crumble, bits of them flaking off with each step as Diaz ascended. As she grew closer she could hear the collective buzz that usually accompanied a crime scene, the conglomerated attention and focus of a half dozen people crammed into an enclosed space.

Arriving at the top landing, she turned a corner to find a pair of officers leaning against the rail. On the right was a man just north of fifty with short hair in a deep widow's peak, his face and paunch both fleshy. A tweed sport coat was draped over the railing beside him, his short-sleeve dress shirt appearing misshapen on his pear-shaped frame.

Upon seeing Diaz, he broke off the conversation he was engaged in, the uniform beside him receding a few steps. Appearing as young and fresh faced as those in the parking lot downstairs, Diaz recognized him right off as token security, told to watch the door and check identification of anybody seeking to enter.

"Agent Diaz?" the man said, using his hips to push himself up off the rail as he extended a meaty hand her way. "Detective Fred Murton."

Diaz accepted the handshake, his grip moist to the touch. "Detective," she said. "Special Agent Diaz, this is Agent Lefranc."

The two men exchanged a handshake as Diaz turned, staring through the door standing open. Inside, the criminalists were already at work, a trio of people in white paper suits going over the room in excruciating detail. Two of them held small vials of fingerprint powder and brushes while a third checked over the carpet in the corner, taking samples for analysis.

Given everything she had seen about the place thus far, Diaz didn't want to speculate as to what might be found attached to the fibers in the room.

"What can you tell me?" Diaz asked.

Murton appeared beside her, taking up the remainder of the doorway. He raised his arm above his head and pressed his forearm against the frame, leaning heavily against it. "Just what I told you on the phone. Maid came in this morning, found him like this. Nobody saw anyone come or go, nobody even heard a gunshot."

"What kind of weapon was used?" Diaz asked. She wasn't especially concerned for the purposes of the present crime scene, but rather that they might yield some evidence for her investigation into Molina.

"Don't know," Murton said. "Entry wounds look small - nine millimeter maybe - but we won't know for sure until we dig them out and have them analyzed."

A flush of heat rose to Diaz's face, bringing moisture to her armpits and the small of her back. "You haven't yet?"

"Waiting for you," Murton said. If he noticed the inflection in her voice at all he didn't seem to show it, continuing to gaze in through the doorway at the techs hard at work. "Told them not to touch the body until you'd seen it."

Feeling more anger rise within, Diaz pushed it down, swallowing heavily. She nodded to him and stepped forward, taking a pair of paper booties from the box by the door and sliding them over her shoes. None of the others inside so much as glanced her way as she walked forward to the edge of the bed, her knees just inches from the bedspread, and stopped.

The room was standard cheap fare, the kind of place that could be rented in increments ranging from the hour to the month. Twelve feet in width and a few more in depth, a single king size bed dominated the space. It was situated against the back wall, a closet on one side of it, a bathroom on the other. Above the headboard was a terrible oil painting that was made even worse by a heavy coating of crusted blood spatter and fragments of brain and bone.

No other décor of any kind, be it even a telephone or a TV.

Diaz gave the place one last glance before focusing on the bed, the reason she had made the drive.

Lying before her was Paulo Gomez, there was no mistake about that. Twin wounds had torn away most of his chest, gunpowder marks and ripped fabric showing the shots had been made from a close range. Very little blood was present on his white dress shirt, just two small streaks, the momentum of the shots knocking him straight back, where he was left for dead.

The shot to the face was most likely done last, a final blow meant to either ensure death or drop a calling card. The lack of gunpowder or any residual burns showed the shot had been made from further back, the blood spatter on the wall proving it had been done before he made it all the way to the mattress.

Imagining it in her mind, Diaz saw somebody enter and put two in Gomez's chest point blank. As he fell backward, the intruder fired again, letting him drop to the bed.

Given the positioning of the body and the lack of blood smears beyond the single pool that was already crusted and beginning to mildew beneath him, it seemed likely that Gomez had been standing in front of the bed as the man entered. Perhaps there was a short conversation, but most likely not as the killer came in, fired three times, and exited right back out through the front door.

Glancing to either side, she looked at the three techs working diligently, shaking her head just slightly. They would no doubt find a mountain of DNA evidence inside the room, but none of it would do any good for what she needed.

Turning on a heel, Diaz exited back out onto the balcony. Murton and Lefranc both watched as she slid the booties from her feet, wadding them into a ball and keeping them clenched in her hand.

"Was the door locked when the maid got here?" she asked.

"Yes," Murton said. "She knocked, then let herself in using a master key."

Diaz nodded, figuring as much. Whoever had done this would want to give themselves as much lead time as possible before the body was found. For what she couldn't be certain, though the thought of Hawk and Lake somewhere in Montana flitted across her mind.

"Tell them to start on the door," Diaz said, motioning over her shoulder with the top of her head. "Anything else they find is going to be from previous guests."

Murton's mouth parted a half inch as he glanced from Diaz to the direction she was pointing. "You sure?"

"Positive," Diaz said. "This wasn't a crime of passion, damned sure wasn't random. It was an execution."

Twice Murton's mouth worked up and down as if he wanted to say something, though no sound came out. "Execution? You sure?"

"Absolutely," Diaz said, already wanting the conversation to end, needing to be off to her next destination.

"Does that mean you also know who pulled the trigger?" he asked.

Chapter Forty-Seven

The Rocky Mountains stretched out many miles below, the top ridgeline running like a railroad track connecting the various peaks. From the central line extended dozens of tiny tendrils, fingers drifting down on either side in varying lengths and patterns. A heavy dusting of snow coated most of it, giving the entire scene a monochromatic palate of grey and white.

The image did little to penetrate Thiago's psyche as he sat and stared down at it. His eyes narrowed, his chin resting on a fist, he thought on everything that had occurred, all that was about to unfold.

The position he now found himself in was not one he was especially fond of. Seated in the captain's chair Molina himself had used just a couple days before as they traveled to Mexico City, he kept himself swiveled around to face forward, not even wanting to look at the other faces around him.

Of the six men crammed into the cabin of the Raytheon Premier 1A, he was the only one on staff with Molina. Seated in the opposing captain's chair was Felipe Soto, a man Thiago had begrudgingly coexisted with in the preceding years, barely tolerating for the length of time possible to make the drop and go their separate ways into the night.

The reasons he had always disliked the man were present even now, his hair gelled into place, his usual sleeveless flannel swapped out for a skintight long-sleeved compression shirt. On the table between them sat an open bottle of Corona, Felipe's second since leaving Palmdale.

Sitting across the aisle was Dante, a man whose perpetual silence and large eyes that always seemed to be rotating without attachment in their sockets was unnerving. Beside him were three men that Felipe had recruited for the trip, their appearances close enough to insinuate some form of familial connection.

All wearing dirty jeans and dusty boots, they each had some form of shaggy hair and bad goatee, more than a few teeth missing from the lot. The night before at dinner, Thiago had watched as all three drank freely from the sangria, taking down pitcher after pitcher. No one had been foolish enough to say anything, though the state of their inebriation was obvious to anybody paying attention.

Unfortunately, he was the only one doing so, his attempt to share his concerns with Molina that morning brushed off. The old man had practically scoffed at the notion, stating Guzman would not have brought them if they weren't capable and any question to the contrary would only be an extreme offense to all parties.

Thiago had not wanted to bring them to begin with, even less so after seeing how they handled themselves at the dinner. Any discussion of leaving them behind though, of letting him pick his team, was summarily dismissed.

Molina reasoned he had made the call to Ecuador to allow Guzman to be an active participant. Denying some of his party would only offend him.

Feeling his head shake from side to side, Thiago continued to stare out the window.

Preservation of the old ways - and more importantly the money they represented - was the only thing his employer seemed to be concerned with anymore. It had clouded his judgment, causing him to place trust where it was not warranted.

The removal of Paulo Gomez was a necessary risk. The man knew too much and presented a direct link back to the organization.

The girl was a different matter, though. Expending such resources on her was nothing more than the growing paranoia of a man that had been marginalized for years and was fearful of ever being pushed to the side again.

Having replayed the incident in the desert over in his mind a hundred times, Thiago was convinced there was very little real damage the girl could do to them. At most she had gotten some pictures of a late-night meeting, raising suspicion but nothing more. No mules had changed hands, no money was even present.

As much as he hated to admit it, any concern law enforcement had with the entire affair could be pinned on Hector. He was a friend, and a good partner, but if the business was willing to cast aside Gomez so easily, they should be willing to do it to Hector as well.

Thiago knew without a doubt that despite his own personal history with the man, Molina would have no qualms doing the same to him.

Instead though, the old man had acted against prudence. He had taken a gigantic overstep to include Gomez and his goons in hopes of preserving a business venture. He had loaded the storage hatch of the plane with enough weaponry to arm a band of Somali pirates for years and sent them on their way, tramping through the wilderness to find one scared girl.

Anger, frustration, animosity, roiling through him, Thiago pulled his phone from his pocket. Ignoring all previous warnings given by the steward, he powered it on, waiting as the implement came to life before calling up the app.

On cue, the same single red pin he had been chasing for days now appeared on screen. No longer was the blue circle pulsating around it, indicating that it appeared to have stopped moving for certain, remaining stationary for the better part of the afternoon.

From what he could tell, the site was just outside of a town named Glasgow in northeast Montana. Not once had he ever heard of the location, the place looking to be no more than a pinprick on the map. Shifting his focus back out the window, he imagined a dusty Main Street with a half dozen storefronts stretched across it, an image right out of central casting, calling back to the John Wayne and Clint Eastwood movies of old.

Just as fast he dismissed the image, one more thing about the entire situation that was utter bullshit. He cast it aside with an angry twitch of his head, turning off his phone and stowing it away again.

"Everything alright?" Felipe asked, the sound of his voice bringing renewed acrimony to Thiago, his eyes sliding shut.

"Perfect," he replied, forcing his voice to remain even.

"Hey, how much longer?" one of the men on the bench asked, his voice nasal, a bit higher than expected and heavily accented.

For a moment, Thiago considered not responding. Any words that passed his lips would no doubt be laced with disdain, his feelings for the entire affair made plain for everyone present.

With one long exhalation, he pushed the notion aside though, rotating to see the three men in his periphery.

Soon he would be walking through the woods with five heavily armed men, none of them with loyalties aligned to him.

"Couple hours yet."

Chapter Forty-Eight

I still had the Glock 17 Diaz loaned me, along with all but the few rounds I fired at Hector Ortega and the man in the red truck, almost four full magazines. In addition to that I had a Smith & Wesson I carried when trail riding and taking folks into the park, something in the event I came across a mountain lion and her cubs or a surly grizzly. What it lacked in speed and accuracy it made up for in stopping power, having the ability to tear away enormous chunks of flesh if need be.

The guns were lined side by side on the kitchen table in my cabin. Both had been disassembled and oiled, put back together to ensure everything was in perfect working order. The extreme cold of Montana had been known to wreak havoc on weapons before, the dry air causing things to freeze up faster than in other places.

That was a risk I could ill afford in the days ahead.

The barrels of the guns gleamed in the firelight as I polished the Winchester, bracing the butt of it against my thigh and dragging the oil cloth the length of the weapon. Fired no more than a few hundred times in total, what little dirt there was on it came away quick and easy, all three items ready for action the moment the need arose.

Arranged in a row on the table, it was far from being a veritable arsenal. The fact was though, I was just one person, unable to operate more than the two handguns or the Winchester at a single time anyway.

In total, I had well over a hundred rounds of ammunition. There was no way I would ever fire anywhere close to that many. Either they would show up and overwhelm me by sheer force of numbers or I would prevail, but in no way would it be for lack of firepower.

Besides, if things went as planned, the weapons would only be needed for clean up anyway.

The door to the cast iron stove in the corner stood wide open, a heavy blaze visible within. Orange and yellow flames flicked upward in misshapen stripes, throwing uneven light over the interior of the cabin, everything taking on a golden hue. The warmth from it filled the space, managing in just a few hours to push aside any lingering cold, heating the room enough that sweat had formed along my brow. It ran down the bridge of my nose and saturated the short hair of my scalp, my Henley sticking to my back as I worked.

There was no way of knowing when or even if anybody would be coming for me, though I had a deep rooted suspicion someone would be arriving soon. They had too much invested in Lake's fate, had made too many attempts on her already, for them to give up simply because we had relocated.

The disappearance of Gomez was only an acceleration of their timeline. They must have known that the connection had been made between the two sides, the discovery of his body now just a formality.

Ensuring that as little evidence existed against them as possible whenever law enforcement did come calling would be in their best interest. With Gomez gone, Lake was the only living soul that could successfully point a finger in their direction.

Everything else was simply conjecture, and every person involved knew it.

The satellite phone on the chair beside me sprang to life, barely drawing me from my thoughts as I regarded it a moment before picking it up, knowing it could be only one of two people.

"Yeah?"

"Hawk," Pally said. There was not a trace of humor or goodwill in his voice, the reason for his call apparent in a moment.

"What did you find?"

"A small private plane just landed at Glasgow International," he said, keeping his tone even, adding nothing more.

"Origin?" I asked.

"Palmdale," Pally said, "which wasn't easy to find. They had to file something to get in the air, but this back trail gives the impression they had no intention of ever being uncovered."

I nodded, the information giving me the answer to the next question already. If the flight had been legit, there would have been a clear paper trail from origin to destination, everything on the up and up.

The fact that so much had been done to obscure this one only confirmed my suspicions.

"How long ago did they land?" I asked, feeling my pulse pick up, glancing around at the cabin. Outside, the first signs of darkness were beginning to set in, long shadows crawling across the floor, kept at bay only by the fireplace in the corner.

"Ten minutes," Pally said, "probably still on the runway as we speak."

I glanced at the clock above the stove, doing the math in my head. Assuming they departed in the next few minutes and loaded up, I had at most the better part of an hour before arrival.

"Thanks, Pally," I said. I could hear the strain in my voice as I said it, making no effort to mask it from him.

After years together, it wouldn't have mattered anyway.

"You got it," he said. "You give a call if you need anything else."

"Roger that," I replied, rising from my seat. "Until you hear from me though, radio silence."

"Yes, sir," Pally said.

The call ended there, no wishing of good luck, no admonishments to be careful. Together we had been through too many instances like this before to bother with such statements, both of us knowing the stakes.

I slid the phone across the table and did one quick revolution, collecting my bearings, aligning everything in my mind. Once I was sure I had a plan, an order for doing things, I set to work.

The most important item was the tracking device, left inside the bottom of the camera bag. I placed the entire thing up on the bed, tucking it away beneath my pillows.

There was no way I could mask the signal, no chance I would want to even if I could, but I needed to ensure it was out of direct eyesight. It was imperative that whoever showed entered and spent a few minutes inside, rummaging if they had to.

Content that the bag was hidden away, completely camouflaged between the two pillows at the head of my bed, I turned toward the woodstove. I grabbed up the last three sticks of wood I had carried in from the pile, white pine that had aged more than a year in the Montana elements.

Completely dried out, it would burn fast and hot, keeping a good flame going for at least an hour.

Shifting a few feet to the side, I grabbed the nightstand by opposing corners and drug it closer to the stove. I positioned it tight against the wall, appearing completely natural, bisecting the space between the bed and the stove.

From there I went back to the kitchen, taking up one of the two creations I had spent most of the afternoon formulating.

The body of it was two propane bottles duct taped together, each one a long green cylinder, sixteen ounces apiece. Around the top was a simple fuse and detonator, the work of nothing more than some wire and cheap wristwatches, everything purchased at a farm supply store in Billings on my way through.

Weighing just over five pounds in total, the entire assembly looked like a miniature scuba diving set painted an odd combination of green and grey. Keeping it balanced across my palms, I used my toe to pull out the bottom drawer of the nightstand, tucking the improvised explosive inside.

Turning back to the table, I took up a second matching device and opened the door to the kitchen stove, placing it on the top shelf like a casserole about to be baked. Given the open flame roaring in the corner, I couldn't turn on the gas to the oven, but knew that once the first was detonated it would engulf the second, igniting the line as well, all in one coordinated sequence.

For a time I had considered placing devices on the other two walls of the cabin as well, but such excess would simply be overkill. The place wasn't large enough to need four explosives, the amount of goods required to build them sufficient to potentially trigger someone's curiosity back at the farm supply shop.

Instead I settled on two, knowing that the twin occurrences of lighting the wood burner and the stove simultaneously would be more than enough to serve my purposes, flash frying anybody standing inside.

Not knowing how many men might soon come rolling up out of the darkness, I needed to leverage what I did have at my disposal. Losing the cabin wasn't something I was overly fond of, but given the situation, it seemed the most prudent.

I had found the tracking device, and I knew how to operate in the cold wilderness far better than a group based in Southern California. I was certainly a long way from infallible, but had to believe the odds were much closer to even than any objective observer might believe.

Certain that everything was exactly as I wanted it, I pushed on a pair of sunglasses to preserve my night vision as much as possible before moving through the place. I flipped on every light I had and started a disc of *Friday Night Lights*, turning the volume up loud enough to be heard without drawing suspicion.

I needed them to believe we were inside. I wanted them to get cocky, to let their guard down as they approached.

Sweat continued to roll down my scalp, burning my eyes, tasting salty on my lips, as I pulled a double knit sweater on over my head. Atop it I shrugged on my fleece vest and canvas coat, the combined garments raising my body temperature, bathing me in sweat as one at a time I took up each of the handguns and stowed them, stuffing my pockets with ammunition until they bulged.

The last items up were the Winchester and the detonator, grabbing them and backing toward the door. Not a single pang of melancholy or nostalgia passed through me as I looked at the place that had been my home for the previous five years.

People were coming to do me harm, to do harm to someone I cared about. To stop them I would blow the cabin sky high without pause, would do anything else necessary as well.

That singular thought filled my mind, pulsated through my body, as I opened the front door and stepped outside, the cold mountain air wrapping around me. Out of pure reflex it brought a smile to my face as I pulled off the sunglasses and stowed them before taking off into the night.

Chapter Forty-Nine

"You realize what you're asking for here, don't you?" Special Agent Mark Mathias said. A thick man, powerfully built, he leaned forward and spread his arms out wide, a learned posture no doubt meant to intimidate anybody sitting across from him.

The stance had no effect at all on Diaz.

"And you realize I'm not asking, right?" she countered, leaning forward in the chair across from him. Her elbows were braced on her knees, her hands in front of her, fingers flexed.

The decision to return to the Santa Ana DEA office had been made on the fly, a snap reflex as Diaz was driving away from the All-Niter. She hadn't discussed the notion with Lefranc, had not called on one single person back at headquarters. Instead she had simply turned south, fighting the heavy early evening traffic to make her way back.

She had just caught Mathias before he departed for the day, most of the building empty as they sat on the top floor. A stark contrast in every way to her office, it was a palatial corner spread, glass forming both outer walls. Beyond it the sun had blinked out from the evening sky, the lights of town just starting to awaken.

The view was completely lost on everyone, though. Mathias had not looked pleased to see them walk through the outer door to his suite, even less so as Diaz pushed her way into his office, Lefranc on her heels.

Now that look was heightened many times over, red blotches on his cheeks giving the impression he was a powder keg just waiting to erupt.

Given the state she was in, Diaz almost wanted him to, just so she had an excuse to reciprocate in kind.

"You have no proof whatsoever that Arturo Molina was involved in that shooting," Mathias said, maintaining his posture, his eyes squinted up tight, appearing too small for his oversized head. All hair was shaved clean from it, the lights above gleaming off his smooth flesh.

Most likely the effect of years of steroid abuse.

Pulling a long breath in through her nose, Diaz rocked back in her seat. She rolled her eyes, letting him see the movement swing her head back in a wide arc.

"Yesterday we brought in Hector Ortega for trying to kill a witness to a drug deal," Diaz began.

"There was no proof of that being a drug deal," Mathias inserted.

Diaz waved a hand at him, not even bothering to humor the statement with a response.

"When we entered him into the system, we found a history of tracking the file by Detective Paulo Gomez," Diaz said, her voice rising. "The same Paulo Gomez who was known to communicate with Molina. The same Paulo Gomez who, just hours after we went to see him, disappeared."

Mathias leaned back a few inches in his seat, his face twisted up in anger. He breathed loudly through his nose, saying everything he needed to without uttering a word.

"And I shouldn't have to finish this," Diaz said, leaning forward a bit more, "but I will. The same Paulo Gomez who was just found executed while staying in a shit box hotel under the name of a popular television character."

She paused there, letting her words sink in, watching as Mathias tried to push them aside. His round head swiveled as he stared everywhere but directly at her, not wanting to concede an inch.

"And you think we've got no grounds to at least bring the man in?" Diaz asked. She let every bit of animosity, of frustration, she felt show in her voice. A scowl played across her features as she did so, her head cocked just a bit to the side.

Despite the fact that she and Mathias were technically of equal rank, she knew she should at least be somewhat careful. Working out of the southwest headquarters office gave her purview over everything in the region, though this particular area was his primary jurisdiction. At the moment, she hardly cared if she torched a relationship, though maintaining some form of working collegiality would be best.

More than that though, she didn't want to take the time to call in for support. Even by helicopter, it would take a couple of hours to get everybody culled together and en route to where she now sat.

The body of Paulo Gomez was just barely cold. She could only guess where Hawk and Lake were and how they were faring. Time was critical, far more so than potentially stepping on a few toes.

"That's just it," Mathias countered. "We've brought him in before. Nothing ever sticks. He'll only disappear for a while, become that much more careful, that much harder to track once he resurfaces."

"So that's it?" Diaz asked. "We just let him skate on this, push everything we have to the side on the chance he might make us look like idiots?"

Leaning back in his chair, Mathias laced his fingers before him. He glanced to the side, shifting his shoulders, his mouth pressed tight into a small dash.

"Look," Diaz said, "we're doing this anyway."

She paused as another flash of anger passed over his features.

"Tonight. You can either get your team together and we make this a joint effort, or I can call in my own crew. Then tomorrow, as the press is hailing the arrest of a major trafficker, they can also be left to wonder why the local office was nowhere to be seen on a bust taking place in their backyard."

Even as she said it, Diaz knew the threat was off-sides, though she didn't much care. The combined effects of everything that had occurred in the preceding days, of the lack of the sleep, of knowing she had put others in danger, pushed any concern for Mark Mathias's ego far from her head.

The threat struck home, the man leaning forward and again assuming his inflated stance. He glared across at Diaz, letting her know he did not appreciate anything that was taking place, before finally shaking his head in acquiescence.

"How many men do you need?"

Chapter Fifty

I heard them long before I saw them.

Just one of the many advantages afforded to me by being on my home turf, the air was so clear, so cold, that sounds carried for miles. There was no ambient city noise, no traffic in the distance, never even a plane flying overhead to muffle anything. Simple things, like tree limbs snapping or guns being fired, could be heard from much further away than was expected.

In this instance it was a car door, two of them in fact, slammed shut one after another.

Hidden one hundred yards away from the cabin, I heard them as clearly as if I was standing beside the car itself. Judging by the din and pitch of it they were a quarter mile out, stopped near the base of my driveway and choosing to walk in on foot.

After leaving the front door of the cabin, I had crossed the small stream running next to it. From there I avoided all remaining snowfall, picking my way through the barren trunks of lodge pole pine trees, using the thick mat of dead pine needles underfoot to mask any sounds and to blur any sign of my passing.

Keeping my breathing even and my ears attuned to the slightest sounds, I ascended up through the forest. Rising at a sharp angle, I made my way just south of the ridgeline overlooking my place. There I found the rocky outcropping I had identified in case something like this happened five years before, the habits of a recently deactivated agent.

A flat shelf of granite, it provided an unobstructed firing lane to the cabin below.

By the time I reached the rocks, the light from overhead was completely faded, the sky just beginning to shift into darkness. With it came a drop in temperature, pulling it down beneath thirty degrees, the omnipresent wind whistling through the pine trees. It shoved dead and barren tree limbs from side to side and shook more needles onto the ground as it went, tugging at the open flaps of my coat, running along my freshly shorn scalp.

Moving fast, I leaned the barrel of the Winchester against the base of a tree and shook my coat off, laying it flat on the rock. I took the gun back up by the barrel and carefully placed it along the edge of the coat before setting the detonator on the rock and easing my body down beside them.

The cool feel of the rock shelf passed through the canvas material, pressing against my entire torso, dropping my body temperature another few degrees. Ignoring it entirely, I drew myself up into a prone shooting position and pulled the rifle in tight to my shoulder, checking over the perimeter of my place three times before covering the end of the scope and laying it down beside me.

Just like with Lake in the desert, I didn't want anybody checking the ridge to see a flash of light against the glass of the scope, giving away my position. Instead I remained completely motionless, watching the world around me grow darker, details of everything disappearing. Overhead, a thick cloud cover blotted out any moon or stars, the only illumination visible coming from the windows of the cabin.

Heat seeped from me as I waited, clearing my mind. No longer did I feel tension or even apprehension about what was to come, all moments of contemplation now long since passed. In their place I felt a steely resolve, the familiar feelings that had been dormant for years coming back. They evened out my breathing, leveled off my heart rate, as I waited.

The sounds of the doors slamming arrived just over twenty minutes after I was in place. A moment later came the familiar din of voices in chatter, at least three or four, before a final voice cut in. I couldn't make out the words that were used, but the tone and delivery of them informed me immediately he was the man in charge, telling the others to quiet down.

The moment he spoke they did as instructed, all sounds falling away.

It took the crew five full minutes to cover the quarter mile down the dirt driveway. As a group they moved in near silence, the occasional broken tree branch or round being jacked into place the only sounds. Keeping my attention focused on the cabin, I fought the urge to peer through the scope, narrowing my gaze, waiting for any sign of them.

My first glimpse of movement came much further away than I expected, a quick burst over fifty yards from the side of the cabin. A moment later a matching figure disturbed the darkness, nothing more than a shape sprinting between trees.

My right index finger ran itself along the edge of the rifle's barrel as I drew the weapon in a little tighter against my body, cocking my head a few inches to the side to see past the scope. I watched as a third, and then a fourth figure emerged, encircling both of the sides of the cabin that I could see.

From what I could tell, the group had fanned out around the place, using the natural backstop of the stream and the cliff rising behind it as the fourth leg of their square. They stayed far out away from the building, all spread wide, nobody making any forward progress on the house.

A feeling of dread welled within the pit of my stomach as I watched them move. The goal was to draw them inside, to get them pinned in, before activating the detonator.

From what I could tell, they had no intention of entering.

What they were doing seemed to be getting into a firing position.

My mouth ran dry as I made the calculations in my head. I could see four men from where I was, had to assume there were at least two more covering the back end of the house. No good view of the weapons they carried could be seen, though assuming they were automatics of some sort with large magazines, there could be anywhere from seventy to several hundred rounds of live ammunition about to be pushed through the walls of the cabin.

The place was well built and maintained, the structure made to withstand a Montana winter. Still, even the harshest wind was nothing compared to a gas projected bullet, the wooden walls and insulation maybe stopping a few, but definitely not all.

The structure itself I wasn't worried about, prepared to blow it away myself at any moment. My larger concern was that their rounds might pierce one of the improvised devices, setting the place ablaze while doing only minimal damage.

From the center of the ring, a white light appeared. Fluorescent and unnatural, it was too small, too pale to be a flashlight of any kind. It floated a few feet above the ground for a moment, too much for me to ignore.

Slipping the lens cover off the end of the scope, I focused in on the sight.

It was a man, his profile too dark to make out any clear detail. In his hand was a cellphone, his action obvious at a glance.

He was checking the tracking device.

The man stared down at the phone a moment before pocketing it and raising his weapon to his shoulder. There it remained less than a second before the first report of a gunshot echoed out, carrying through the night air.

On cue, a handful of other weapons barked, bright orange muzzle flashes illuminating the men holding them. Each one carried an assault rifle as they stepped forward, the sound of glass breaking and wood splintering mixed in with the metallic buzz of the weapons.

Moving slowly, they continued stepping inward, hundreds of bullets smashing into the place.

In that moment, I had a decision to make. It was only a matter of time before one of the rounds struck something vital, sending the place up in a fiery pyre. From where they were now standing it would be impossible to know how much damage would be incurred, though assuming the deaths of every man would be foolish at best.

For a brief time earlier, I had held the upper hand. I had created a trap that was meant to lure them in, get them to do as I wanted.

It was time to take that back.

Lowering my eye down to the scope, I took aim on the closest man to me, his entire silhouette visible against the backdrop of the house. Aiming for center mass, I squeezed the trigger, the massive crack of the weapon rolling down over the hill.

Less than a second later the man's arms rose by his sides, his weapon flipping into the air. He crumpled to his knees as I instantly shifted my aim a few inches, the man beside him glancing over, seeming confused.

Without pause I squeezed a second time, the velocity of the round striking him in the upper body, lifting him from his feet and dropping him onto his shoulder.

A harsh ringing settled into my right ear as the group stopped moving forward, the gunfire slowing. Shifting my attention, I could see the other two men turn in my direction, their muzzles pointed toward the ridge above.

They now knew where I was.

Shucking the spent shells from the gun, I shoved two more in and locked the bolt into place. Going straight up the line, I remained motionless as the closest target fanned his aim over the cliff, spraying bullets sporadically. Not one of them came within fifty yards of me as he took a step forward, trying to determine what had cut his cohorts down.

I allowed him to take one more step, his entire body exposed from behind a tree, before pulling the trigger.

The shot skimmed just past him, smashing into the tree he had emerged from, his entire body dropping into a crouch. He duck-walked a few paces away while keeping his attention in my direction, all shooting aimed at the house ceasing, another pair of shadows coming into view.

They knew nobody was inside. I had the high ground, but they had the advantages of numbers and supplies. They could wait me out, knowing the cold would eventually cause me to do something stupid. Each time I fired I gave them a direct bead on my location, the flash of my muzzle acting like a flare for them to follow.

As much as I didn't want to give up my vantage, the odds were still too heavily weighted in their favor to try and pick them off one at a time.

Once more I ejected the spent shell casings, the smell of gun powder and burnt metal drifting up to my nostrils. I drew it in in long breaths, feeling the acrid scent enter my lungs, muscle memory kicking in as I returned the weapon to my shoulder and peered through the scope.

Four shapes were visible, spread in a zigzag pattern through the trees along the side of the cabin. The one with the phone seemed to have an arm extended wide, barking instructions at the others, who started to drift out in a looping arc.

The further they got from the cabin, the less effective my explosion would be.

If ever I was going to send the place up, it had to be now.

Shifting my rifle's aim out wide to the right, I fired once, a round not meant to hit anybody but to herd them back. I waited a moment, watching as the men started to inch further away before again squeezing off the final round in the rifle.

On impact, the men reacted exactly the way I wanted them to, jumping back several feet, no more than ten yards from the side of the cabin.

Dropping the gun down onto my coat, I reached past it to the detonator lying on the cold rock face. I snatched it up and pulled it over in front of my chest, rising up onto my knees and elbows, preparing to make a move.

A pair of muzzle flashes erupted from my opponents, rounds crashing into the rocks far below me as I hit the detonator, sending the entire cabin upward in a twisted cyclone.

Chapter Fifty-One

There were two ways Mia Diaz could play things.

The first was that she could put her front headlights to flashing and go screaming through the night, letting the sirens announce her arrival ahead of time. She could hit the driveway going fifty miles an hour and slam on the brakes, leaving a trail of fresh skid marks and the scent of burnt rubber in her wake.

She would be the first one out, Lefranc on her heels. Mathias and his team, more than a dozen agents strong, would pull in right behind her. They would park in a haphazard arrangement across the front lawn, blocking any path to escape, presenting a show of force.

As theatrical as the entrance might be, it would also present the wrong impression to every person inside. Arturo Molina was no doubt a man with security on hand, the kind that would have experience with weapons, would not be afraid to engage in a firefight.

From her position out front she would be exposed, forced to run for cover, the entire affair escalating into a melee. It would pull in curious onlookers, people more drawn by their desire to see what was playing out in the neighborhood than to maintain any form of self-preservation.

People would get hurt. Fellow agents, innocent civilians, maybe even herself.

As delicious as the thought of taking out Molina, of not letting him anywhere near the convoluted court system, was, she couldn't allow that to happen. She was forced to go with option two, which involved pulling up along the front curb. She, along with Lefranc and Mathias, would walk calmly to the front door, and they would put Arturo Molina under arrest for suspicion of murder. They would also grab every other person onsite, holding them at least through the night as they scoured the grounds and questioned every last one of them.

No doubt, within an hour of being brought in Molina would lawyer up, but that would do little to insulate him. He had not pulled the trigger, had not even been anywhere near Pasadena, but there was enough of a causal link to connect him on conspiracy to commit.

The fact that it was a police officer - no matter how dirty - would only escalate the charges.

Every fifty feet a street lamp threw down a cone of yellow light, illuminating the neighborhood as Diaz wound her way through it. Behind her in the rearview mirror a half dozen cars followed in order, each one with a pair of agents, all instructed to make themselves visible without being threatening.

The goal was to appeal to Molina's ego, making him believe that he was untouchable, that he had nothing to fear from the people knocking at his door in the middle of the night.

"You good?" Diaz asked, glancing over to Lefranc in the passenger seat. Of everyone in the division she could choose to be riding shotgun, he was nowhere near the top of the list, having been thrust into it more by default than anything else.

Had Diaz ever dreamed when first assigning him duty over Lake Pawlak that it would come to this, she never would have dared give him the task.

"Good," Lefranc said, checking the slide on his weapon for the fifth time of the drive over. It was the first word he had said since leaving the Santa Ana station, his left leg moving up and down in a constant pattern.

For a moment Diaz considered telling him to breathe, that they were just going to pick Molina up, but she let it pass. Every agent she had ever worked with had dealt with things in their own manner. She had to let Lefranc do the same.

Easing her foot back off the gas, Diaz pulled up to the address of Arturo Molina. She sidled up to the curb and parked directly in front of the walkway leading to the front door.

Turning off the engine, she left the keys in the ignition and climbed out, keeping the car between herself and the home as the other vehicles came into position around her. She waited as Mathias climbed out, meeting her by the rear bumper, both of them turning to assess the situation before them.

The house was two stories tall, constructed in white stucco with a red roof of Spanish tile. The front façade was cut into sections, giving the house depth, a spotlight providing contrast between pale and shadow.

"So this is the home of a major drug dealer?" Mathias said, peering up at it. "I expected something a little bigger."

A handful of cracks passed through Diaz's mind, but she let each pass, knowing they would only build ill will, adding to the tension of the moment.

Behind them each of the remaining cars got into position, forming a wide arc, encompassing the entire front of the property. Eight men and two women climbed out, joining the three of them in the space formed between the vehicular motorcade.

For a moment, all thirteen stood in silence, each one staring up at the house. A shadow passed behind a second floor curtain and a door closing could be heard from somewhere inside, but otherwise there was no movement of any kind.

The neighborhood remained quiet and subdued as they prepared to move, the late evening hour pushing everyone inside, the remainder put off by the overwhelming show of force gathered in the street.

"Okay," Diaz said, turning to face the others, standing shoulder-to-shoulder with Mathias. "Everybody ready?"

A handful of terse nods were the only response, people casting each other sideways glances as they positioned themselves along the street, ensuring they were seen. Diaz waited until they were all aligned before turning to Mathias and nodding, neither saying anything as they moved for the front walk, Lefranc in line behind them.

The grass underfoot felt soft and uneven as they cut a diagonal across the lawn, the turf fresh and not yet taken hold, the smell of it strong. Diaz could feel cool dampness rising from it, hitting her bare ankles, could see the moon shining down from above. The sensations brought with them a sense of calm, her senses leveling out as she walked to the front door.

Every part of her wanted to reach for her hip, to run her fingers over the butt of her weapon, to reassure herself and whoever was watching from inside that she was prepared.

Beside her she could sense Mathias doing that very thing, unable to beat back the urge, his breath coming out in ragged puffs as they walked forward.

In an even triangle the three approached, nobody saying a word, ten agents on their heels prepared to open fire. Every person present had been briefed twice on the man they were coming to bring in, told in excruciating detail what they could expect.

The man was believed to have killed at least one cop on the day, would not hesitate to take down more. He was known to be the head of a conglomerate controlling no small part of the cocaine business in Los Angeles and had security on the payroll, all with proficiency in handling weaponry.

The sound of the front door opening stopped Diaz and Mathias halfway across the front lawn, Lefranc almost bumping into them from behind. They stood poised in place, their hands just inches from their weapons as the entry swung open, a trapezoid of light shifting out onto the front lawn. A moment later a shadow appeared within it, nothing but a rounded head atop a pair of shoulders, starting in the distance and moving steadily closer.

Of everything Diaz expected to encounter upon pulling up, it was the last thing she actually expected to see.

Arturo Molina, alone, standing before them.

Chapter Fifty-Two

T he force of the blast reduced the cabin to splinters instantly, sending most of the rubble skyward in a fiery twist. A moment later, a deafening echo rolled out over the grounds, pushed out with so much force I even felt the warmth and wind on my face high on the ridge.

Just as fast, most of the initial flame dissipated, thick smoke billowing upward, disappearing against the darkened night sky. The smell of it hung thick in the air, mixed with the scorched remains of pine and the slight scent of charred pork.

An aroma that could have only originated from human flesh.

Using the scope on the rifle, I scanned the grounds once more, everything much brighter through the fiber optics, the entire scene glowing in the firelight. Swinging the front end of the gun in a quick arc I could spot what looked to be the remains of two men, their shapes twisted and misshapen, unmoving on the forest floor.

That left two more unaccounted for.

The blast was much larger than I anticipated, discounting how much gas was left in the tank attached to the stove. The two small bombs I made would have barely been enough to bring down the structure, the plan relying more on the wood burner to create a flash fire than anything.

The scent drifting over the air, growing stronger, told me that had been true to no small degree. Even more jarring was the sheer destructive force that the gas had caused, obliterating much of the structure, bits of it still landing as they sifted through the trees, the sound of them crashing to earth just audible.

Staring down at the macabre scene, I could remain where I was, put a round in each of the bodies I spotted, and wait for the last two to show. It bore to reason that finding me was no longer their primary worry, the blast at the very least wounding them, if not worse.

From here on out, their chief concern had to be self-preservation. Four of their comrades were killed. They were most likely hurt. They were in a wilderness they were not prepared for, and they were at least a quarter mile from any means of evacuation.

Finding me perched high on the cliff wall was not an active fear.

It also told me that never would I have a better chance to end this.

I opted against putting a shot in each of the bodies I could see, figuring I could do that on the spot if need be. Instead I scanned once more, and seeing no movement, lowered the rifle back to the ground.

Using my knees and elbows, I reverse crawled away from my position, waiting until I was tucked away on the trail, obscured by thick forestation, before rising to my feet. Keeping my knees flexed, I drew both handguns, keeping the Glock with the larger clip and better accuracy in my dominant hand. I reserved the Smith & Wesson for my left, a last resort when tearing an enormous hole from up close was the primary concern, hoping it didn't come to that.

The thick carpet of dead pine needles masked my footsteps as I ran as fast as my crouch would allow, the downward grade propelling me forward. What had taken the better part of five minutes to cover earlier passed by in less than half that, the smell of smoke growing stronger as I moved. It settled in my nostrils and burned my eyes, tears and snot rimming both as I pressed forward.

Each step brought me closer to the fire, sweat enveloping my body. It formed along my brow and upper lip, saturated the back of my shirt. My nerves tingled as I became hyper aware of every sound, my head jerking toward each noise, weapons held at a forty-five degree angle from my body.

At the bottom of the cliff I paused, watching, waiting, for any sign of movement.

Less than twenty yards from me, the remains of my cabin burned fast and hot. Most of the roof had been ripped away, the remainder a blackened mess twisted into an angry heap. It stood jutting toward the sky on the far end like the half-opened lid of a soup can, just barely visible against the horizon.

Beneath it most of the wooden exterior was gone, the walls rising no more than waist high. They formed a jagged line around the perimeter of the place, my sofa, dining room table, and bed providing fodder for the fire within.

Just outside the scorched grass surrounding the cabin, I could see all four bodies clearly outlined, their unmoving forms illuminated by the flames.

The other two were still nowhere to be seen.

Skills obtained a lifetime before surged to the forefront as I stood and assessed the scene. A renewed calm flooded through my system, heightening my senses.

Twisting back in the opposite direction, I stayed at the foot of the cliff and followed the stream for over forty yards, moving fast. My breathing remained even as I jogged forward, rising up onto the balls of my feet, making no sound as I found a narrow point in the waterway, well beyond the edge of the firelight.

Splashing wasn't as much a concern as making myself a silhouette. For a moment they had taken control of the situation, but now I had it back in a big way. So long as I didn't get hasty, used my resources to my advantage, there was no way they could seize it again.

Without the step stones I had used to cross before, I had no choice but to put my foot directly in the water. Stepping out over the thin layer of ice lining the bank, I placed my boot straight down, waiting until I knew I had a firm foothold before pressing my weight on it.

Icy water swirled to mid-calf, causing the air to seize in my lungs, my foot immediately starting to burn. Within seconds it would be numb, my only choice to get across as fast as possible.

The second step was even worse than the first, the water rising to me knee. Every nerve ending in my body clenched in unison as I clamped my jaw shut, willing my teeth not to chatter as I took another step forward.

Four steps were all it took to get across the stream, the effort pulling all feeling from my entire lower body. Adrenaline coursed through me, urging my nervous system to look past the numbness, but it didn't eliminate the fact that I had to move quickly.

My window of advantage was narrow, growing more so by the moment.

My feet and ankles seemed to lock themselves in right angles as I set off in a loop to my right, keeping the cabin in my periphery. My steps were not nearly as quiet or precise as I would have liked, ice crystals already forming on the outside of my jeans and the tops of my hiking boots. I could feel the articles clenching as I moved, only begrudgingly allowing me the freedom to push on.

Stiffness settled into my knees, causing me to give up on the crouch as I moved forward. Instead, I bent myself forward at the waist and came up on the scene at an angle, careful not to look straight toward the fire, preserving my night vision as much as possible.

The sound of wood crackling echoed through my ears as I approached the first body, smoke so thick it burned my nose. Darting from tree to tree, I slid up alongside the man with guns raised, watching my surroundings for any sign before nudging the man onto his shoulder.

His clothing was warm to the touch as he rolled over, his head flopping to the side. In less than a second I processed what I saw, the face one I had never encountered before. A baseball-sized wound had torn away most of his chest, pine needles clinging to the blood already beginning to congeal.

Leaving him in place, I took three quick steps to the man beside him, his body twisted onto its back. Most of the hair was stripped away from his head, and a great deal of debris - charred wood bits and singed chunks of pine - had fallen onto his body.

Despite all that, it was clear at a glance that this man was Felipe

Soto, one of the people Lake had photographed less than a week before.

Resisting the urge to empty the Smith & Wesson into his body, I moved away toward the other two.

The force of the blast had driven them both backwards, chunks of shrapnel lodged in their bodies. The pieces stuck out at odd angles along the length of them, buried in their flesh.

Side by side, the men looked as if they could have been related, though it was impossible to be sure, the heat of the blast having seared a good deal of the flesh on their faces. Both were about the same size, with seemingly brown skin and dark hair, their eyes staring open at the sky above.

Remaining on a knee between them, I crouched down as low as I could, peering through the trees. No more bodies could be seen from where I was, no signs of movement showing that someone was trying to get away.

Pressing my toes against the soles of my boots, I tried to keep them in working order. Regaining feeling was out of the question, but I just needed them to be functional for the next few minutes.

I had two more to find.

Chapter Fifty-Three

I t felt like my body was split into two distinct halves. The top half was completely wet with sweat, my shirt soaked through, droplets visible on the backs of my palms. Long rivulets started up high in my hair and ran down my head, crossing over my face, dripping from my nose and jaw.

A combination of nerves, adrenaline, and the fire burning nearby, I could taste it on my lips as I inched forward.

The bottom half was a different story, feeling like I was still standing in the stream. My quads burned as they fought through the chill, everything from my knees down numb. Every step felt foreign to me, my feet registering nothing as I moved through the woods.

Keeping the cabin on my left, I walked with both guns extended from my shoulder, pointed outward ninety degrees from one another. With my head on a swivel I checked for any sign of movement, the flickering flames sending shadows dancing, my gaze sweeping back and forth.

Holding my pose, I moved forward along the side of the cabin, the back end slowly rounding into view. Resisting the urge to move straight for it, I crouched to a knee and checked the areas out to the side first, making sure nobody was waiting to ambush me before going on.

It was there, kneeling on the forest floor, that I happened to spot what I was looking for.

Blood.

Just a thin trickle, it stretched in an uneven line over the ground, already turning dark and starting to harden. Within ten minutes it would be firm, the pine needles it was splashed atop crusted solid.

Raising my knee from the earth, I moved a few feet to the side of the trail, pushing myself into the shadows, and began again. I used the trunks of trees for cover as I went, the trail the easiest tracking I had ever done.

Whoever had lost the blood was not in the least bit worried about being followed. There was no attempt at obscuring their steps, the pattern clear. Where there weren't fresh droplets there were heavy trenches cut through the dirt and needles, the result of feet dragging in uneven steps.

This person was hurt, and they were running.

Clearing the corner of the cabin, the trail bore to the left, circling around to the back end. It headed past the driveway, bypassing the way they had come in.

The combination of the blood, the haphazard pattern, the complete lack of care, told me this person had been injured in the blast. Most likely they had been burned badly, heading for the only place out here where relief existed.

The stream.

Raising myself upright a few more inches, I increased my pace just slightly, not as concerned for watching my surroundings as a dark silhouette came into view. Firelight danced off the water behind him, making his outline stark and obvious against it, sitting like a misshapen boulder on the bank.

In another life I would have announced my presence. I would have told them I was a federal agent with the DEA, demanded they discard their weapons and raise their hands above their head.

This was not that life. I had no interest in reading this man his rights, no authority or way of arresting him even if I did.

The smell of his baked skin made its way to my nose as I came closer. It mixed with the scent of the smoke in the air, turning my stomach. As I went forward I could see steam rising from him, his body hunkered down.

I kept going until I was less than twenty yards away before turning my body perpendicular to the stream, my right arm extended. Without pause I squeezed the trigger three times, all three rounds slamming silently into the man, his body jerking with impact. After the third shot he teetered for a moment before falling to the side, his body moving with the stiff awkward movements of a man that was already dead.

The realization hit me too late.

In an instant I knew I was in trouble, the body having been used to lure me into the open. On instinct I began to swing back in the opposite direction, facing out into the forest, but was stopped by a voice behind me.

"Nice shooting," it said, a male's tenor. It was even and pained, not containing a single bit of mirth. "Drop the weapons. Now."

In any other position, there was no way I would have done as instructed. If I was even a few degrees further in my turn I would have had the man in my periphery, would have been able to at least attempt to wheel and fire. The odds of hitting him would be low, but it would distract him enough to maybe get myself moving, give me a puncher's chance in a firefight.

By turning to get a better angle on the body by the river though, I had taken myself out of position. I had showed him my back, enabled him to get the ultimate jump on me.

Every fiber in my being told me not to release the weapons in my hands, but I had no other options.

The weapons thumped audibly against the ground as they landed on either side of me. I kept my hands at shoulder level and slowly turned, making no attempt to mask the malevolence I felt.

The look was matched many times over by the man standing across from me. The right half of his body was Latino, the same man I had seen outside of LAX, the very same one driving the black truck in San Bernardino.

In an instant I even recognized him from the images Lake had taken, not from his face but from the Heckler & Koch 416 in his hand.

Beyond that, there was very little to even recognize him as a man, the left side of his body a matted mess of bloody clothing and burnt skin. Bits of shrapnel extended from his thigh and his outer arm, holes torn into his jeans and thermal. The entire sleeve of his shirt had been burned away with the blast, along with the hair on the left side of his head. In their place was an unending streak of pink, the tissue stripped bare, gleaming in the firelight.

Every bit of him was dripping with water, having thrown himself into the stream to try and ease his burns.

"Where's the girl?" he asked, his mouth misshapen, wounds tugging at the corner of his lips.

I watched as he attempted to take a step forward, his body stiff and rigid, like mine had been after exiting the water, only much, much worse. Combined with the effects of the burns, it appeared he might keel over at any moment, anger and adrenaline the only things holding him up.

"She's not here," I said, lowering my hands a few inches. "In fact, she's a long, long way from here."

I wanted to smile at the man, to let him know that he had been bested, but I didn't. I needed to keep him at bay a few minutes longer, already recognizing what was going on.

"Where is she?" he asked, taking another step forward, closing the gap between us to just over ten yards. If he was surprised I had duped him, or even registered that I had used his own device against him, he didn't let on.

In his state, he had one concern only.

"Why should I tell you?" I asked. "The second I do, you're just going to shoot me."

"I'm going to shoot you either way," he said. "You tell me, and I'll aim for your head instead of your knees."

The first sign of what I was looking for appeared on the barrel of the gun. It was faint, almost indiscernible, but it was unmistakable. I stared at it a long time, making sure I knew exactly what I was looking at, before letting a small smile form over my face.

"Her name is Lake," I said. "She's a nice girl. You should have left her alone."

I let my hands fall down by my sides, watching as anger surfaced. It registered on the side of his face unmarred with burns, his body quivering. "I don't give a damn what her name is, just tell me where to find her."

I let the smile grow a little larger. "You should have dropped the gun when you went into the water."

Bending at the waist, I grabbed each of my weapons up from the ground. I kept my gaze raised to him as he pointed the HK and shook it in my direction, pulling on the trigger, the weapon doing absolutely nothing in his hands.

Despite the sweat bathing my body, the ambient temperature was below thirty degrees. Once he dipped the cold steel into water, it took no more than a couple minutes for the thing to begin freezing. Not solid, but enough to disrupt the firing mechanism.

I had known it the moment the droplets on the underside of the stock froze stiff, forming a row of clear beads along the grip. Once I saw the fire reflected off of them, I knew the weapon in his hand was nothing more than a club.

That's what he got for using a German gun.

I gave the man one extra moment. Not for him, not in some misguided attempt to let him plead for his life or swear allegiance or offer penitence.

I did it for me. I did it so I could envision Lake sitting in that hotel room, no longer having to fear this monster showing up at her home or trying to track her down on the freeway.

So I could picture Alice, sitting on that front step beside me, trying to understand why sometimes I had to do what I did.

The thought remained in my head as I raised the Glock and fired every last bullet that remained.

Part Five

Chapter Fifty-Four

It took three phone calls for the Billings field office to believe a word I was saying. Even after I explained to them that I was a consultant charged with protecting a witness, even after they checked in the system, saw my prior service, saw that I was assigned to active temporary duty, they didn't seem to buy anything I told them.

Instead they burned up the better part of an hour attempting to reach Diaz in California, who was tied up with her own affairs. After that they tried to reach the Boise office, hoping that someone there could corroborate my story, but as to be expected couldn't reach anybody in the dead of night.

It wasn't until they put in a call to Washington D.C., rousting an old colleague of mine from his sleep, that they were told I was legit and to assist in any way I asked.

Given the looks on their faces and the sideways glances they gave after they did arrive, I could only imagine the call had been a little more colorful than that, though I let it go.

Having your home destroyed and being left sitting in your truck, blasting the heat on your toes, trying to fend off frostbite, has a way of removing any inclination to gloat.

Once they did arrive, they went straight to work. They brought a small army to process the scene, three different men asking me the same exact set of questions three different times. When they were content that everything checked out just the way I described it, they cut me loose.

Dawn was less than a few hours off as I climbed into my truck and drove away, the remains of my cabin now just a smoldering pile. Of everything I had there, only the three guns and the satellite phone survived, otherwise my entire worldly possessions reduced to the duffel Diaz had retrieved in California and whatever odds and ends I had lying around the office in West Yellowstone.

The thought of driving straight back to Idaho Falls crossed my mind, was even the prevailing focus as far as Bozeman, before basic physiology won out and I pulled off to check into a hotel. Whatever adrenaline had fueled me through the night had long since bled away, my entire system easing itself into auto-pilot, my vision starting to blur, my reflexes behind the wheel becoming a half second slow.

Staying close to the freeway, I checked into the cheapest chain I could find, a Motel 6 with a sign announcing vacancy at $39.95 a night. I wasn't sure what that meant for somebody coming in at eight in the morning, but I hardly cared as I plunked my credit card down and stumbled to my room, not to be disturbed until Diaz called the satellite phone five hours later.

After a brief conversation I brewed a pot of hotel room coffee and drank it all, followed by a hot shower over a half hour in length. Upon climbing out I had another pot of coffee, more for the warmth than the caffeine.

I made it to Idaho Falls just after seven o'clock, arriving with a couple of pizzas in hand. The two agents from Boise both looked relieved to see me, watching as Lake leapt onto me the moment I passed through the door, sending the boxes flying. After prying her loose and retrieving the pies from the floor I offered for them to stay, but both begged off joining us for dinner before almost sprinting from the room.

What had transpired in the preceding day and a half I wasn't sure, reasonably certain I didn't want to know.

That night we both slept soundly until dawn, the first uninterrupted rest I had gotten since Diaz called me a week before. The two pots of coffee were no match for the pillowtop mattress as I bypassed REM sleep and fell straight to darkness, my body in the same exact position nine hours later when I awoke.

The drive back to Los Angeles from there was uneventful, my backside beginning to ache from the time spent behind the wheel, the drive starting to feel a bit monotonous. The idea of the impending return trip somewhere in the near future didn't enthuse me much, though I pushed the notion aside as I continued watching the mirrors for any sign of lurkers, never once finding anything suspicious.

Diaz was waiting for us in Los Angeles as we made our way south, directing us to bypass the headquarters for the Santa Ana office. She also whispered something under her breath about politics and bureaucracy that I didn't quite catch, not bothering to push it.

I accepted the directive without comment and followed the instructions laid out for us, pulling into the facility exactly one day after arriving at the hotel in Idaho Falls. I parked in the underground lot and took an elevator to the top floor, expecting the office to be near deserted at the odd hour.

To both our surprises the place was alive with activity, a full staff plus a few extra people running to and fro as we exited the elevator. We stopped on the thin carpet just inside and stood watching the chaos, barely noticing Diaz as she emerged from an office and strode our direction.

"Thanks for getting here so fast," she opened. She stopped just short, looking like she might try to hug one or both of us, before pulling back.

"What's all this?" I asked, jutting my chin out toward the room.

Rotating at the waist, a faint smile crossed her face. "You've got a lot to be filled in on."

I glanced in her direction, matching the smile. "Likewise."

The smile fell away as she motioned with the top of her head toward the office. "I hope you're up for sharing. We've got some folks in here just dying to hear every last word we all have to tell."

I knew instantly what Diaz was referring to, having been through the process too many times to ever forget it.

329

Unfortunately, my young charge was not quite yet as versed.

"Why?" Lake asked. "Who's waiting in there?"

"Prosecutors," I said. "Apparently, they think we now have enough to bring charges."

She gave a slow nod as if she understood, though she had no idea.

We were all about to embark on the longest night any of us had had in the past week.

"There better be food in there," I said, following Diaz as she led the way.

"On the way," she replied. She paused beside the door, standing off to the side so I could see the team of lawyers inside. All in their mid-forties, they wore full suits and dour expressions, the late hour doing nothing to penetrate their harsh façade.

"With coffee," she added. "Lots and lots of coffee."

Chapter Fifty-Five

Thirty-six hours after arriving on American soil, Daniel Guzman extended his legs before him, reclining in the same captain's chair he had ridden up in. The twin engines of the Gulfstream purred evenly as it pushed the plane down the runway, lifting the small craft from the ground, the city of Los Angeles growing further away with each passing second.

After being folded up on the uncomfortable wrought iron furnishings at Molina's for the better part of two days, the overstuffed chair was a welcomed change as it enveloped his body. His back let out a low series of pops as his spine relaxed, his body already yearning for the morning's swim, the tension of the evening easing away. It brought with it the realization that he was both hungry and tired after all that had transpired, two things he would fast remedy the moment the stewardess was told she could move about the cabin.

"What a terrible plan," Rafa muttered across from him, his bulk wedged down into the opposite end of the wraparound bench that he had used two days prior. One thick arm was folded over his face, Guzman seeing only his nostrils peeking out from beneath the crook in his elbow. "The audacity."

Behind him the first light of morning crested in the east,

appearing through the open windows of the craft. For the time being it was nothing more than a straw-colored glow, but within half an hour the sun would be well above the horizon, bright light illuminating everything.

"I agree," Guzman replied, letting his eyes slide shut, his head reclined on the seat back. "Audacious is the perfect word for it, but it was not our place to argue with him."

"Yeah, well..." Rafa mumbled, his voice already growing thick with sleep, tailing off before finishing the thought.

Guzman nodded, feeling the exact same way, content that he would never be subjected to the shortsighted dealings of Arturo Molina again.

The plan, as thin as it was, had been concocted in haste the night before. As best Molina could tell, the encroaching effort of the DEA was nothing more than a stab in the dark. With the removal of Paulo Gomez, and the contingent that was sent north to dispatch the girl, there were no witnesses that could vouch for a single thing against the organization.

The property holdings under pseudonyms, the half-trails of phone records, even the enormous financial holdings that could not be entirely explained by the assortment of legitimate business holdings, would not be enough to make an arrest stick.

He reasoned that nobody had ever seized an ounce of product or discovered a single dollar exchanged. No mules would ever dare say a word and Hector Ortega knew to just bide his time before being released.

Taken together, Molina was convinced he could use the entire incident to humiliate the DEA. He would make a public spectacle of how little evidence they had, go straight to the papers and claim that his rights as a citizen were being trampled on. By the time he was finished, the DEA would have no choice but to walk away from the case, the court of public opinion crushing them far beyond any rehabilitation a court of law could provide.

The moment that was accomplished, the organization could return to doing things just as they always had.

There was merit to some of what Molina had said, and Guzman

did applaud his counterpart's deterrence to armed violence. Succumbing to such would have most likely done in every person at the home, would have at the very least landed them all behind bars.

At the same time, he neither agreed with nor appreciated the cavalier nature of the entire undertaking. It was clear by the time Molina presented the plan that a decision had already been made. There would be no mutual discussion, no determining what the best course for all involved was.

Molina thought he knew what was best and was going to act on it, input or logic from others be damned.

In that moment, Guzman realized that his counterpart had become too antiquated for his own good. His reliance on the old ways had inhibited him from changing, even when necessary.

The old man had practically cackled with delight as he described what was about to take place, foreseeing the entire event as a chance for them to make the DEA look foolish. So convinced was he of the idea that he insisted on turning himself over the moment they arrived.

He never once paused to realize that just because he had skated by in the past, he was now being scrutinized by a different system entirely. The DEA had more than enough to hold him, would continue digging until they found whatever else they needed. The court of public opinion would never be employed to embarrass them, it would be used to make a spectacle of him.

Guzman had known all of that at the time, had watched in silence as every bit of it came to pass. Never once did he offer a word of contradiction though, accepting his role as a guest by remaining on the sideline.

In truth, the situation had presented itself as the perfect out that he was looking for. Interviews for a proper replacement could be set up within a week.

Less than an hour after leaving the home in Maywood, a call arrived confirming everything Guzman suspected. Routed south from Montana, it was reported that the expedition to look for the girl was a colossal failure.

The pilot was being detained, all others were dead.

With everybody crammed into the Lexus SUV, aimlessly circling the city as they avoided the house and waited for Molina to contact them, Guzman held out a hand for the driver to stop. He waited until the car was safely pulled over alongside the road before rotating in the front passenger seat.

"Right now, I need an answer," he said. "If you're in, you will ride to the airport and head back to Ecuador with us. If not, we will drop you at the nearest bus stop, no questions asked."

Neither Rafa nor Sanchez seemed surprised by the statement, having seen the situation play out more than once before. Both met his gaze as he stared past them into the rear, knowing his inquiry was not aimed in their direction.

The old ways dictated that he at least extend the offer to Molina's people, just as they dictated that Molina never utter the name Daniel Guzman to another living soul.

For all the man's faults, he still believed in the ancient rules.

As his final act as part of the partnership, Guzman would extend the same.

Between the two holdovers of Molina's stowed in the back of the car, Guzman didn't much care what Jasmine decided, extending the invite to her a mere formality. She presented no special skills and held no true value to him, though she did possess a certain look that would always be useful in their line of work.

It was what had garnered her the role with Molina, would serve her just as well in South America should she choose to come along.

The bigger get would be Declan, a soldier every bit as capable as Rafa without the added baggage of fifty extra pounds and fifteen extra years. If anywhere as capable as suspected, he would provide for a seamless transition of security measures for the organization, allowing Rafa to move into more of a management role.

The entire structure of things needed to change with whomever they chose to work with in the future.

Declan could be a first step toward that.

Opening his eyes in the cabin of the Gulfstream, Guzman saw Jasmine sitting across from him. Still wearing the cocktail dress and ridiculously tall shoes from the night before, she had Sanchez's jacket draped around her shoulders, both of them sitting on the remainder of the wraparound not occupied by Rafa.

Neither one met his gaze as he looked them over, both content to stare straight down at their laps.

He didn't really need two assistants, but had no doubt he could find roles for both. In the meantime, Sanchez could train her to Guzman's liking, making her something far more useful than just the bit of eye candy Molina had kept her around to be.

Using the toe of his shoe, Guzman shifted his chair to the left, the entire leather seat rotating on the steel pole beneath it. No sound escaped the well-oiled metal as he moved, coming to a stop looking directly at the profile of Declan.

His eyes were open, his face awash in early morning light, as he stared out the window. Striated tendons and veins could be seen running the length of his neck, even with his body at ease.

Much like Jasmine, the man had been wasted in the employee of Molina. The only fault the old man had greater than his inability to adapt was his loyalty, causing him to put so much faith in Thiago Ruiz.

Pursuing the girl was a waste of time, had been from the first minute. Guzman had just never said as much because he knew in the end it would give him a clean exit, just as he wanted.

Just as the old ways dictated.

Chapter Fifty-Six

The early morning sun was strong, reflecting off the mirrored glass facades of the buildings rising around us. After nine hours tucked away in the timeless environment that was the fifth floor conference room, the piercing light seemed especially potent, penetrating my puffy eyes, causing me to lift a hand to shield my face.

Beside me I could sense Diaz doing the same, a low groan rolling out as she twisted her body a few inches to the side.

On the far end of our little procession Lake appeared oblivious to it, her body seeming to have settled into a state of walking comatose, beyond reproach from external stimuli.

"Well, then..." I muttered, the glass doors at the front of the Santa Ana DEA station swinging closed behind me. They landed back into place with a small sound, none of us bothering to turn around.

"Bet you miss nights like those, huh?" Diaz asked, settling a hand along her brow, using it shield the early morning glare.

A wan smile pulled at the corner of my mouth as we drifted a few steps away from the building and formed into a loose cluster. Around us the first few employees started to slide by, ready to begin a new day, coffee cups and breakfasts in paper sacks in hand. A few of them glanced over at us as they went, their expressions showing every possible permutation of disinterest.

"There have been a lot of things this past week I haven't missed much," I replied.

"Like all that hair?" Diaz asked, the same wan smile growing on her features.

My eyes bulged a bit, the grin growing larger on my face. "Or getting shot, having my home destroyed, almost losing my toes..."

"Oh, come on," Diaz replied. Despite the obvious fatigue she was under the smile grew a bit larger, the look appearing a bit out of place alongside the dark circles beneath her eyes. "The bullet barely grazed you and we agreed to build you a new hermit hut."

Pressing my lips tight, I shook my head and glanced away, the bright sun having moved a little higher, now fully reflected in the windows across the street. I remained there a moment, letting her see my shoulders quiver with suppressed laughter.

"And you do look better without all the hair," Lake added, causing all three of us to openly laugh for the first time in days.

On face value the joke wasn't that funny, though in some small way it felt cleansing for all of us. A week ago, Lake was just trying to scrape by, Diaz was off working on some other case, and I was getting my Winchester ready for the summer season. In the time since we had all been through a whirlwind, each in our own respective way, each with a few new scars.

Conversely, we were each still standing, all the stronger for it. Diaz had scored a major get for the agency, a man that thought he was so untouchable he practically handed himself over.

Lake had stumbled into the dark underbelly of society and made it out the other side. She was a little shaken, most likely would be for quite a while, but she was standing. In time, she would come to discover that was all that truly mattered, the entire affair providing her with more strength than she ever thought possible.

As for me, the benefits weren't quite so clear, but in their own way even more meaningful. While I had been shot, had lost my cabin, had spent a week without sleep and pumped full of adrenaline, faith had been placed in me and I had confirmed that it was well founded. A young girl had been in need and I had done everything I could to ensure her safety.

Just like I'd promised.

"So what's your plan from here?" I asked.

Shoving her hands into the pockets of her slacks, Diaz raised high up onto her toes, shrugging her shoulders toward her ears. She held the stretch for a moment, pushing a puff of air out through her nose, before settling back down flat.

"Sleep," she said, not a hint of irony in her voice. "I'm going to drive us back down to headquarters, and we're both going to sleep. If anybody in that building dares wake us, there will be hell to pay."

I offered the perfunctory smile to let her know I caught the joke, though remained silent.

"After that, we'll work with the prosecutors to get everything nailed down, hopefully get Arturo Molina and Hector Ortega put away for a long time."

I nodded, knowing exactly how much went into the word *hopefully*.

After listening to the team of lawyers upstairs for most of the night though, I felt cautiously optimistic that things would play out the way we envisioned.

She glanced over to Lake and said, "Now that charges are pending, we'll be able to get her under protective custody for a while. In the meantime, we'll monitor if any additional danger exists..."

Her voice fell away there, not needing to go any further. I understood how the system worked, knew that once Lake testified, she could either remain under protection or the two sides could agree it was safe for her to leave.

None of that Diaz bothered saying, not wanting to get too far into it while standing on the sidewalk, people drifting by on either side of us.

"And you?" I asked. "This time they might make you take a promotion, drag you to Washington kicking and screaming if you even try to turn them down."

A wry smile crossed her face as she looked at me, the exact reaction I had expected. "Yeah, well, they'd have to find me first, and luckily I know a guy that's pretty good at keeping people hidden."

At that she stepped forward and slid her arms around my shoulders. I returned the embrace as her face settled against my neck.

"Thank you," she whispered. "I won't forget it."

I gave her one last squeeze before we both released, not bothering to respond to her comment in any way.

There was no need to.

"Just remember," I said, "we open up our summer schedule next month for tours into the park. If you ever decide on a vacation, I'm sure we'll be able to fit you in."

She smiled and leaned forward at the waist, her gaze tracking to the ground as she nodded, backing away. "I'll remember that."

"You do that," I said as she drifted on toward the parking garage, facing us for a few steps before turning and making her way out of sight.

Lake waited until she was gone before turning to look at me. A tremor passed over her face as a veneer of moisture appeared on her eyes, her upper lip quivering.

I knew exactly how she felt. So much had transpired in the preceding days, so many things that we both had to be thankful for, so much we had each been through, infinite things we both could say.

In the end, neither of us uttered a word.

Lake remained rooted in place a moment before stepping forward and sliding her hands around my waist. She pressed her face into my shirt and cried softly, her entire body trembling, her tears soaking through the thin cotton. Her hands grabbed at bunches of cloth as she stood, letting every bottled emotion of the past week flow out of her, ignoring the open stares of people passing by.

I slid my arms around her shoulders and pulled her closer to me as she did so, lowering my face to the top of her head.

In that position we remained until Diaz pulled out of the parking garage, Lake eventually releasing her grip on me and backing away. I stayed where I was as she jogged toward the car, stopping along the curb just long enough to wave before climbing into the passenger seat.

I remained on the front steps and watched as they turned away from the building, standing still until they hooked a left at the end of the block, disappearing from sight.

For a moment, I considered taking myself into the parking garage and retrieving my truck before thinking better of it. Instead I descended the stairs and crossed the street, my boots clicking against the asphalt as I fell in line with a loose gaggle of foot traffic headed toward the coast.

I had a fourteen-hour drive and five months of staring at mountains ahead of me.

I could sacrifice a couple hours to enjoy the beach.

Epilogue

I remained silent as we ascended, drawing in deep pulls of the cold mountain air. The calendar said it was now the first of May, spring already beginning to give way to summer in most parts of the country, though the park was still shrugging off the effects of a long winter.

Spots of snow dotted the ground around us, the earth firm as we walked on. Our hiking boots scraped against the solid dirt as we made our way forward, the icy breeze hitting me full in the face, telling me we were getting close.

Elephant Back Mountain was one of my least favorite hikes in the park. Most times of the year the trail was teeming with tourists, all taking advantage of the relative easy accessibility and the views afforded at the top.

Given the early date on the calendar though, the park was still closed to the public. As a guide I was granted access, allowed to bring along personal guests only.

Another three weeks and I would take great pains to dissuade all customers from going near the place, though in this instance I was more than willing to overlook it.

The climb had been easy, the two of us moving in silence, making our way up the mountain. She had kept up with me every step to that point, though the combined effects of the cold and altitude were beginning to take hold.

I could see them on her face, hear them in her pained breathing.

Tell by the fact that not a bit of conversation had taken place since we left the trailhead.

The ground leveled out as we covered the last two hundred yards of the hike, the forest opening up. No longer did we have to lean our bodies forward to compensate for the incline, my feet resuming their normal position inside my boots.

Bit by bit, the only reason for my even tolerating the hike came into view. Off to our left was Fishing Village, the Yellowstone River drainage combining several smaller tributaries like fingers coming together at the palm. From there it wound through open meadows, the ground still generously splashed with snow, before depositing itself in Yellowstone Lake. Almost fifteen miles across, the lake stretched the breadth of most of the horizon, the late afternoon sun striking the water, irradiating upwards in hues of gold and orange.

A smile crossed my face as I walked to the faded wooden signpost demarcating the top. I pulled my ski cap from my head, feeling the chilly wind run over my sweat-stained scalp, and rested an elbow along the top of the sign.

Behind me, I could hear Lake's footsteps slow as she came up alongside. The new camera that had been purchased for her by the DEA hung from her neck, swinging by its straps from one side of her torso to the other as she moved. Leaving it in place, she raised a hand to her brow, framing her blonde hair now outlined with sapphire streaks, narrowing her field of vision as she looked out at the scene.

"Wow," she whispered.

"Yeah," I said, gazing out in the same direction, the smile still on my face.

Together we stood like that for a long time, neither one acknowledging the chilly breeze, too preoccupied with the vista below to much care. Our breathing slowed and our heart rate's receded, two people alone in nature, fully content.

"You know, I never really thanked you for everything you did," Lake said.

My smile grew into a small chuckle as I leaned forward, dragging the sole of my shoe against the ground. "Yeah, you did."

"No," Lake said, turning to face me. The smile faded from her face as she regarded me, pulling in a shallow breath. "I mean, you *are* only like five years older than me."

I knew what she meant even before she parroted my own words back to me, but my previous answer still remained. Instead of offering it again, I jutted my chin toward the horizon, my eyes squinted up against the sun. "Aren't you going to take any pictures?"

The change of subject was poor, but it was the best I had. I could sense her gaze on me a moment, realizing full well what I had done, before turning her attention back to the lake.

She raised her hands and gripped the camera on either side as if she might finally use it, but never lifted it. Instead she dropped her hands away, letting them fall by her side.

"Diaz told me what happened," she whispered. "Before. Your wife and daughter."

The smile faded from my face, my mouth drawing itself into a tight line as we stared out at the scene below.

"She said she thought that was why you helped me. It wasn't some sense of duty to the DEA, wasn't even really about doing a favor for her."

Why exactly I had done everything I did was something I had spent a great deal of time chewing on in the preceding months. I liked Lake, despised Molina and everything he stood for, so keeping the two apart wasn't a hard sell once I was brought in.

The bigger question, though, was why I had come onboard to begin with.

Diaz was right. I hadn't done it out of duty, and while I did feel like I owed her, it wasn't about that either.

It was about sitting on that front porch with Alice years before. About the last conversation I had with her and the promises I'd made.

About the bond a man has with his daughter, more sacred than anything else that can ever exist in the world.

"You know," I said, my voice so low and soft even I could barely hear it, the wind carrying it away the moment it left my mouth, "I never thanked you either."

"For what?" Lake asked, her tone matching my own.

"For helping me keep a promise."

I didn't bother going into any further detail. I just stood and watched the sun move in a gentle descent toward the horizon, standing in place until the last of it dipped below the far banks of Yellowstone Lake.

Thank You For Reading!

Again, I must first start by saying thank you for taking the time to read my work. Depending on which numbers you choose to believe, there are up to a million books published each year in the United States alone, and I truly appreciate you selecting this novel. I enjoyed bringing back Hawk and Diaz, as well as revisiting some of my favorite places, and I hope you did as well.

Please know this is my least favorite part of the entire writing process, but again I would like to ask a favor. If you would be so inclined, I would greatly appreciate a review letting me know your thoughts on *Cover Fire*. I know it is generally frowned upon to read reviews, but I continue to do so in an ongoing effort to gauge how my work is received and to hopefully improve upon it. Everything that is written is taken quite seriously. If you would prefer to let me know your thoughts directly instead, please feel free to email me at authordustin-stevens@gmail.com.

Much love,

Thank You For Reading!

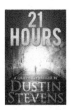

Free Book Offer

Sign up for my newsletter and receive a FREE copy of my first
bestseller – and still one of my personal favorites – *21 Hours!*
dustinstevens.com/free-book

Bookshelf

Works Written by Dustin Stevens:

Reed & Billie Novels:
The Boat Man
The Good Son
The Kid
The Partnership
Justice
The Scorekeeper
The Bear

Hawk Tate Novels:
Cold Fire
Cover Fire
Fire and Ice
Hellfire
Home Fire
Wild Fire
(Coming 2019)

Zoo Crew Novels:
The Zoo Crew
Dead Peasants
Tracer
The Glue Guy
Moonblink
The Shuffle
(Coming 2019)

Ham Novels:
HAM
EVEN

Standalone Thrillers:
Four
Ohana
Liberation Day
Twelve
21 Hours
Catastrophic
Scars and Stars
Motive
Going Viral
The Debt
One Last Day
The Subway
The Exchange

Standalone Dramas:
Just A Game
Be My Eyes
Quarterback

Children's Books w/ Maddie Stevens:
Danny the Daydreamer…Goes to the Grammy's
Danny the Daydreamer…Visits the Old West

Danny the Daydreamer…Goes to the Moon
(Coming Soon)

Works Written by T.R. Kohler:
Shoot to Wound
Peeping Thoms
The Ring
The Hunter

My Mira Saga
Spare Change
Office Visit
Fair Trade

About the Author

Dustin Stevens is the author of more than 40 novels, the vast majority having become #1 Amazon bestsellers, including the Reed & Billie and Hawk Tate series. *The Boat Man*, the first release in the best-selling Reed & Billie series, was named the 2016 Indie Award winner for E-Book fiction. The freestanding work *The Debt* was named an Independent Author Network action/adventure novel of the year for 2017 and *The Exchange* was dubbed a fiction novel of the year for 2018.

He also writes thrillers and assorted other stories under the pseudonym T.R. Kohler, including the *My Mira Saga, The Hunter, The Ring, Shoot to Wound,* and *Peeping Thoms.*

A member of the Mystery Writers of America and Thriller Writers International, he resides in Honolulu, Hawaii.

Let's Keep in Touch:
Website: dustinstevens.com
Facebook: dustinstevens.com/fcbk
Twitter: dustinstevens.com/tw
Instagram: dustinstevens.com/DSinsta

Made in the USA
Columbia, SC
16 March 2021